CONQUEST

UNICORN & DRAGON™

VOLUME II

Other Avon Books by
Lynn Abbey

UNICORN & DRAGON

CONQUEST

UNICORN & DRAGON ™

VOLUME II

LYNN·ABBEY

Illustrated by
Robert Gould

A BYRON PREISS BOOK

AVON BOOKS ◆ NEW YORK

CONQUEST: UNICORN & DRAGON VOLUME II is an original publication of Avon Books. This work has never before appeared in book form. This work is a novel. Any similarity to actual persons or events is purely coincidental.

AVON BOOKS
A division of
The Hearst Corporation
105 Madison Avenue
New York, New York 10016

Editor: David M. Harris
Book and cover design by Alex Jay
Cover painting by Robert Gould
Cover title design by Alex Jay and Robert Gould

First Avon Books Trade Printing: August 1988

Printed in the U.S.A.

OPM 10 9 8 7 6 5 4 3 2 1

CONQUEST

UNICORN & DRAGON™

VOLUME II

usk had settled over the secluded valley. Mist rose from the rain-moist ground, but the sky overhead was clear with the promise of pleasant weather. A solitary rider broke away from the muddy track and guided his horse uphill to a patch of forest overlooking Hafwynder Manor.

The woods were quiet except for the patter of droplets blown down from the branches. It was too early in the season for birds and insects. The land had not yet felt its last wintry frost, and though the shrubs and trees were showing new growth, most animals still heeded nature's warning to take shelter through the night. No eyes took note of the black-haired man unbridling and hobbling his horse before he entered a dense juniper copse.

Ambrose did not think of nature as he set his lantern on a sarsen boulder and withdrew a middling-sized leather sack from beneath his cloak. Insofar as he or his teachers understood the words, Ambrose was a rational man: a man who understood that humanity stood at the apex of creation, far above the constraints of primitive nature.

He would prove that before this evening was over.

Stakes, lime chalk, and silken twine, withdrawn from the sack, were used to create a perfect circle on the freshly sodded ground in front of the boulder. Then, through the aid of knots tied in the cord, an equilateral pentagram was marked off along the faintly glowing circumference. Finally, using the first stake-hole he had made, Ambrose set a small silken packet into the earth.

It had become dark. The ground mist had grown palpably thicker. Ambrose's black hair glistened in the lantern-light where the mist touched it. His hands grew chafed and stiff. A part of him cried out for a fire—preferably in a proper hearth in a proper room; but Ambrose was as accustomed to denying his physical wants as he was to ignoring the discomforts of nature. He closed his mind to the aching,

I

pressed a teardrop-shaped crystal between his palms, and sat, stiff-backed, on the boulder.

A crescent rose above the trees on the opposite side of the valley. The young sorcerer felt the mist become silvery in the moonlight. He shut his eyes and concentrated entirely on the contents of the little packet at the center of the pentagram. Discipline was the key to the esoteric mysteries he'd studied in Byzantium—not sensitivity, and certainly not moon-induced ecstasy. Ambrose's will, channeled through tongue-twisting mnemonics and the clear quartz crystal, would make his sorcery.

Ambrose had known before they'd buried Lady Ygurna that he'd need to meet with her again. He'd taken tiny amounts of hair, skin, and blood from her corpse, infused the motes in myrrh, dried them, then wrapped them in silk and carried them against his flesh throughout the winter—all in preparation for this moment.

Ygurna, a priestess of the old Cymric gods as well as chatelaine of the manor in the valley below, would answer his summons. There was arcane art between them— rival arts. The microcosmic bit of her earthly body merely made her return easier, and might make her more amenable to his suggestions.

The moon rose above the mists and trees. It shone onto the grave at the center of the juniper. The mist became opaque and viscous. The copse became still: beyond naturally quiet as if time itself had been stopped.

Ambrose lowered the crystal and opened his eyes.

"So, you have wrought your will against nature, have you?"

There was no mistaking Lady Ygurna. Tall, steely, and slender, for all that her form was greenish silver mist. The voice was hers too, although Ambrose could not have said if she spoke or if he simply felt her thoughts within his mind.

"Mankind always stands opposed to nature. It is not fitting that we be ruled like sheep; we are rational as nature is not."

2

The mist-figure smiled. "Rational, are we? More's the pity of it. You're sitting out here in the damp talking to a woman long dead. Only a man . . ."

"You're not long dead, Ygurna. It is scarcely three months since the Black Wolf threatened and you walked your circle across the snow. You are still very much bound to this earth, very much in the thoughts of the living."

Ygurna wavered as if thought or doubt cost a measure of her substance. She tilted her head like a cat or dog listening to a far-off sound. "No. No, it is over. Long over. We have peace now." She retreated to the rim of the lime-drawn circle.

"It's about Alison, Ygurna," Ambrose whispered before she tested the limit of his power to hold her here.

She had devolved into a column of swirling mist, but her niece's name brought her back. Her eyes took form again once the mist touched the silk at the center of the pentagram.

"Alison? What about my sister's daughter?" Her voice was still an empty breeze through the branches.

"She has not undone what she did."

"And you want me to do what she will not?" Ygurna's personality had waxed strong again; her voice was a cackle full of knowledge and spite.

"You could." Ambrose forced himself to stare into the mist as she grew more cronelike. He was only a mortal man despite his discipline; his flesh had an instinctive fear of death. He channeled his remaining faith into the geometria he had scraped into the turf. He *wanted* to be fearful, but a Zoroastrian magus did not *need* to be fearful.

The mist caressed itself, sounding like twigs scraping against each other—or bones. "What was done will be done, and cannot be undone. My sister's daughter has become a player in her own game. The best sacrifice is made by the holy or the innocent."

The sorcerer's concentration faltered as he realized that the ghost he had conjured was not alone in the mist.

4

Ambrose's human curiosity asked who, or what, might have accompanied Ygurna into his circle; he stifled it and strengthened his will against nature, death, and evil.

The mist recondensed into the woman he had known.

"Stephen does not belong here," he explained patiently, as if to a child.

"What was done is still done," Ygurna explained, twisting uncomfortably. "Alison has been accepted, and she has accepted him. They have become a part of something much larger. She will not be allowed to undo it."

"But you could."

Ygurna looked away, seething with some unexplained turmoil.

"Surely Stephen is not the one *you* would have chosen for her . . ."

The ghost snapped upright, moving more solidly than Ambrose had anticipated. And the other presence, the one that had spoken through the sound of scraping bones, was with her again.

"He is, after all, not one of your kind, not of your blood," Ambrose added quickly as his own fears finally freed themselves.

The mist spoke in a voice that came from every corner of the copse. "It has happened before; it will happen again. There is no native blood in Britain—only what blood has conquered. First there were the Celts who pushed the Picts to the edge of the land. Then the legions who conquered the Celts and lived among them until they were both abandoned by Rome. The world grew small again, but the Cymry—the Romans and Celts intermingled—remembered. The English came: Saxon, Angle, Jute, and Friesian. They conquered in blood again, but the Cymry still remembered their promises and survived. We were hidden, but not forgotten. We made the sacrifices still. The English were accepted; the land stayed green.

"Then the Vikings came—who cared only for the sea and glory. We could not accept them, and our bond with the land has grown weak. The promises are forgotten; the sacrifices are forgotten. Our land is naked—ripe, again, for conquest. But the Cymry remember. We will try one last time. A new hero will be chosen; blood will make the land fertile again."

Ambrose was afraid of the mist, but not its prophecies. Sorcery and magic weren't necessary to know that England would soon be enveloped in catastrophic war. The island's native dynasties had all failed, and her riches caught the eyes of other ambitious rulers. Harold Godwinson, who held the throne since Christmastide, might have been born on English soil, but he was no more an *English* king than Harald Hardrada of Norway or Duke William the Bastard of Normandy.

"I will have Stephen back," the sorcerer warned the evanescent pillar.

But the mist did not hear him. It grew brighter, and Ambrose, on his rock outside the circle, could feel the gathering power.

"He comes," Ygurna cried, seeking to free herself from the pentagram. "He comes. The green king comes. The land shall be reborn in blood!"

Power swept through the juniper. It rasped through the trees and sucked up the mist. It obliterated the circle and pentagram beneath a shower of winter-killed twigs. Then it was gone, and the moon was behind the treetops, sinking toward morning.

Ambrose tried to stand, but he might as well have been part of the boulder beneath him. He was numb from the buttocks down, and no amount of discipline could restore him. He pushed and fell to his knees where the pentagram had been. Ambrose could no longer deny the pain and fear. He was shivering and sweating as he dug the knotted square of silk out of the wet grass. He placed it inside his tunic and moaned as the cold thing slid across his chest.

Knowing he would not stand until he had been warmed

by the sun, he crawled to the back of the rock where his cloak lay as he had left it. He forced his legs straight, then rolled himself into the thick, fur-lined wool.

Dawn could not be that many hours away.

tephen found Ambrose's horse nibbling grass. He recognized the trees and the junipers within them. He called his friend's name several times before dismounting and leaving his own horse ground-tied. There were a hundred places he'd rather be, a thousand things he'd rather do; but he forged past the damp evergreens and stared at Ambrose sleeping beside Ygurna's grave.

"Look alive, now," Stephen commanded, giving Ambrose's shoulder a shake.

The sorcerer groaned, opened his eyes, and did not recognize the face staring down at him. Stephen snatched his hand back and, standing up, turned away.

"For the love of God Almighty, Ambrose, why this place?" There was weariness and despair in his voice, but not enough to endanger their friendship.

"God Almighty, I think, had very little to do with it. Here, give me a shove or I'll never unwind myself from this thing."

Stephen helped him out of the cloak and then to a seat on the boulder. "Did my lord uncle know, or was this his idea in the first place?" Stephen asked as he gave Ambrose's cloak a vicious snap to remove the dew.

With a loud sigh, Ambrose wrapped the cloak around his shoulders and declined to answer the question. There had been a time—several years ago in France, while Stephen was still a child—when sorcery had not stood as a wall between them. Then Stephen had found his tutor's mysterious behavior to be a fine source of adventure in an otherwise constrained, predictable world. But now that his education as a feudal warrior was complete, Stephen was an unwilling party to his friend's secrets.

"Shall we say Lord Beauleyas did suggest I might scout ahead before we arrived at the manor."

"And did you find anything?"

8

CONQUEST

"Hafwynder Manor is much as we left it: preoccupied with its own problems and unaware that a stranger was riding on the hill above it. Their ewes are dropping early, and the men have been dispersed to the high fields. The rest would not interest a man of the world like you or your uncle."

Stephen stared at the shapes scratched across the turf and the debris that littered this copse but nowhere else. He knew why and how the Lady Ygurna had died; he had been the one to find her lying dead in this very spot. He knew as well not to ask questions for which he did not truly desire answers.

"If I bring your horse, will you be able to ride from here? I left the men before dawn, and surely they are not far behind me."

"I guess I shall have to, won't I? I think I'll be fine once we get moving."

"You need someone to take care of you, you know," the younger man remarked once they had cleared the copse and his friend was walking on his own. He was smiling as he glanced at Ambrose; then the smile vanished.

Everything had been simpler before Stephen had made his way to his mother's half brother, Jean Beauleyas, and Ambrose had accepted service to the same man. Friendship overcame the inequalities of their ages, experience, and inclinations. They had been encouraged to rely upon each other. Stephen was the sole heir to his father's many manors. He'd need a strong arm to keep the peace among them and a trustworthy steward to manage them. Then Stephen's father had been slain in a pointless skirmish and his mother had been forced to marry a neighboring lord with no use for a raw lad who was none of his blood. Not when he had three sons of his own—each older than Stephen—and not enough land to keep them from each other's throats.

Now his mother was dead as well—poisoned—and he had gone skulking to her remaining relatives, hoping for some change in fortune that would lead him and Ambrose back to France.

Or Ambrose hoped. Stephen hadn't mentioned his lost patrimony since Christmas. He was at an age when young men are apt to be smitten, and Alison—with her deep blue eyes; long, golden hair; and innocent manner—was just the sort of woman to produce a powerful smile. Magic need not have been involved at all—but it had been, though Stephen refused to believe that.

The sorcerer, who took great pride that he had never tampered with a freeman's thoughts, despite the ability to do so, considered Alison an affront to all magical arts. He clung to her act of immortality, keeping it always as the focus of his outrage lest he slip into a sort of professional jealousy; for, try as he might, he could neither undo nor mitigate the changes she had wrought. He had not, however, the faintest notion that Alison had changed him, without recourse to her magic, far more than she had changed Stephen by using it.

"Are they well?" Stephen asked when they reached the horses and Hafwynder Manor could be seen below in the valley.

"Well enough," Ambrose replied quickly, knowing there was no *they* in Stephen's mind, only Alison. Because of Alison, and Alison alone, Stephen had risked his uncle's wrath to lead this return to Hafwynder Manor. Ambrose hoisted himself into the saddle without assistance and was of that much grimmer countenance when he faced Stephen again.

They rode just within the trees, following deer trails, until the curve of the land put them beyond the sight of the manor's lookouts. Not that either man expected the English to be alert for strangers. The English were unaccustomed to the suspicious habits of the French. Neighbors here were generally friendly, and a man might reasonably expect to die in his bed, as King Edward had done the past Christmas. Such tranquillity and trust would serve these people poorly in the months to come,

and gave the few land-poor Normans already on the island a sublime sense of superiority.

Stephen touched his spurs to his horse's flanks, broke
from cover, and led Ambrose on a fair ride across the
downs to the narrow track where they rejoined the other
men from his uncle's stronghold, Torworden. If these
five oath-bound men had questions about the comings
and goings of the one they called the Greek—and they
did—they kept them to themselves. It was not for them
to question the decisions of Lord Beauleyas, not when
the lord's word was law, and law was the edge of his
sword. Especially when opinion was still divided about
Stephen's prospects at Torworden. The smarter men,
veterans like Hugh de Lessay and Alan FitzAlan, who
rode with Stephen now, appraised the young man's style
beneath his inexperience. They wagered the old man
would make Stephen his heir once William took the island in hand, and placed their bets accordingly.

The escort fell in silently behind Ambrose and stayed
that way until the track wound its way to the foot of the
hill where Ambrose had passed the night.

"Break out the pennants," Stephen commanded.

Two of the five tied strips of embroidered cloth to their
spears; then they moved forward to provide more tempting targets than either Stephen or Ambrose. They were
much relieved when the assembly gong was struck and
the gates swung open to greet them.

The early spring rains had not erased the marks of the
battle that had been fought within Hafwynder Manor's
yard. Charred timbers still outlined the byres that had
been set afire. The whitewashed sides of the hall and the
nearby stone tower were scarred by those same fires; the
manor lacked the manpower to bleach them anew. Raw
mounds of earth marked new household graves on the
slope behind the hall itself. There was a similar but larger
mound farther downstream, outside the manor stockade,
where the Black Wolf and his outlaws shared a common

grave. The most noticeable scars, though, remained on Hafwynder's people and on Godfrey Hafwynder himself.

The lord of the manor stood in the doorway of his hall, flanked by his two daughters. His hair and beard were freshly combed, his braes hung loosely around his legs, and his embroidered tunic was brilliant in the morning light. But his movements were flaccid, and there was no glimmer of recognition in his eyes when Stephen led his horse up the path to the hall. Alison took her father's hand.

"Stephen, Lord Beauleyas's nephew, is here, Father."

Obediently the blue eyes focused where Stephen stood. The youth smiled awkwardly and extended his hand, which the lord of Hafwynder Manor ignored. Disappointment showed clearly in both young women's faces. Alison gripped her father's hand more tightly, and Wildecent, the petite, dark-haired sister, hid a tear behind her sleeve. Stephen pulled his hand back and trapped it in his belt as if it, and not Godfrey, was the source of their discomfort.

"He has not recovered at all since your last message?" Ambrose asked in a detached but not unkind way as he came up the path after leaving his horse with one of the manor's servants. His English was good, as were his French, Latin, and Greek. He learned everything quickly and completely. Most feared his sorcery, but his mind was his sharpest weapon.

"Some days we think he knows us," Alison answered quickly, looking up into eyes that did not know her today.

"And the other times . . . he is like this?" Ambrose took Godfrey's hand into his own and squeezed hard. There was no reaction in Hafwynder's face.

Alison hesitated, then shrugged a tentative agreement. "We have done all that could be done," she said with a trace of defiance in her voice.

The blond heiress had cause to be defensive. She had spent the night before the Christmastide battle practicing the earth magic of her maternal ancestors. The ancient powers had noticed both her and her aunt, but they had not protected the manor. Wildecent and Stephen had found her in an exhausted stupor beside Lady Ygurna's corpse. Stephen had carried her back to the manor. For the better part of a day and a night, Alison had lain beside her father before the hearth in the great hall. The family that had protected the valley for generations had seemingly abandoned it.

With Ygurna newly dead and Alison reckoned among the dying, the wounded turned to Wildecent, the other sister—a timid child of unspoken birth. Wildecent herself had been injured; a broken arm was bound against her breasts. She'd turned to the foreign sorcerer, Ambrose, and used him as her hands. They'd worked with quiet skill throughout that very long afternoon, but with every wound they stitched, every bone they splinted, the manorfolk looked to the raised pallets where the Hafwynders lay, and their sense of hopelessness grew.

When Alison had recovered she blamed herself for all that had happened and tended her crippled father with obsessive concern.

"To do more would be to call upon black arts," she warned, staring hard into Ambrose's black eyes.

"Assuredly," Ambrose agreed.

He would have said more but their five Norman companions, still clad in heavy hauberks and conical helms, came up to the doorway asking if the horses should be set in the English stables or in a separate line. They did their asking in Norman French, and the alien words pierced the shield surrounding Godfrey's mind.

"Outlaws! Traitors! Murderers!" the blond man shouted as he shed his daughters and shouldered his way to the enemy.

Godfrey had been a strong man before his injury; his daughters' care had kept him from becoming a weak invalid. Whatever he saw standing behind Stephen, he had the strength to kill it with his bare hands. The surprised soldier fell backward and saw his death upon him.

Wildecent screamed, Alison raced for the stables, and Stephen struggled to pry Godfrey loose without further injury to anyone. The manorfolk gathered, shaking their heads in worried silence, unwilling to lay hands on their lord, however mad he might be. Not so the Normans, who struggled to separate the combatants. Stephen ordered two of his men, Hugh and Alan, to restrain the English lord. He felt the manorfolk's distrust focus on him and was supremely relieved when Thorkel Longsword, the manor's steward, charged up the path from the byres.

The Viking's face was grim; his hands and tunic were smeared with blood. Stephen took a long step backward before a single word was said, and signaled his men to release their prisoner.

"My Lord Hafwynder!" Longsword shouted, taking Godfrey's hands between his own. *"Friends,* Lord Hafwynder. These men are our *friends!"*

The fire faded from Godfrey's face. His arms fell back to his sides and he stood empty of thought or reason. The Norman escort relaxed. There was no insult in a madman's assault; there was no honor to be gained in reprisals against the befuddled gentleman who now sat meekly on the bench where Thorkel put him.

The man Godfrey had attacked was bleeding. Hugh de Lessay offered him a cloth, and after a nod from Stephen, led the Torworden men away.

"This has happened before?" Ambrose asked, suspecting he knew the answer.

Alison spoke first, a single shrill no!, but a glance from Longsword, whom Jean Beauleyas had left in charge here, made her quiet.

"He knows us, all right, after his own lights—but strangers set him raving. See to your lord father now," Thorkel added with a curt nod to the young women.

The sisters hurried to straighten his tunic and wipe the traces of blood and spittle from his sandy hair.

"The good brothers at the chapel think he's still fighting the Black Wolf and seeing those men come through his gates. Myself . . ." The tall man paused, thought better of his comments, and only shook his head. "There's problems with the ewes in the byre," he said after a moment. "You can follow me down there."

An adult lifetime spent on the English island hadn't touched the Viking core of the man who had stood at Godfrey's right side these last five years. His thoughts could be guessed by any man who knew the Viking ethic: Godfrey Hafwynder should have died in his final battle. At the very least someone should have prevented his softhearted daughters from bringing him back to this unmanly madness.

No one knew where Thorkel Longsword had been before he appeared in Godfrey Hafwynder's service. He was a mercenary, but he had no use for gold. And Stephen, now following him down to the sheep-byre, was keenly aware that there was no aspect of life in which he felt he could match the Viking strength for strength. No area save one: Longsword had no affinity for leadership. He dominated the crippled manor, but Stephen—who had been taught to command men as he was taught to ride or hold a sword—could see that it languished without direction.

The thought put steel in Stephen's stride. He stood before the sheep-byre and looked straight into Longsword's eyes. "I've come on Lord Beauleyas's orders to bring Hafwynder's treasure to Torworden," he began.

"That—and to fetch your fine stallion back?"

Stephen grinned and inwardly admired the man who had guessed the argument with which he had won his uncle's permission. Sulwyn's injuries—and his own—had been the first strands in the ties that now bound the English manor to the Norman stronghold of Torworden in the North. The seven-year-old chestnut was Stephen's most valued possession. Beauleyas might know in his heart that his nephew was dangerously smitten with the English heiress, but he could not deny the young man the opportunity to retrieve his prized horse.

"I'm looking forward to riding him home."

"Today would be soon enough for me, but I suppose you'll be wanting to wait a few days to see everything's counted properly." Friendship faded from Longsword's voice.

Stephen knew something was not as it should be or as his uncle had said it would be. "What's wrong? You've told my Lady Alison and her sister, haven't you?"

Thorkel made a dismissing gesture with his hand, then swooped down to grab the ewe that was trying to escape. "They won't like it. They'll make a man's life a misery with their whining and pleading; he won't get a decent meal for weeks. So why tell them? They'll go anyway." His hands probed through the unshorn fleece and then, satisfied that there was no bleeding, let the mother join her snow white lamb in the far corner.

"It's not the women," he began again as he stood straight. "There's been a muster called. Godfrey held this land from the Godwinsons. Harold Godwinson's lord and king both; he asks for men and supplies. We've sent enough of each and we'll have to send more when planting's over. You should be grateful the herald had no eye for horseflesh or your beast'd be gone to carry the king."

Buried in the speech—an exceptionally long one for the Viking—was the notion that the English king was putting a claim on Hafwynder's treasure. Longsword would not have been able to deny Harold's messenger the men and gold that had been demanded. And Jean Beauleyas would find that he could deliver that much less to his own lord, Harold's enemy: William the Bastard, Duke of Normandy.

"Aye, it will need counting, then," Stephen agreed, already wondering how he would explain the loss to his uncle. "Is that the worst of it?"

CONQUEST

Something very like rage passed over Thorkel's face; Stephen stiffened, fearing he had awakened the dread *berserkerang* that lay in the heart of every Viking.

"The worst is watching a good man cry for death. His body knows, and what's left of his mind. That's why he sees traitors and outlaws in every face. The ladies, though, they'll see none of it. It's just as well to a woman to have a man with his head in her lap. Just as well until the reavers come to the gate and there's none to protect her or her pretty things—"

"Are there reavers about, then? My lord uncle will want to know."

"Reavers of the worst sort: good men intent on wardship. It's a lot of land to leave this way. The girls take care of their father: whoever takes care of the girls has all this valley at his beck and call."

"We'll take care of Alison and her sister: myself and my uncle. We'll have them gone from these parts soon enough; then all you must do is defend the land—which oughtn't be difficult if the king's summoned the *fyrd* for the summer season."

Thorkel snorted a veteran's derision, completely unimpressed that the Frenchman knew the native term for the king's summoned army. "You leave the worrying and planning to Lord Beauleyas 'til you've some meat under your belt, lad."

Stephen fought a blush of discomfort. "I'd like to see my horse," he mumbled.

The Viking pointed to another byre. Stephen heard Longsword's peal of laughter as he hurried away. Twin fires of shame and anger burned in his cheeks. He was grateful that the English had kept Sulwyn apart from their own beasts and that no one saw him bury his face in the stallion's mane.

"I should have known better than to tell him what to do or how to do it."

His fingers locked in the coarse hair and pulled hard

against it. Sulwyn rumbled with surprise and swung his head, teeth bared, around to investigate.

"He missed you. I have an apple for him. He likes them."

The voice, unmistakably Alison's, was right behind him. A slender arm came between him and Sulwyn. The stallion relaxed and took the fruit delicately from her steady palm. Stephen lost his tongue between the excitement of having her close by and the outraged betrayal of watching Sulwyn eat from her hand.

"He'll bite," he managed after an awkward moment.

"Not anymore. We've had enough time to become friends," Alison assured him.

"He's *supposed* to bite! I trained him not to trust strangers."

Stephen glowered at Sulwyn, who stared benignly with bits of russet stuck to his lips. A plowhorse—a cud-chewing cow—could not have looked so harmless. Stephen had a good mind to put his fist into a solidly muscled, coppery shoulder, but Alison was watching, so he confined himself to a friendly pat.

"Oh, he tried a few times, but I guess I remind him of you," Alison said, letting the stallion rub his face against her.

Stephen saw no point in telling her that he never took such liberties with the animal, which had bitten him many, many times. Now that she was standing beside him, he had no desire to talk about Sulwyn at all.

"I am glad to see you well recovered. We were sore worried for you when we returned to Torworden," he mumbled, wishing he were glib enough to sound friendly and well-mannered at the same time.

"I've missed you," she replied in her forthright way. "Nothing is as it was before you arrived, and if it must be different, then it is better to have you here. I'm certain the manor will seem happier now that you've returned."

He shrugged. "I'm honored that you held me in your thoughts, my lady, but in truth it is my lord uncle's thought that Hafwynder Manor is no safe place with England's throne usurped and challenged. He has sent us—me—here to fetch you north to Torworden, where you'll be better protected—"

Alison's artless friendship vanished. "Just me?" she asked.

"Nay, we would bring your sister, Wildecent, as well. And a serving woman, perhaps, for Torworden is not yet so civilized as your English manors. And such treasure as is moveable and can be loaded into carts for the journey—"

"And my father? You mean to bring my father to safety as well?"

Stephen's mouth hung open. His uncle's orders had been blunt and specific: the sisters, the treasure, and such folk as the women would need to attend to them; Godfrey Hafwynder was to remain on his manor. With Alison tucked out of sight behind Torworden's walls, the Norman claim to Hafwynder Manor was secure no matter what happened to her father.

"I will not leave my father," Alison insisted, correctly interpreting Stephen's lengthy silence. "He will die without me. The wolves will tear him limb from limb. You must know that, Stephen. You *must!* You must help me!"

Her voice went shrill and her eyes burned so bright with blue fire that Stephen wished to look away; his thoughts seemed disconnected from his body. It came to him that she was probably right and his uncle terribly wrong. Godfrey Hafwynder should not be abandoned to his fate, even if that meant defying Torworden. There might even be—the notion came to him the longer he stared into Alison's beautiful eyes—wisdom in challenging his uncle. He would be his own man then and, having defended Alison, her manor, and her father, he would be welcomed by Harold when the English king gave come-uppance to the Bastard Duke of Normandy.

An image grew in his mind, an image of sitting in Hafwynder Hall and ordering his Norman uncle back to France. His muscles thrilled with a sense of power, then shuddered. Beauleyas would strike off his head in a moment. He was succumbing to some forlorn English dream and shook himself free of it—but not of Alison. Convincing the young heiress that her future lay with him alone, to the exclusion of her past and family, would not be easy. But, as the woman who haunted his every dream, she was definitely worth his efforts.

"Of course I'll help you," Stephen replied, daring to take her cold, trembling hands in his own. "But I can best help you at Torworden, and *you* must learn to trust my judgment on your behalf."

"I won't lose my land. I won't leave my father!'

"Your father hardly knows you," Stephen explained, doing his best to sound compassionate, "and leaving your land to stay at Torworden is hardly losing it."

Alison shrank away from him. Her face mirrored a stunned surprise. Stephen thought he heard her whisper, "You're supposed to do what *I* want!" but she had fled from the byre before he could demand clarification.

ildecent was in the buttery choosing cheeses for their supper when her sister raced into the kitchen. She didn't see Alison's face, but the sound of both the outer and inner door slamming against the wall told Wildecent everything she needed to know about Alison's mood and destination. The former was stormy and the latter was their bedroom in the tower above the pantry.

"It's that Frenchman," Bethanil, the cook, shouted when the door at the top of the tower stairs slammed shut.

Wildecent bit short a barbed reply. In the months since their aunt's death, she and Alison had been responsible for the daily life of the manor. Lady Ygurna had seen to it that they were capable of doing all that needed to be done—but there was, they had discovered, a great difference between knowing how something should be done and seeing that it *was* done.

The manorfolk did not resent the sisters, but for generations the folk of Hafwynder Manor—be they free, slave, or somewhere in between—had done what they were told to do. They waited to be told even now when they each knew more about their tasks than their mistresses did. It was the time-honored way; and the folk of Hafwynder Manor were honorable.

Lady Ygurna had treated the young women as equals when she taught them the responsibilities of the manor, and so it was as equals that they attempted to replace their aunt. Solemnly they had divided their aunt's keys and sworn to accept each other's word where it applied. Then they had discovered that manor life did not lend itself to neat divisions. Meals got served, and the pantries were maintained, but the manorfolk were choosing sides— and the side they most often chose was nostalgia.

Before their aunt's death Bethanil would never have

dared express her opinions, much less shout them across the kitchen. Then again, before Lady Ygurna's death Alison never would have excused herself from her chores and gone trysting in the byres. And although Wildecent had become much more certain of her abilities since Lady Ygurna's death, she was in no way ready to tell Alison what the latter should or should not do. Though their aunt had never shirked her responsibility for their behavior, her death had not shown the sisters their responsibility for each other.

Alison was throwing things. The sound echoed down the stairway into the suspiciously quiet kitchen.

Taking one of the yellow wheels from its shelf, Wildecent laid it on its side and attacked it with the cleaver. Her back was to the kitchen. No one could see the flush burning across her cheeks. All her frustration, even the frustration she would not acknowledge, was transferred to the knife as she whacked it through the hard crust.

Just like them, Wildecent thought as she delivered another stroke to the cheese. *All smiling to themselves. Laughing at her. Laughing at* me *because I don't know what to do about it.* Something hit the upper door and fell to the floor in pieces. *Our bowl! She's gone and broken our washing bowl!*

The cleaver wavered in her hand. She had half a mind to storm up the stairs herself, but the other half—the half that envisioned the smirks and chuckles that would follow her exit—won out. She separated the sloppily cut wedge and returned to the kitchen, doing her best to imitate her aunt.

"What about bread?" she inquired slowly and evenly. "They'll expect more than a loaf for each man. Do we have enough?"

"Only black bread, with husks, my lady," Bethanil replied, looking properly attentive. "It's the end of winter, you know."

Of course she knew. The manor was lucky to have any flour left after sharing their stores with the cottars who'd been burned out by the Black Wolf at Christmastide. "It's better than they'll have seen for many a day—"

Alison descended from the tower, blond plaits and forest green cloak streaming behind her. She didn't notice them staring, but they, from Wildecent to the lowliest half-wit drudge, saw the 'high color in her cheeks. She flung the outer door open and did not bother to close it behind her.

"She's going to the weaving solar," Wildecent whispered, unaware she'd spoken aloud.

"Likely enough."

Wildecent whirled around, gesturing at Bethanil with the point of the cheese. "You worry about the bread," she commanded. "What my sister does is none of your concern!"

Momentarily cowed and contrite, the stout woman took the cheese into her own ample hands and held her tongue as Wildecent sped out the door. "Close that door," she barked at the drudges.

Alison had been more careful with the solar door; it was both closed and relocked. But it was one of the few locks for which both young women possessed keys, though Wildecent, shaking with nervousness, made several false starts before she got it unlocked. Her sister had heard the fumbling and was unsurprised when Wildecent finally pushed through the door.

"It's about time."

"You weren't acting like you wanted, or needed, my companionship," Wildecent replied. "You were doing quite a good job of destroying our bedroom without any help."

Alison had no time for the gibes which had become a regular part of their conversations. "He's taking us to Torworden," she shouted, knowing it would explain almost everything.

And it did. Thorkel Longsword mentioned the Norman lord's proposal each and every night. The men were virtually unanimous: with Godfrey Hafwynder crippled, his manor was no place for his unmarried heiresses. A woman could own her own property but a man believed he owned the woman. Two attractive heiresses in a lordless manor were a dangerous temptation to any man.

Wildecent sank onto a spinning-bench with a sigh. "All of us?" she asked. "When?"

"No, not all of us. That's the worst of it. Just us; our lord father's to remain here—"

"God's will be done," Wildecent muttered reflexively.

"No it isn't. It's those shave-necked Normans up at Torworden. It'd serve their purposes right well to have me under their thumbs."

Wildecent's timidity masked a quick mind; behind her shyness she was an astute observer—especially of Alison. She wagered silently that there was something more to her sister's anger, and that something was, as Bethanil had suspected, Stephen. Throughout the long weeks since their aunt's death, Alison had assumed that Stephen would do as she wished.

She had also noticed that Alison said *me,* not *us*—and that was cause for concern. Wildecent had nothing of her own; she and Alison were not blood sisters. Wildecent's only claim to the privileges she enjoyed had come from Godfrey Hafwynder's generosity. What little might be known of her true heritage, if she had any worth mentioning, was locked in her lord's addled mind. No matter how bad Alison's position might become, Wildecent's could become much worse. Rather than dwell on how much she stood to lose, Wildecent decided that Alison, in her self-centered frustration, had simply misspoken and forced the thought from her mind.

"What did Stephen say?"

"Nothing."

"Then it was Longsword who told you?"

Thorkel Longsword had sworn an oath to Torworden's Norman lord while Godfrey yet lived. It might have been expedient, even wise under the circumstances, but it could have the Viking declared an outlaw if the new king, Harold, heard about it. King Harold could make both young women his wards, if he chose, and then Wildecent would suffer nothing worse than an honorable marriage to a man she might never love or like.

"No," Alison admitted, visibly reluctant. "Lord Stephen told me. He's come himself to see that everything valuable, including us, is loaded into carts and hauled to Torworden."

"And our lord father's not valuable enough?"

Strength was important in the higher strata of English society—as it was everywhere. An older man, even a physically crippled man, might get by on the strength of his personality, but a man without his mind, as Godfrey Hafwynder had become, was a lamb among the wolves. The love the young women felt for him was irrelevant, and a danger to all it touched.

"They don't know what they're doing," Alison murmured, her voice full of hidden meanings. "If they knew what's good for them, they'd leave me alone."

Then—while Wildecent was torn between a desire to console her foster sister and an equal desire to know her secrets—a hardness came to those sky blue eyes. An ugly grin stole across Alison's face, and Wildecent no longer wished to share the mysteries that Ygurna had revealed to one girl but not the other.

"They *do* know," Alison swore. "Why else send Stephen and the sorcerer? They know, and mean to do it anyway."

"Do what, Alison?"

"Ambrose knows that I am the last priestess. He seeks to control me and my choice!"

Wildecent rolled her lower lip inward. At times she wondered if Lord Godfrey were the only one whose wits were addled. "Don't talk like that," she said, gripping her sister's upper arms gently. "Our lady aunt said the time was past and forgotten when the land was made fertile with a hero's blood. No matter what happens, there's not going to be a blood sacrifice . . ."

Alison wrested free. "Lady Ygurna didn't know *everything.*"

Alison had been with the Cymric gods. They spoke to her in her dreams and, although she couldn't remember their words when she was awake, she knew she'd promised to do something important: something wondrous and terrible. But a *geas* had been laid over the promise and she could neither discuss it with anyone nor remember it herself.

"What are you going to do?" the dark-haired girl asked fearfully as Alison lifted a section of the mosaic floor.

"If we're leaving, this has to go."

Wildecent blinked. The threatening fire was gone as if it had never existed. Alison was herself again and speaking sanely. Of course their pharmacopoeia would have to be included among the valuables of Hafwynder Manor—included or destroyed.

But because this was Alison and Alison had a wild magical talent, which she was apt to use whenever it suited her, Wildecent hesitated before descending into the earth-walled bolt-hole. She checked her most recent memories: what she had said, what Alison had said, and how they had stood while they spoke. Alison could alter a person's memories; she could add a notion or take one away. Wildecent was the only one who understood the extent of her sister's power, and the only one with conscious defenses against it. There were no gaps—this time.

"While you're about it, we should make something up for our lord father," Wildecent said as she descended the wooden ladder into the bolt-hole.

A questioning look came into Alison's face then vanished. There was no way they could serve dinner to their guests and have their father at the table with them. "I feel guilty somehow, whenever I do this," she admitted, reaching for a glazed jug. "He drinks it readily enough, even knowing that he's going to fall asleep and wake up in a little locked byre . . . but I wouldn't want it done to me."

"You begin to sound like Thorkel Longsword," Wildecent said recklessly. "It's a sleeping draught or some of Ygurna's black poison, you know that."

Alison's hands trembled a moment, then were still. "They'll not have our lord father," she said. "His mind will be restored when this is over. I will see to it." She filled a small vial and put the jug back on the shelf. "Here, take this over to Bethanil. We've a lot to do."

"It will take us 'til summer," Wildecent remarked, looking at the cluttered shelves and boxes.

"He wants to leave as quickly as possible," Alison said flatly.

"Alison!" It was just another kind of madness to think the effects of a prosperous and ancient manor could be made transportable in so short a time. "Why, we haven't nearly enough chests and boxes, and our carts are scattered all over the manor—"

"I'd guess it's different in their precious Normandy."

"Surely Stephen—"

"Lord Stephen's mind will not be changed."

Wildecent was curious—achingly, silently curious—to know what had passed between them in the stables. Alison must have used her talent on him as well as more ordinary female wiles; and it must have failed spectacularly. "I guess we'd best get started, then, and hope that when the Frenchmen see what a big task it is, they'll think better of the whole thing," she said with false cheerfulness.

"We can always hope and pray," Alison agreed, though her tone implied that she expected little success. She looked at the heavily laden shelves and appeared defeated by them. "Maybe you'll have more luck than I have."

Alison waited until Wildecent was off the top of the ladder, then climbed it herself. Had she ever been able to confide all the successes and failures of her talent, she would have been able to do much to reassure Wildecent.

She might even have been able to lance the festering sores of doubt that had grown within her, for the *geas* was not always comforting and it did not always make her strong.

That December night, when her aunt had pushed her deeper into magic than she'd ever gone before, Alison had welcomed the embrace of the Cymric gods. After surrendering herself to them she'd wrought a protective sphere over the manor—a sphere that failed only because the Greek sorcerer had confounded it. But the failure of her magic hadn't undone the promise that lay beneath the *geas*.

When Alison had awakened in the great hall of Hafwynder Manor, her father lying mindless on the next pallet and her aunt with the other corpses in the sheep-byre, she had not known herself. There was no smooth bridge of memory across that bitter-cold night. Her childhood had been severed and her magic was tainted by something she could not understand.

Not vanished, Alison admitted to herself, but changed and unreliable. Strange thoughts lingered from her dream-wracked nights—lustful, unmaidenly thoughts; bloody thoughts. She sensed she had the power to send a man to his death, but she could not alter Stephen's simplest desires.

Alison pressed her knuckles against her eyes and convinced herself it was the raw weather that made them water so. Each night she slipped a little further into the *geas* world.

Some night, any night now, she would overcome the *geas* and confront the promise she had made. Alison feared that night because some echo of her childhood said she would go mad when she set foot on that path. Not the generally benign madness that blanketed her father, but something terrible and beyond absolution.

"You coming or not?" Wildecent called from the kitchen door.

Alison turned the key and hurried across the yard before her sister called again. There was suspicion in Wildecent's face, but she said nothing and Alison was grateful for that small blessing.

Pleasant aromas had spread from the kitchen to the nearby hall, luring visitors and residents alike. Since Twelfth Night at the end of Christmastide and their muted celebration of Harold Godwinson's coronation, Hafwynder Manor had been a solemn place, but the Normans expected a welcoming feast.

The trestles were set in a formal U with a high table set between two longer rows. The high table, which was, in fact, no higher than the others, was covered with linen and graced with chairs rather than simple benches. The nobility could come and go at their individual pleasure and did not have to sit thigh-against-thigh with their companions.

All too soon it was time for Alison, as her father's legitimate daughter and recognized heiress, to sit in the most ornate of the chairs and signal the beginning of the meal. She perched on the edge of the hard wooden seat, looking as uncomfortable as she felt—or as uncomfortable as Wildecent in the chair beside her. Stephen sat on her other side and she spoke politely with him, as a chatelaine was expected to do.

"You seem to have recovered well enough from your wounds. Do you still have any pain?"

Stephen looked away from his bread, giving her his full attention. "None at all—hardly. I shall be able to begin work with my sword once we return to Torworden. My uncle's men are well impressed with your English herbals. You'll be much appreciated—you need not worry on that account."

Inwardly Alison wilted, though she made a brave show of graciousness. The last thing she wanted to do was practice herb-magic at Torworden, but she dared not say that. Instead she asked simple questions about France and watched him eat.

His manners were as good as any Englishman's, certainly better than the other Frenchmen—though he claimed that practically no one at Torworden was French. He was from the south, while his uncle was a Norman. The French were those unfortunates who had a Capetian king as an overlord. Alison paid scant attention to his catechism; all she noticed was that he was different, and not because of his continental habits. He watched her with a measure of distraction, of obsession. She had not meant for him to love her like this when she first laid her image over his fantasies. But now, as it had turned out, she needed him, and she meant to control him.

"I've spoken with my sister," she said after the meat was served. "She says that, even without Father, if we are to transport our valuables it will take considerable time to prepare them. And the tracks, of course, are treacherous at this time of year. I cannot see us coming to Torworden before summer." She smiled artlessly.

It didn't work. Stephen took a sip of cyder and said, "Then you'll come without your dower goods. I'll have you out of here in two days. You're more important than your father's gold."

Alison wanted to shout that her father's wealth was more than gold; that marriage had never been in her thoughts when she tampered with his fantasies. She didn't. Everything she said, no matter how she said it, with or without her talent, was only making matters worse.

She did not look forward to telling her sister that their situation had gotten more precarious, and she dreaded the dreams that would come this night.

"You needn't look so glum," Stephen chided, to no avail.

It was not much better on Alison's right, where Wildecent found herself sitting next to Ambrose. Wildecent had tried not to think about the sorcerer during his absence. Now that he was beside her, she lost the battle completely. Ambrose was a door to what Lady Ygurna had denied: a key to the arcane arts that depended on dedication, not wild talent. Ambrose was also Ambrose: dark, mysterious, and sensually attractive.

He was the personification of everything that could tempt and ruin her. Wildecent had the sense to fear him, but she no longer had the strength to put him out of her thoughts. She was glad he did not seem to mind that she was so obviously ignoring him. The dinner passed in awkward silence.

"I wish it were over," she whispered finally to Alison.

"You too? We can take care of *that,* at least."

Alison proclaimed it was time for the bard to take up his instrument and begin the night's entertainment. In the next breath she ordered another round of the manor's potent cyder, and with the third she demurred that her guests and her own men would enjoy themselves more if they did not have to worry about their manners in the presence of ladies. Then she and Wildecent, the only two in the hall who could possibly claim that distinction, retreated.

CHAPTER FOUR

'm sorry," Alison snapped impatiently once she and Wildecent were in the bolt-hole. "You know I didn't mean to do it."

"I know you didn't mean for it to fail."

Wildecent could spare little compassion for Alison. She had been unhappy to learn that they could not wait for their baggage to be loaded onto carts before going to the unknown world of Torworden. Skillful mismanagement would have kept those carts unfilled for months. "You never think," she complained. "You just go ahead and *do*. Well, how long do you think we have? A week, a fortnight?"

"We leave the day after tomorrow, I think."

"Lord God Almighty have mercy on you, Alison. We'll barely be able to get our clothes loaded in a day. What about all this—" She gestured at the shelves. "We'll have to destroy the whole lot of it. Lady Ygurna will rise out of her grave if we leave her legacy where some fool can stumble onto it."

If she hasn't risen already, Alison thought, after failing utterly to calm Wildecent with her magic. "I'd almost rather leave our clothes chests behind. I don't even know what kinds of plants grow near Torworden and . . ."

"And what? Come on, Alison. What else went wrong? What else did you do?"

The blond girl could endure only so much guilt before pride got the better of her. "I didn't do anything. We all had a hand in healing Stephen, didn't we? I guess our plants don't grow in Normandy, or if they do the women there don't know what to do with them, because I got the sense that we're going to have our hands full of bandages once we get to Torworden." She saw Wildecent's brow rise higher and preempted whatever her sister might be thinking. *"Egede,* Wili, it's hardly my fault that we saved his life."

Whether it was the truth of Alison's words or the

crackle of anger in her voice as she spoke them, Wildecent swallowed her own indignation. In the days to come they would only have each other to rely upon. Truly, her sister had never precipitated more disaster with her talent, but just as truly she had never admitted her defeats so readily.

"This is of our own making, then," she agreed sadly, convincing herself that it was no longer relevant who had done what in the past with the uncertain future looming before them. "We'd best be getting on with the sorting and packing if this is the only full night we'll have."

Alison set the first of many containers on the work-table. "We'll take what's needed for healing; Stephen won't balk at that. And what we know can't be replaced in England. The rest we'll destroy or hide."

Wildecent was already gathering the most basic medicines and laying them carefully in a deep basket. From time to time she or Alison would trudge up the wooden ladder with a heavy basket or fetch bits of carded wool to pack between the delicate vials. Travel by oxcart was not a gentle experience. They'd consider themselves fortunate if half the bottles survived. Leaves and powders were less fragile, but it seemed that those herbs that would travel best were also those that would likely grow within easy distance of Torworden.

At last, long after midnight, when the hall had grown quiet and they'd replenished their lamps many times, they faced half-empty shelves and the hardest of the night's tasks.

"I can't bear it," Wildecent complained, struggling to pick her way toward the stables with an overflowing armful of fragrant herbs. These were the exotics, the ingredients of magic. They opened no doors for Wildecent, merely gave her a headache. But they were the heritage of ancient England and everything a Norman presence threatened.

"Then don't think about it," Alison snapped as she heaved her burden onto the manure and thrashed it with a nearby pitchfork.

As if either of them could *not* think about it. Laying Lady Ygurna in the earth beside the junipers had not been nearly so hard or so final. Yet they weren't finished. Not everything in the bolt-hole pertained to healing or the Old Ways; some of the earthen jars held poisons, which they poured into the frigid waters below the fish weir—believing that the swift-running water would render the fatal liquids harmless. They vowed that they would take none of the noxious drugs with them, save those that were diluted to produce purgatives, pain-killers and sleeping draughts, yet each hid a tarry lump in her sleeve. One never knew what the future—especially a Torworden future—might hold.

The bolt-hole was nearly barren then, its bare earth walls exposed and stripped of its scents and mysteries. Alison picked up a necklace made from apple seeds, blew away a cloud of dust, and sank down to the floor. There should have been two of them, she remembered. When they had been very young, not long after Wildecent had first come to Hafwynder Manor, Lady Ygurna had treated them with complete equality. They'd both worn seed necklaces one early spring night when she'd led them to the forest to watch the rebirth of the greenwood.

A night almost exactly like this. Wildecent had been cold and miserable, and more than ready to believe she saw green giants moving through the mists. Lady Ygurna had smiled and embraced her but, of course, it had been a mistake. The world never came to life for the dark-haired orphan.

"It's so hard to imagine leaving here," Wildecent said. "I can barely remember any home but Hafwynder Manor, and I can't imagine Torworden at all."

"Stephen says it's on a high hill," Alison answered absently, not looking away from the necklace. "He says that when the sky is clear, you can see a horse a half-day's ride away."

"I won't like it then."

Wildecent didn't like heights, didn't like the squat

stone tower Lord Godfrey had built to contain their bed-room and the food pantries, and she was nearsighted. She had trouble seeing from one end of the great hall to the other, much less seeing a horse a half-day's ride away.

"You'll come back here," Alison continued in the same dreamy voice. "We'll both come back here someday."

Wildecent brightened, unaccountably relieved, though her sister's gift for prophecy was a chancy thing at best, observed most often in the breach. "Then we don't have to destroy all this! We can just leave it here."

"Huh?" Alison shook herself free of mental cobwebs and remembered what she had just said. She tucked the necklace into her sleeve as she got to her feet. "It's not that simple."

"You said we'd be back, Alison. I was looking at you. I saw it in your eyes. You *said* we'd be back."

Alison didn't deny her prophecy but could not explain the complex web of gods and sacrifices that lurked be-neath the *geas*.

"Alison . . ."

The bolt-hole had never been that important to Wil-decent. She'd learned the herbcraft, all right, better per-haps than Alison, for she relied on hard memory, not intuition. It had been different for Alison, marked by her aunt to be a hidden priestess of an almost-forgotten tra-dition. Herbcraft was the least of the skills Alison had learned in this subterranean room.

For ten years their status had been clearly defined: equal sisters in ordinary tasks, incomparable in all others. That balance had been subtly altered in the months since their aunt's death. Wildecent had proved herself stronger and more capable than Alison had imagined a head-blind woman could ever be.

Alison had not felt threatened by her foster sister for many years. Wildecent had been called her *half* sister when she'd first arrived. For several years Alison endured the suspicion that her beloved father kept a mistress some-where. She also believed it was her father's Saxon blood that endowed her magical powers. She wasn't told the truth until Wildecent proved resolutely head-blind.

The orphan was no kin to anyone on the manor, and magic was the Cymric heritage of Alison's mother and aunt. There'd been Cymry in France, Lady Ygurna had explained, justifying her own behavior. There'd been a wild hope that the dark little girl had been *sent*, but she had only been found.

Alison's love for her father was no longer compromised. Wildecent could be loved but need never be feared. And wild magic was Alison's alone.

You and you alone will become the priestess, Ygurna had said many times, *a guardian of the Cymric ways, and because of that you must learn compassion as well as strength.* Alison knew she had more mastery of strength than of compassion. But she tried, when she remembered; and this time she remembered. "Well, we can't just leave everything sitting on the shelves. Without someone to watch them, sooner or later they'll collapse. We must set what's left on the floor and conceal it." She watched a smile of relief soften Wildecent's face. Compassion had its own rewards.

They worked together emptying the shelves. Their exhaustion abated as ancient objects revealed themselves, objects Alison herself had never seen.

"Who are they?" Wildecent asked when they had three ferocious-looking plaques on the ground between them.

Each was a wood carving, though each was a different wood: that in itself gave Alison a clue. Traces of paint still clung to them; their faces had been green, their eyes had been crimson. Their expressions were fierce, almost grotesque. They might have been the faces of imaginary animals, but they weren't.

"The tree kings," Alison explained. "The Oak King—see, he has acorns in his hair. The Holly King, the one with thorns. And the Ivy King, with those little curly things."

Wildecent let her fingers run lightly over the age-dark

wood. They were masks, she realized, with holes above their ears for thongs that had long since disappeared. No one had worn them in her lifetime, she was certain, nor for a good many lifetimes before that.

"Shouldn't there be four of them?" she asked after another moment's thought. Numbers had power in the Cymry myths. Everything had its appropriate number, and four was the number for green, living things.

Head propped against the heels of her hands, Alison seemed to give the matter thought, though actually she was only determining what she could say. She had never seen the masks before; she recognized them from her nightmares. "The fourth king has no face," she answered in carefully measured words. "He takes his head from the hero."

"You're talking about blood sacrifices again . . ."

Alison sighed. "It happened."

She expected more questions, but mercifully, Wildecent seemed satisfied—or sufficiently disquieted—with what she had already learned. Alison's heart had almost returned to its normal rhythms when Wildecent reached for a rickety basket they'd rejected earlier in the evening.

"I think we should bring them with us—"

She's head-blind! Alison screamed to herself. She had decided to leave the horrific things behind and now her sister—her *head-blind* sister—was doing the *geas*'s work. She said nothing as Wildecent buried the leering, toothy faces beneath loose coils of rough-spun wool.

Wildecent had experienced no supernal revelations. No voice had told her to bring the kings to Torworden, except they set her fingers tingling when she touched them. They were like Ambrose's crystal: talismans for storing power, though it was certainly odd to find such things here. Natural magic resided only in living things: it could be enriched, but not increased; shared, but never taken. This was the dichotomy that made all sorcery repugnant to Alison and Lady Ygurna.

The masks possessed power no piece of wood should

rightfully possess. They emanated sorcery, yet they were here, in the bolt-hole. Wildecent hefted the basket, then set it down again. "Maybe we should burn them instead."

Their eyes locked across the lantern-light.

"Why would you say that?" Alison asked cautiously.

"Because of what they are," her sister replied with equal caution.

"What *are* they, then?"

"Magical."

"The seed necklaces are magical." Alison held the necklace out. "You wouldn't think of burning this, would you?"

"No."

"Then why these?"

Wildecent swallowed hard. It was one thing to know that Alison had replaced Lady Ygurna, but quite another to be interrogated by her. And yet, as her thoughts and reflections expanded, it was not so bad after all; Alison had, as usual, led the way earlier when she'd admitted how she failed with Stephen.

"It is sorcerous," Wildecent said calmly.

"How would you know?"

"I'd know."

Alison sat back on her heels not quite surprised, not quite shocked, and not at all certain where she was going from here. She knew instantly how her lady aunt would have reacted; she knew how she should react. It took a little longer to discover her own reaction.

Across the pool of light, Wildecent also waited. With a simple statement she'd declared herself anathema to all that the Cymric heritage represented. She, too, knew how Lady Ygurna would have reacted—and would never have volunteered the information. Alison, though, was her sister in everything but blood. They weren't as close, perhaps, as they'd once been, but love, trust, and a common past had to count for something.

"When? How often? With that foreigner Ambrose, right?"

Wildecent breathed more easily. That wasn't hostility in Alison's voice, but something more like the conspiratorial curiosity of their childhood.

"Only once, the night before—well, you know before what. I knew from the way you were acting that you and our lady aunt were up to something, but I was afraid for you, for both of you. I didn't know what you could do. I think, I honestly believe that all I wanted to do was help.

"Ambrose had already said he could teach me sorcery. I went to him, meaning to ask him to help, or to show me how to help. But he was already working his own rituals." Her hazel eyes misted. Even in front of Alison, she couldn't escape a thrill of excitement. Ambrose had drawn power through his talisman; an ordinary man with extraordinary power: the memory was tinged with guilt but no less delicious for that.

"Oh, Alison, he'd made a miniature of the manor and set his crystal above it, then he concentrated his thoughts through the crystal, into the miniature and into the world. He drew the Black Wolf to the manor—because he wanted victory, not protection, I guess. But I could feel it, Alison—like I never felt anything that you or Lady Ygurna could do.

"And then, later, when I understood what had happened, when I saw your circle beyond the stockade, I used the miniature myself to learn what had happened to you."

Alison found her hands were shaking. Compassion. Where had her compassion been, or her aunt's, when they'd given Wildecent a glimpse behind magic's curtain, then condemned her to wait forever on the outside? How much temptation could love withstand? Alison lowered her eyes, knowing she would succumb to temptation more completely than her sister if her gifts ever vanished.

When Alison looked away, Wildecent's doubts overwhelmed her. "I've thought about so much since then. I still don't know if sorcery itself is evil, but I keep thinking: what if I'd gone to that room for him instead of his sorcery? What if he hadn't crossed your circle? I feel myself being weighed for what I did that night. I felt my judgment when I sat beside him at the high table tonight—and I wanted to run away."

"I don't think you did anything wrong," Alison began, speaking to her own distress as much as her sister's. "Our lady aunt knew what she was doing. She knew what Ambrose was and what he could do. She took the poison with her; I saw her take it. And I don't know—I just don't know—if anything could have made any difference.

"We can't burn the masks," Alison said after a long pause. "We can't even leave them behind. If we hadn't seen them— No, there are many paths, but home is always home . . ."

Wildecent smiled weakly, remembering how many times Ygurna had muttered that proverb under her breath. Then she carried the broken basket up the ladder and put it with the others. The rest of the night, what little of it remained, went by quickly. Alison unveiled another of their aunt's secrets when she pulled another panel from the ceramic tunnels of the old Roman hypocaust and fitted it into place beneath the mosaic. Then she scattered broken bits of tile and loose dirt across the panel until, if the uninformed or unsuspicious had by chance lifted the mosaic, it looked like the nearly ruined foundation of any other structure that had endured since the Roman Empire had abandoned the British Isles. It was not necessary to conceal the bolt-hole; merely to make it seem uninteresting.

Pale pink streaked the eastern horizon when they emerged from the weaving solar for the last time. Cocks had already crowed, and it would not be long before the manorfolk woke up, if they were not already awake and assembling in the kitchen. The nobility, warriors and landowners, could drink cyder, ale, or mead until mid-

night and sleep until well past dawn. Not so those who supported them.

Unfortunately for Wildecent and Alison, the only path to their tower bedroom lay through the sure-to-be-rousing kitchen. Taking care to keep her keys from jingling, Alison reopened the door and searched through the baskets. She found a handful of fresh mistletoe and gave half to her sister. They smeared the sap on their hands and tucked the broken leaves in the soles of their boots.

Thus invisible, or at least unnoticed, they tiptoed across the courtyard, eased the kitchen door open, and crept stealthily to their rooms.

"I'll sleep until noon," Alison proclaimed once the door was bolted behind them. "I don't care what anyone thinks."

luxurious morning of sleep was not, however, what fate held for them. It seemed they had only just fallen across the bed when something heavy pounded on the door. Alison stumbled across the wooden planks, suddenly mindful of light streaming through the shutters, and the mounds of clothing they'd left strewn across the floor.

"What?" she grumbled, unwilling to open the door.

"It's time you two were awake. There's work to be seen to, and that Frenchman wants to speak with you. And your father's poorly for waking up without seeing you!"

Only the last persuaded Alison to face the obviously irate Bethanil, but she braced the door against her shoulder. "Tell everyone we'll be right there."

"As you wish, my lady."

There was nothing particularly servile about Bethanil's manner as she trod heavily back down the stairs. The cook knew that they were to be taken north to Tworden, and she might well guess why neither of them was up and about for breakfast.

She'll run the manor once we're gone, Alison mused, and run it better, no doubt. "Come on, Wili. I know you're awake!" She took her frustration out on the blankets Wildecent clutched tight around her. "No rest for the weary. You know that."

"Wha'd she want?" Wildecent asked through a body-shaking yawn.

"The day of eternal judgment."

Wildecent had already caught the mood of the day, and shared it to the extent that she didn't want to talk or move either. Still, it wasn't fair to blame Bethanil for their problems. On any manor there was always one person—usually a freewoman, often the cook—who stood between the chatelaine and the manorfolk, just as the noble lord always selected one man to be the chief of his housecarls. Bethanil depended on the sisters; she did not dare, or want, to usurp their authority, but her anger was justified when they failed to perform their duties.

"You heard what she said about father?" Alison asked as she laced a single layer of hose beneath her linen undertunic.

"I'm hurrying, Alison." Wildecent shoved her foot into the nearest boot—it didn't matter which—and craned her neck to catch her reflection in the polished bronze mirror. There were dust smudges on her cheek; she wiped them as best she could on her sleeve. Alison had, after all, broken their washbasin. Her hair, she knew, should be rebraided, but there was no time for that.

"Do you want me to go to our lord father or deal with Stephen?"

"Talk to Bethanil first." Alison thrust an arm down the sleeve of her tunic. A broken fingernail caught on the hemstitching. Both the nail and the embroidery ripped loose. "Oh, bother it, do what you want. Talk to Stephen first; he seems to be making all the decisions around here anyway."

"You take care of our lord father, then."

Wildecent was still fumbling with her sleeve laces when she reached the kitchen where Bethanil, fists on hips, was waiting for her.

"We've got to know how many's for dinner and if they're wanting meat. I'll not have Godeshalt wringing necks for no good reason. Leeks 'n' eels is good enough unless they complain."

The thought made Wildecent's stomach turn. "I'm going to talk to them now—"

"And what shall I do until you're back?"

Was this truly what their aunt had endured every day? Dozens of people unable to move until someone made their decisions for them? "Lord God Almighty and all the holy saints, Bethanil, it's *your* kitchen. You know

44

what's needed here better than I do. Count the fish in the salt-house for all I care. I'll be back as soon as I can."

She blinked as she entered the bright morning sun, then noticed how it highlighted all the tracks they'd made the night before in the soft mud. Groaning inwardly, she hurried across the line of paving stones to the hall.

Thorkel Longsword, Stephen, Ambrose, and the rest of the Torworden visitors were seated on benches and stools contemplating a still-cold hearth. Her groan became a low growl as she realized none of them would ask to have the fire rekindled, much less get down on their knees to do it themselves. Piercing their circle, Wildecent approached the hearth.

Men spent half the year campaigning, traveling, or hunting. Surely every one of them was more adept at prodding the embers to life than she was, but no—men ruled in the great hall and those who ruled had no need to work. Folding her skirt so only the underside touched the ashes, Wildecent took up the fire tools.

"Nay, we're comfortable as it is," Ambrose interrupted.

He was lying—a social lie, a civilized lie that was supposed to soothe everyone's feelings. But then, perhaps they hadn't noticed—men were notoriously indifferent to comfort. Wildecent got to her feet and slapped the gray dust from her hands, noticing as she did that there were two empty stools at the bottom of the circle. Ambrose gestured toward them with his eyes, but Wildecent continued to stand.

"We had expected both of you," Stephen began, gesturing more broadly for her to be seated. "But perhaps it's just as well that you've come alone. Last night Lady Alison said you made the decisions"—which was a great surprise to Wildecent—"and so surely you would be the one she'd listen to—if you were convinced of our good intentions."

Time had come to do as she was told. Wildecent took her perch and stared back at them. Stephen was clearly as uncomfortable as she was, but that was apt to be a small satisfaction in the end.

"We English count sensibility as a virtue in women," she replied, smiling as she imagined Alison might.

Stephen muttered something under his breath and passed the initiative to Ambrose, who spoke dispassionately. "When first we spoke of Torworden and the need for you and Lady Alison to be brought there you seemed understanding enough—"

"It is not the leaving that upsets either of us," Wildecent replied, stretching the truth a bit. "Merely that Lord Beauleyas has not extended his hand to our lord father; nor will his nephew extend it on his behalf. Surely a daughter's devotion to her father is not another isolated English virtue?"

"*Deus aie,*" Stephen swore. "Hafwynder nearly went berserk when he heard three words of Norman French. Even if I wanted to overrule my uncle, how could I possibly bring your lord father to Torworden?"

"Then leave us alone. We're safe enough here. We'll care for our father and see that the crops are put in—"

"I warned you," Thorkel cut in. "There's no talking to an Englishwoman when her mind's made up. Just put them in a cart and take them away—if you think your French fortress is ready."

Stephen gave the Viking a dark look. "Wildecent, please, you're only making matters worse for all of us. No one wants to take you away from Hafwynder Manor against your will—"

"You just want us to change our minds, to set aside everything to become Norman hostages?"

"No one mentioned hostages," Ambrose said mildly.

"No one needed to," Thorkel said.

A faint ruddiness stained Stephen's cheeks, and Wildecent wondered if Thorkel Longsword had the truth of it. But Longsword was a risky ally. He followed his own path and let no one walk beside him, not even those to whom he'd given his oath. Regardless of Alison's dire dreams, there was no small risk in leaving the crippled nobleman in Longsword's care.

Stephen caught her staring at him; she lowered her eyes and waited for one of the others to speak. If her few childhood memories were right, she was already a hostage of sorts sent to England by people who were long forgotten for purposes no one here had ever known.

Stephen cleared his throat and turned to his companions. They spoke in rapid French, shutting out the Viking and Wildecent. Longsword did not seem to care, but Wildecent, hearing her name spoken several times, resolved to learn Norman French as quickly as possible.

Finally Stephen addressed her in the competent English he'd acquired courtesy of Alison's intrusions into his private thoughts. "I have decided to leave Alan FitzAlan, Serlo, and Gauche-Robert here. Alan will guard your father; Serlo and Gauche-Robert will ride with the baggage train. You and your sister, though, will leave with us tomorrow after breakfast—I trust that gives you enough time?"

Wildecent blanched. "Your offer is most generous, but there is so much to do. I just do not see how we can be ready in less than a fortnight," she began, and watched Stephen's face shift from hopeful to angry. "Three generations of Hafwynders have lived here," she explained. "And a dozen families dwell in our cottages and use our oxen. Even if we could sort through everything here in a single day—which we cannot do—there's much of value beyond the hall . . ."

Stephen glanced at FitzAlan. The taciturn man shrugged, then nodded. "I do not think my uncle meant to strip the manor bare. He needs to protect at Torworden only those things likely to tempt an honest man. It does not matter if the baggage is delayed until the oxcarts can be brought here. If you will show Alan FitzAlan that property which should be loaded, he will see to the details."

Wearily, Wildecent conceded defeat. These men would

not lose sight of their goal. She and Alison were going to leave their home in less than one day; there was nothing to be done about it. "I will show your man through the storerooms—"

"Don't forget the cook," Ambrose interjected.

"Yes, and we're to bring your cook. There's no cook at Torworden to compare with yours. My uncle would have her prepare our food for your pleasure and his."

Wildecent nearly lost her balance from surprise. Bethanil was a freewoman, not a chattel to be bartered back and forth between manors. "I cannot command Bethanil to go to Torworden. Her family is here. She has every right to remain here whether we stay or not. She's a freeborn woman with property of her own."

"I'm sure Lord Beauleyas will pay her a good wage, enough to house her family in the village," Ambrose suggested. "Explain to her how much he liked the food she prepared and the order of her kitchen. Perhaps she'll be flattered and agree to come of her own accord."

Wildecent envisioned how Bethanil would react to the proposal that she trek halfway across England to cook for a foreigner. She was so caught up imagining Bethanil's indignation that she paid no attention to Stephen's final words and found herself standing alone with FitzAlan before she had properly collected her thoughts.

"We must go to the kitchen first," she informed him, and led the way from the hall.

She paused at the door. Bethanil was scolding an unfortunate drudge who'd dropped an egg.

"Perhaps if I waited in the hall?" FitzAlan suggested.

"Perhaps you should," Wildecent agreed. She watched him go, but then, instead of confronting the angry cook, she headed for the back of the manor yard where byres sprang haphazardly between the great hall and the stockade.

Alison had Godfrey sitting in the sun and was carefully combing sleep-tangles from his hair.

"Did they relent?" Alison asked without looking up from her tasks.

"Did you expect them to?"

"I . . . I had hoped Stephen might see things differently this morning."

An honest hope, or had her sister been, despite her previous disasters, trying to influence the young man's thoughts again?

"He did, a bit. He did say we could ride rather than travel in the carts. So that's something. But, other side of the coin, he insists there's no need to wait until the carts are back. He's leaving three men behind; they'll oversee the loading of the baggage and protect our lord father until we can make our appeal to Lord Beauleyas. And we're to bring Bethanil, if she'll come. They said Jean Beauleyas will offer her enough wages for her family to have a house in the village."

But Alison, for once, was thinking more deeply than her sister. "A house in the village? What sort of place are we going to, where the cook's family lives someplace else?"

She smoothed her father's cornsilk hair until it concealed all traces of the still-ragged scar above his ear. There was some truth in Thorkel's accusations. In health, Godfrey had never been overfastidious about his appearance. His comfort had mattered more than his cleanliness, though he seemed not to mind the constant attention his daughters now focused on him. If he even knew they were his daughters. He smiled when Alison called him Father, but he didn't say her name; he hadn't said anyone's name since his injury.

The little boy who sat in the dirt at Godfrey's feet, caring for his body's needs and such minimal wants as he still had, took up his post. Godfrey smiled again and patted the lad on his tawny head.

"Do you have treasures?"

The boy dug deep into the pouch slung inside his braes and produced the crushed remnants of a bird's egg.

49

"Oh, treasures indeed!"

Alison spun around. "He won't even know when we're gone," she said in a tight, husky voice.

Wildecent laid her arm around her sister's waist, but Alison stepped free, shaking her head as her shoulders hunched forward.

"I'll be in the gallery with FitzAlan, the man Stephen's left as overseer," Wildecent said softly. "When you're ready."

She felt the pain of Godfrey Hafwynder's decline differently than Alison did. Indeed, though she would not admit it aloud, Wildecent thought Longsword might be right. Almighty God had simply forgotten to gather Lord Godfrey Hafwynder into his arms. The arcane arts—Ambrose's sorcery and Ygurna's magic—had made the divine oversight possible. No wonder the Church stood against the arcane in every form, decreeing there was no difference between sorcery and the magic so carefully preserved beneath the manor's weaving room.

The Church was many things in eleventh-century England—and none of them all-powerful. Some clerics said that Joseph of Arimathaea had fled to Britain with the Holy Grail in the first century; certainly the Irish had brought Christianity to the Saxons not long after they'd conquered the Cymry. There were Frenchmen who preached that the English church, having fallen away from Rome and into the influence of the Irish, was scarcely better than no church at all. At Hafwynder Manor they kept a chapel a half-day's journey to the north and kept the rest of religion further away than that.

Wildecent pulled her thoughts back to the problem at hand and headed to the hall, where FitzAlan was mending his boots. He bit off the thread and followed her up the stairs. The first of the storerooms she unlocked was filled with bolts of cloth, boots, and other articles of clothing. A lord had a responsibility to keep his men fed, housed, and clothed. Most of the housecarls had already been summoned by King Harold but, in Wildecent's mind at least, so long as there was a Hafwynder Manor this particular room should remain untouched.

"These remain as they are," she said slowly and clearly.

FitzAlan shrugged. "It's gold and the like we're interested in, my lady, not your house goods."

No wonder the Normans expected the women could pack their valuables in an afternoon. Hafwynder Manor was comfortable and secure but hardly one of England's great estates. Many of its treasures were sentimental rather than valuable. So she led him to the one room where such treasures as had been given to Godfrey and his ancestors by *their* lords and masters were stored.

The door had just swung open when Alison ran up the stairs to join them. "You'll take him into our treasure room?" she demanded.

Wildecent was stung by her sister's accusatory tone. "I don't think I have a choice. It's our gold they want—"

Alison stood between FitzAlan and the door. "You'll have what remains of our king's gift. And you'll trust us to prepare it for you."

The Norman was accustomed to taking orders. He gave one of his many shrugs. "As you wish, my lady. Set the coffers before the door." He turned and disappeared down the stairs.

"He'll be in here the moment we're gone," Wildecent objected once they were alone.

"I'm not leaving them with the keys."

The women had the keys to every casket and coffer, but neither of them had had the time to learn what each box contained. There were some secrets their aunt had never shared. They knew what was in the coin chest—or, more properly, what wasn't in it since Harold's men had extorted an extra levy—but there were another half-dozen chests piled beside it.

"I'd like to take it all and bury it in the forest," Alison complained. "If this doesn't belong to us, then it should belong to our English king, not to some French bastard.

But we owe Torworden for Christmastide, and it will go hard for our people if anything comes away missing.''

It was barely midday when they arranged a stack of heavy boxes outside the storeroom door. Alison removed a key from her ring and handed it to FitzAlan. ''You may place the treasure in the weaving room.''

FitzAlan's eyes never left the keys she did not give to him, but he said nothing. The locks could be broken once the women were gone. ''As you wish, my lady,'' he told Alison as he strung the key on a thong of his belt-pouch.

Then it was time to face Bethanil, who reacted to the Norman proposal much as Wildecent had imagined she would.

''Wages,'' she sputtered. ''Wages as if I were some forsaken day laborer with nothing to call my own? See Godeshalt groveling for work in some muddy dunghill village? See my children run off with ne'er-do-wells and Frenchmen?'' Her cleaver slammed through a half-dozen leeks, then swept the pieces into the stewpot. ''I'll ride with the baggage carts,'' she told them as she lined up another handful of leeks. ''I'll do that for Lady Ygurna, for her soul's rest, and I'll talk to your French lord, and maybe I'll take up his kitchen for him. But my family stays here on Hafwynder land—you tell him that for me.''

''I can't wait to see the look on his face when we do,'' Alison whispered as they left.

CHAPTER SIX

y late afternoon the sisters had done all that could not be entrusted to lesser hands. There was nothing left to do but wait. They watched as journey-bread was baked, and took careful note of the way the setting sun lit the great hall's thatched roof. Their melancholy became contagious, infecting all who gathered for the meal. There was neither singing nor boasting from either the English or the French. The eels were consumed in gloomy silence.

Only the kitchens and the byres, where the manorfolk dwelt with their families, produced laughter that night. But, then, lives were not changing dramatically in those places. The valley was fertile; it would always attract a protector, and a protector always needed common men to do common work. Benign master or harsh, their lives changed little so long as the land grew green each spring.

"We leave at sunrise," Stephen said in a low voice that nonetheless carried through the hall. "Everyone should get some sleep."

Benches and stools scraped through the rushes as men rose with the same lethargy that had marked the entire meal. Englishmen shuffled forward to say their flat good-byes to Alison and her sister. They had endured enough already, and saw too much more on the horizon, to let emotion creep into their farewells. Alison mumbled the right responses, but she, too, was numb—wishing that it were over, that it was next spring and all this a fading memory.

The young women left the hall and carried a torch across the garden to the door that led to their bedroom tower and the kitchens. Wildecent held it open, but Alison shook her head.

"I want to be alone, I think," she said. "I'm too tired to sleep. I'll just go sit someplace."

Wildecent nodded and watched as her sister headed toward the stream. She felt tired enough to sleep forever. But her drowsiness vanished once the upper door was closed and the candlelight flickered over the compact bundles they had made of their belongings.

The bed was unchanged, the aroma of sweet grass and their perfumes still hung in the air, but the room was no longer theirs. Wildecent draped her riding cloak over her shoulders and closed the door. Her first thought was to join Alison. But Alison wanted to be alone, and she herself had nothing in particular to say. The dark-haired woman wandered among the byres instead.

Standing outside Lord Godfrey's quiet byre, Wildecent thought she could hear him snoring. Alison had cried when they brought a dinner tray to him. She'd gotten down on her knees and begged him to say her name—all to no avail. Wildecent had hung back then, as she did now. She remembered no father but Godfrey Hafwynder, yet she felt very little pain on leaving him.

Her memories of a life before Hafwynder Manor were dreamlike paintings without life or movement. The strangers, her true mother and father, who wandered though her past meant less to her than the heroes of the sagas they sang in the great hall. Her parents had abandoned her, anyway; she owed them nothing. Yet the knowledge that she had been cast adrift once before worked to cut her free again. She felt nothing for her lost past; she would not let herself feel anything for the present.

Wildecent was appalled by her own coldness. She summoned despair, hoping to turned the emptiness into grief. She summoned pleasant memories and ruthlessly reminded herself of what she was losing, of the unknown she faced.

You won't find any place better than this. You've had love here, and comfort. Without Lord Hafwynder, you're nothing. A bastard, an orphan; no fortune, no name. And manorfolk won't take you in. You're not one of them: your hands are clean. They'll cast you out, and you'll die along the road some-

place and go to an unhallowed grave. Wildecent's stomach finally tightened. The sadness of every bleak moment hardened into an iron knot. She'd created her own nightmare, and suddenly she no longer wanted to be alone.

Moonlight guided her to the soft banks of the stream. It ran swift with snow-melt. An unsuspecting person could be swept away; a despairing young woman could disappear forever. Alison's footprints descended to the water's edge—and then moved on. Wildecent followed the trail until it vanished in the straw-covered dirt by the animal byres. She searched each one, convinced that only by sharing her sister's grief could she bear the internal pain she had so foolishly called into being.

The weaving solar was empty, the bolt-hole just as they'd left it the night before. Nor had Alison returned to their bedroom. The great hall leaked the sounds of men sleeping or talking in low, uncatchable voices. Holding her breath until it hurt, Wildecent stole along the back wall and up the stairs into the gallery. But the storerooms were locked and silent, as they should be. She went back to Godfrey's byre and opened the door far enough to see that Alison was not there; then she went to the pens where the weakest lambs and ewes were kept.

Wildecent was on her way out of the manor, to Lady Ygurna's grave—the only remaining place she could imagine Alison visiting on her last night at Hafwynder Manor—when she saw a flash of light from the ruins of the old hall.

The old hall had burned down in Godfrey's youth—a not uncommon fate for wooden buildings that sheltered large, unvented hearths. Most everything salvageable had been removed long ago. Only the mews were there now, far from the distractions of the manor. It was just possible that Alison had gone to see her hawk.

And while Wildecent was ready to go beyond the stockade in search of her sister, she was grateful to have somewhere else to look inside the walls. She was rewarded and stunned in the same heartbeat. Alison was in the mews, but not alone and certainly not grieving.

"There is more to this world than one manor," Stephen was staying. "I want to show it to you. I want you to be with me, at my side, just the two of us, forever."

Wildecent leaned against the old, flaking timbers, unable to approach them or to leave.

"I love you." He took her hand between his own and brought it to his lips. "You're everywhere—in my dreams and memories. It's as if I've always known you—or wanted to know you."

Alison shivered, and he held her tighter. She could no more undo what she had done than return a plant to its seed. She was sure of his love, but she would never know if it had been given freely.

Stephen was hardly the man her father would have chosen for her—or one she would have accepted just a few short months before. He was aggressive; he sang love ballads that made her ears turn red, and he kept close friendship with a sorcerer. At the same time, Stephen had fire and strength. He made her feel alive and her skin tingled when he touched her. Alison did not intend to set him free. She would not risk losing him—or angering the gods she and her aunt had awakened at midwinter. But she was not ready to surrender to him, either.

"It's too soon," she hedged. "I could love you, maybe I do love you, but now everything is turned upside down. I do not want to make a promise I might regret." She was honest, at least, and keeping an unusually short rein on her need to *make* him understand.

"That will be soon enough for me." He brought her hand to his lips again, then dared to clutch her tighter. "I can wait to show you the world," he said after he'd kissed her.

"I do not want to see the world," Alison insisted. His ardor unnerved her. "I've never wanted anything more than this manor. I . . . I'm my father's only living child. I'm his heiress. He raised me to love this valley.''

"My father's lands were in a valley, too. The hills were golden, the flowers sweet, and the summer never ended.''

Alison shook her head. She had seen those landscapes when she'd invaded his mind and rashly scattered her image across his fantasies. His pulse throbbed against her fingers; she wondered if she could ride its rhythm back into his thoughts. She had replaced his other women, she could replace those golden hills with England's misty greens. It would be very easy to do.

She realized that she touched his mind in just such a way while she dreamed. The *geas* lifted for a moment and she saw Stephen lying in a spring green field. Dead. Then the *geas* closed. Alison could still feel his pulse and, though her talents ached to be set free, she pulled her hand away.

"You can't understand, Stephen. I have obligations you cannot begin to imagine.'' She shivered. *Obligations I do not want to imagine*.

Alison thought she saw her aunt's ghost hovering in nearby moonlight. She begged for forgiveness, strength, and understanding, never guessing that she sent her appeal to Wildecent's shadow.

"I understand more than you imagine,'' Stephen protested. "I have been Ambrose's friend for many years. I've seen the sacrifices that sorcery can demand.'' He felt her shudder in his arms and, misunderstanding her reasons, pulled her tightly against his chest. "I know him to be a good man,'' he reassured her, "for all that he willingly travels a path where weaker men might be damned. Surely you are no less than he is.''

Wildecent watched her sister slowly relax in Stephen's arms. When they kissed, the dark-haired girl felt a tear slip down her cheek. She rejoiced that Alison had found, by whatever means, that most precious of all things: a man who would cherish her. At the same time the core of despair she had brought to the ruins throbbed larger with each beat of her heart.

She knew she should turn away—each moment she remained made the agony worse—yet she could not leave. Every gesture Stephen made was burned into her memory. Only when he released Alison and they began to speak too softly for her to overhear was she able to wrench herself away. Wildecent leaned against the charred doorway, clutching her stomach, reliving what she had seen.

"Were you truly surprised?"

Wildecent jumped upright. Her hand went to her sleeve, where her knife rested in an embroidered sheath. It sounded like the sorcerer, but she could not locate him in the darkness.

"Lovebirds among the hawks; appropriate, don't you think?"

"Ambrose?" She peered into the deep shadows, cursing the darkness. "Ambrose, is that you?"

"It seems we were both wondering where our friends had gone." A hand wrapped over her arm, urging her further from the doorway. She followed her arm and marveled that he moved so quietly.

"Do you understand what your sister has done?"

Her body moved through indecision: nodding, shaking, and shrugging, all of which he felt rather than saw. "It's her life," she whispered. They had stopped. She could see his silhouette against the moonlight but no detail of his face.

"Then you don't understand. You don't know what is going to happen. Stephen is not free."

That, somehow, brought Wildecent back to one mind and one place. She snapped her arm downward; he wasn't expecting a move and she broke free. "If he's not, then she was right to interfere. Alison might act before she thinks, but she didn't act with malice."

"Well put—but not what I had in mind. Stephen isn't free to marry her; that's all. He cannot make Hafwynder Manor secure for either of you. He hasn't told you about

Eudo; he hasn't told you much about Torworden at all, has he?"

"He doesn't talk to *me*, anyway."

Ambrose overlooked the irritation in her voice. "My young friend has lost his patrimony in France. He came to his uncle with no more than the clothes on his back, his weapons, his horse, and me . . . and now I serve Jean Beauleyas and not Stephen. He needs his uncle's support if he's to try to regain his lands; in turn he must support William the Bastard's designs here, because that's one of the conditions Beauleyas put before him. The other is more subtle. Beauleyas never got children from his wives—he got a bastard, though, Eudo, and Eudo's none too pleased to have distant kin throwing a shadow over his dubious rights.

"Beauleyas's a canny old wolf. He's never made his will known. He won't split what he's got to give; he'll wait to see who survives to claim it."

"He can't mean that," Wildecent protested. The memory of the Norman's scarred grin played in her mind and she knew the old warrior could do that, and more, if it pleased him.

"Eudo thinks he does—and that's really all that matters. Whatever other little games you, your sister, and your aunt might have played, whatever you think of me—and I have never compromised Stephen as your sister has—you should know that Eudo's cunning, and I'd not wager against him. And tell your sister as well that we may yet have to run for France with our tails dragging—and no room for a woman."

Wildecent swallowed hard. The more she heard of Torworden the less she looked forward to being there. "We'd be better off here," she muttered. "You'd be better off here."

"Stephen won't hide behind a woman—and woe betide the woman if he did."

"Why are you telling me this?"

"Because you're sensible and I hope you can talk your

sister into releasing Stephen before it's too late for both of them."

A nervous laugh made its way through Wildecent's clenched teeth. "There's much *you* don't understand. I've told you we're not sisters, and I can only convince Alison to do something she already wants to do. Besides, she couldn't release Stephen now if she wanted to."

She heard him shift his weight from one foot to the other and imagined chagrin settling on his face. Still, she expected him to say something, if only because she believed his willful sorcery to be the equal of Alison's wild magic. When the silence lengthened she grew uncomfortable.

"Is it that bad? I know Alison, and I know that it's gotten beyond her somehow. She hasn't been herself since . . . that day. I don't think she can control her magic anymore. Can't you do something? It never really was Alison's fault. She'd never put someone in danger like that."

"Especially herself, you mean? And yes, it's that bad. I'd been trying to convince him to return to France before he took that accursed message for Pevensey." The confidence had faded from Ambrose's voice, replaced by a frustration Wildecent could well understand. "We should have taken our chances in Sicily."

"Does he know you care this much for him?"

"Does he know—yes. Does it matter—no, or worse than no. He thinks he can beat Eudo in a fair fight—or an unfair one, if it comes to that—and he does not think it at all strange to find his every dream absorbed by the woman he loves. He knows how I feel, and dismisses my fears out of hand."

His last words could have been her own and so, when Wildecent answered, she spoke as much to herself as to Ambrose. "Eventually you have to decide—choose—whether you follow them wherever they go or whether you run."

The moon had risen further, casting faint light into their cul-de-sac. Wildecent watched him plunge into his own thoughts, staring and measuring. But he was no more surprised by her words than she had been.

She was like Thorkel Longsword, with no sense of place in the world, no roots. Only a sister's friendship with Alison. Would she stay beside Alison, quiet and patient, now that she was no longer needed, hoping that someday her situation might improve? Did she cut loose and look for another English noble to befriend her? Or was that impossible as well? Was it the convent or life in Alison's shadow?

"It's late. I'm going back to the tower," she said.

"Let me escort you through the dark."

It was brighter now than it had been when she'd picked her way across the manor yard to the ruins. And she had half a mind to tell him that—or just less than half a mind, for she allowed his hand to slide under her arm. In fact, everything seemed divided into equal or nearly equal parts, so that her own decisions were random and surprising, even to her.

"What will you do?" Ambrose asked midway to the tower.

The choices hovered in her mind, none better than the other. But they were all influenced by the feel of sinewy strength beneath her sleeve. "I don't know," she replied, and heard an unwelcome plaintive note in her voice.

"You could learn to take care of yourself."

Sorcery. She could take care of herself with sorcery—if she dared to ask. Wildecent clamped her mouth shut, determined to keep her turmoil strictly to herself. Ambrose sensed something, maybe the sudden tensing of the arm he supported or maybe something else, and brought them to a stop, face to face.

"I could teach you what you'd need to know."

"Why?"

"Do I need a reason?"

A thrill of danger shot down Wildecent's spine. "I will," she whispered, and ran from him across the yard to the safety of the tower.

ildecent was asleep when Alison finally returned. She closed the door quietly and envied her sister's peaceful breathing, confident that she herself would lie awake until dawn, remembering what had—and what had not—happened in the mews. But sleep came quickly to Alison as well, and she was untroubled by nightmares. They were both resting easily when Thorkel Longsword put his fist against their door.

"Be time you were awake and eating!" the Viking shouted.

Alison rubbed her eyes and gave Wildecent a poke in the ribs. The tower room was dark as night, without the least hint of dawn in the shutter cracks. She stubbed her toe getting out of the bed, then barked her shin against the clothes chest while groping for the lamp. All in all, not the best way to start off what she firmly believed would be one of the worst days of her life.

"It's not even morning yet," her sister complained, eyes watering in the dim light from the oil-lamp.

"You'll get no sympathy from me," Alison replied in a voice that invited none in return.

Wildecent rubbed her eyes and walked slowly into the garderobe. She stared at the heavy wool of her hose as if she'd never seen it before, and needed several tries to get one cloth bound smoothly against her leg. The thought of dealing with the other strip overwhelmed her, and she sat with it draped over her calf.

By then Alison was washed and nearly dressed.

"They aren't going to leave without us," the wide-awake sister snapped. "You'll just annoy them—so hurry up!"

"I'm doing the best I can."

"Will you want anything for breakfast?"

"Anything warm."

Alison was gone, and Wildecent tackled the remainder

of her clothes. She was still yawning when she reached the bottom of the kitchen stairs.

"She's gone to see the horses," Bethanil informed her. "There's gruel on the sideboard."

Wildecent gripped the wooden mug with both hands and took a noisy sip of the steaming liquid.

"You're welcome, my lady," Bethanil grumbled.

"I'm not awake."

"You're lucky to be going off with the Normans and not to a convent!"

Wildecent shrugged and, cup in hand, left the warm kitchen for the stables. Daylight was a pale gray band along the eastern horizon; the hens and roosters were still sleeping. The stables, however, were busy, as riding horses were saddled and pack animals loaded. She scratched the forehead of her own little brown mare and gazed into eyes nearly as befuddled as her own.

"Didn't you bring our bundles down?" Alison asked as she led her mare down the aisle.

"I don't remember you asking me to."

"I didn't think I'd have to *ask.*"

Muttering to herself, Wildecent trudged back to their bedroom. She shouldered as many of the waterproof sacks as she could and went back to the stable.

Wildecent was almost alert when the traveling party gathered in the yard. Five tall Norman horses, including Sulwyn, who hadn't been ridden for months and who fought Stephen's every command, overshadowed an equal number of English ponies. Two squires, one a Norman lad, the other a towheaded English boy, would ride atop pack animals while Eodred, the hawkmaster, rode a mule and carried two hooded birds on a roost that fitted against his saddle.

Eodred's presence was a surprise to Wildecent, though remembering where Alison and Stephen had spent the evening, she guessed she knew what had happened. At least they were bringing her bird as well.

Most of the manor turned out to say good-bye, save,

of course, Lord Godfrey himself, who had not yet shrugged off his sleeping draught. The Norman party had been split apart as Stephen promised, with three men remaining behind. Those three—Alan FitzAlan, Serlo, and Gauche-Robert—embraced their departing comrades with a fervor more often found in the final hours of a hopeless siege.

Both women put on brave faces as they departed the manor—which was expected of them. The facades crumbled the moment the familiar stockade was lost to sight. To his credit, Stephen tried—without notable success—to cheer his charges. He sang verses from the sunny lands of Aquitania, but their meaning was lost to everyone but Ambrose, who seemed immune to their humor this morning. Stephen's efforts were further hampered by the need to control his froth-flecked horse.

"You should have left him behind," Ambrose shouted after he had pulled his own horse beyond the reach of the chestnut's teeth.

"He'll settle down," Stephen insisted as he shortened the reins.

Ambrose muttered something about stallions, mares, and springtime, then dropped back to leave Stephen and his fractious horse in isolation at the head of their party. Stephen considered the entire situation with a stream of curses in a half-dozen dialects. He had recovered from the arrow wound, but his shoulder ached from the task of keeping Sulwyn on the muddy track. Had it been possible he would have preferred the placid gelding he'd ridden from Torworden to the manor, but he had secured Beauleyas's permission to lead the group because of his horse, not the heiresses, and he did not dare return without them all firmly under control.

He braced the reins between his left hand and the pommel, and rubbed his sore shoulder. Sulwyn felt the change in pressure and balance. The stallion clamped down on the bit and bolted away from the track. All eyes turned toward Ambrose.

"Leave him go," the sorcerer said. "He won't go too far—I hope."

Hugh and Guy, both veterans in Beauleyas's service, were as skittish as Sulwyn when it came to taking Ambrose's orders, but in this case they stood down. The group drew closer together without Sulwyn's disrupting presence and moved more quickly to the junction of Hafwynder's track with the ancient Icknield Way.

Stephen returned after midday while they rested the horses and ate from the provisions Bethanil had prepared. His tunic was muddied from shoulder to hip, and Sulwyn's bright coat was dull with sweat, but man and beast seemed to have reached a truce. They were winded, though, and Sulwyn needed to cool down before he could eat any of the grain they carried. It was well into the afternoon before they were remounted and continued west.

Foreigners were not generally welcome in England, and the Normans were the least welcome of all. The men of Torworden lived off the land when they traveled, making camp in the abundant ruins that dotted the countryside or taking refuge with those few of their countrymen who had survived a general purging of French influence some twenty years earlier.

They could hardly expect the young women to share their primitive camps. More civilized accommodations needed to be found on this journey. Alison suggested several of their neighboring peers but the Torwordeners, to a man, rejected guesting with the native aristocracy. The choice was narrowed to those freeholdings and inns that might, for a price, provide a night's rest for strangers.

"There should be a path to a freehold not far beyond the bridge," Alison assured them as the late afternoon sun shone into their eyes. "Our lord father stayed there."

Wildecent glanced sideways at her sister. "Not when he could help it, he didn't," she hissed.

Alison shrugged, and guided her mare behind the others as they headed down the spur.

CONQUEST

The freehold might have been a pleasant manor a long time ago. Now it was a sullen place whose pointed-timber palisade was its most noteworthy feature. The yard within was a sea of mud—complete with pig wallows—and the hall itself was dilapidated, with a dozen or more alcoves sprouting out beneath its eaves.

Except for the animals, the place seemed deserted; no one responded to a shouted summons. The two squires were dispatched to rouse the innkeeper. The boys sank into the foul-smelling muck. No one came forth to open the doors, and for a moment Wildecent thought they might be reprieved. Sleeping in her cloak could only be better than venturing inside this place.

Then the doors were pushed open and a balding, filthy villein stepped out. He gave them a looking-over and was less than enthusiastic about having Frenchmen and their women under his roof. But, he explained, it was early in the traveling season, so he reckoned they could settle in two of his alcoves.

"If you've got coin enough," he added.

"We'll give you your coin," one of the Norman men-at-arms snarled, rattling the chain fittings of his scabbard. "Right down—"

"We'll give you your coins," Stephen interrupted. Among his uncle's army orders was an admonition to keep the peace and give the natives no cause to hate the Normans more than they already did.

It was just as well Stephen had a full coin purse riding next to his thigh. The night's lodgings and food were expensive—doubly so because the owner accepted coins only and nothing in trade. Or nothing in trade from Frenchmen.

The squires were directed to the stables, a line of open stalls whose timbers had withstood at least one sizeable fire. Alison and her sister were helped from their horses and escorted into the hall. There was no threshold, so the mud continued some three paces into the dark and fetid room. Wildecent fought a surge of panic as the doors swung shut behind them.

"We'll die here," she whispered to her sister.

"Well, we won't eat anything—that's for certain."

Once he had his coins—and perhaps because he'd seen how many more there were—the villein insisted they sit at the table nearest the pit-hearth and sang the praises of his goodwife's cooking and beer. And though the English would have preferred a simple request of bread and cheese, the Normans, who were paying for the feast, called forth the best the kitchen could provide.

While Alison searched her trencher for bits of unspoiled meat, Wildecent contented herself with chunks of bread soaked in the flat, bitter beer. Even at the end of winter the lowliest drudges and slaves ate better at Hafwynder Manor—or at least they knew what they were eating. It was this uncertainty that kept the Hafwynder folk cautious when another bowl of the greasy brown stew was placed on their table. None of them had ever eaten at a table that did not belong to Lord Godfrey or one of his peers in the shire. Not so the Normans.

"Stephen did say they wanted us to bring Bethanil," Alison mused as she and Wildecent watched him grab a gristly wad of meat from the common bowl. It was not his table manners that distressed her—they all brought their own knives to the table and got their food from the common dishes to their own trenchers as best they could—but his gusto eating a meal that turned her stomach.

"And if they don't have their own cook, perhaps they're not used to better," Wildecent added without much conviction.

Only Ambrose displayed any reluctance to take a third helping of the stew the slovenly drudge brought from the unseen kitchen. Alison was grateful when he called for cheese and received a creamy wedge that surely had been cured somewhere else.

"Here, take as much as you want," he offered when

he noticed how little they'd eaten. "I thought you said you'd traveled this way with your lord father?"

"We traveled from one manor to the next, never on the tracks and never staying in freeholds," Alison admitted.

He pushed the rest of the cheese between them. "Eat it all. It's apt to get worse before it gets better."

Which it did, and sooner rather than later. Once the meal was over they were shown to the alcoves where they were expected to sleep. The mud shifted beneath the rush-covered planks when they entered the cramped chamber. Alison's hair brushed against the steep roof, and the beds were little more than straw heaped in a corner. The doors had no locks and there were, of course, no windows. The men generously agreed that the sisters would have one alcove to themselves and that two of them would sleep on stools propped against the closed door. They seemed quite satisfied by the arrangement, which kept two of them away from the filthy straw. Neither Alison nor Wildecent could say the same.

"I can see it moving," Wildecent murmured after the door was shut.

Alison took the tallow-lamp from her sister's trembling hand and held it closer to the straw. "Not quite."

"I can't sleep there. Oh, Lord God Almighty, the angels and the saints—why is this happening to us?"

"Lady Ygurna would know what to do."

"Our lady aunt would never *be* in this position, Alison. No one would have dared to move her off the manor."

"That's not what I meant. She'd know what to do about the fleas and whatever else is in that straw."

"She'd burn it—and this whole place around it," Wildecent said with a faint, bitter laugh.

Alison paused and chuckled herself. "She might," she agreed. "She'd get that kitchen into shape, she or Bethanil herself. But what I was thinking of is—"

"Left behind at Hafwynder Manor waiting for the oxcarts, Alison. There's nothing we can do."

"I could try, Wili."

"The last time you *tried* something, as I recall, we found ourselves in a worse way than we'd been before."

Alison made a grim face and set the sputtering lamp on a crude shelf. "I don't deny it, but I've been feeling, well, different—better—since we left the valley." She held up a hand to cut off Wildecent's rejoinder. "No, even you know what it's been like—as if there were something in the air, something more than our lady aunt's death or our lord father. I've seen it in your face."

Grudgingly, Wildecent agreed that leaving Hafwynder Manor had not been as hard as she'd expected it would be. She was homesick and heartsick, but those emotions were directed toward a home that had ceased to exist after Christmastide. The gray depression of the last three months was already fading.

"I don't feel a heaviness inside me anymore," Alison continued. "It's as if—well, you wouldn't understand, but I think I could make those bugs *want* to go someplace else."

But Wildecent did understand, though she was not reassured. "I'd still rather you didn't try," she said after a long sigh. "Not with everything packed away. I don't want to think of what would happen if something went wrong . . ."

"No, Wili, it'd be just like leaning on anyone else, just a little push. There's no danger," Alison replied in her firmest voice, though she was well aware that what she had in mind was like nothing she'd ever tried before. There was no sense of mind, or even identity—as there would be in a horse, cat, or cow—swarming through the straw. Instead the bed radiated a more primitive sense of life. Alison imagined a wall the vermin would not care to breach and was eager to create it.

Lady Ygurna would have done it differently: through pungent herbs and incense. She and Wildecent would have been as irritated by the aroma as the fleas and lice. This would be so much more effective, easier, and quicker. She rubbed her hands together then extended them, palms downward, over the straw. She closed her eyes and erected the first course of her wall.

Her flesh began to tingle as the mental energies were channeled out of her body. There was warmth at her fingertips, then nothing, as her wrists were forced apart and down to her sides. Alison opened her eyes and glared at her sister.

"No," Wildecent commanded. "It's not right for you, Alison. It's not *natural.*"

Alison's indignation emerged slowly from her magic-tinged relaxation. "What do you mean: not natural? Everything I do is *natural.*" She saw the questions in her sister's troubled eyes. "Just because our lady aunt couldn't do something doesn't mean that it's sorcery, Wili. I can do things she couldn't do, but it's just what's inside me—nothing more or less."

Wildecent felt her sister pushing at her mind, emphasizing with her very unnatural abilities just how natural and ordinary she truly was—and, especially, how her power was untainted by sorcery. For a moment Wildecent grasped the opposite—the naturalness of sorcery shone against the wildness of Alison's emotional power. Then that notion became absurd; the insight vanished.

Her sister was innocent—a unicorn who savored peace, harmony, and purity for all that it was also the invincible champion of the forest.

"I only thought . . ." Wildecent mumbled, releasing her sister's wrists and shaking her head in an effort to remember just what she had been thinking.

"You meant well," Alison assured her. "From the outside it's easy to get confused. Trust me."

While Wildecent held the lamp and silently watched, Alison held her hands over the straw again. Nothing changed. There was no aura of light or rustling as the bugs abandoned the straw, only Alison's soft assurances that all had gone well.

And it had. Alison was satisfied that her magic was once again under her control. Wildecent had forgotten, for the moment, that there was any reason to suspect her sister's powers. They slept peacefully, spine against spine.

he sisters were more refreshed than their companions, none of whom had slept well. Each man, including Ambrose, displayed welts where he'd entertained the freehold wildlife. They slapped and complained their way through a cold breakfast. The young women began to hope that the living conditions at Torworden might be better than the food.

After breakfast they bought a wedge of cheese and some sausage that, like the cheese, had not been made at the freehold. Their horses were waiting in the yard, as eager to be gone from the place as their riders.

"We've enough food to ride straight north from here," Stephen said as he mounted and led the way through the gate. "Unless someone wants to try another inn?"

"Be needing to soak my head after this one," Hugh de Lessay said, agreeing with him.

"Your inns are better in France?" Alison asked.

"Better in Normandy."

Alison was disinclined to believe him, but not at all sorry they would be traveling cross-country. Compelling the vermin had given her new insight into the workings of her own talent. Among the English she understood the unspoken words connecting one thought image to the next. Most often she worked her private magic through subtle rearrangement of those silent words. She understood only a few words of French and was unable to manipulate the foreigner's thoughts unless, as she had done with Stephen, she actually descended within their memories. With the vermin, however, she'd simply forced her desires upon the outer world. She believed she could push Ambrose and Stephen apart in a similar way—but to do so she wanted the informality of an open-air camp. She looked back over her shoulder, smiling as she appraised Ambrose, and he, not knowing the source of her satisfaction, smiled back.

They continued along the Icknield Way. The track followed a natural ridge across the landscape and provided an easier course than any other they'd find until they cleared the Uffington Down. Men had been walking or riding along it since there had been men in England. Centuries of use, rather than Roman engineering, had determined its course through the forest.

Stephen had good cause to remember this portion of the Icknield. In December, wolves had attacked him not far from here, drawn by the blood frozen to his shoulder. It crossed his mind that it was too far between the Uffington chalk carving and Hafwynder Manor for an injured man to have traveled on a bitterly cold night; that he and Sulwyn should be nothing more than a jumble of mouldering bones. He remembered praying that night for sanctuary. He'd reached a sanctuary—and not the infested barn where he'd just passed an uncomfortable night—but he couldn't convince himself that God had heard his prayers. Ambrose and now Alison insisted they watched over and protected him. Stephen had always dismissed such words as utter nonsense; now he was less certain.

Anything arcane, even magic that might have saved his life, made Stephen uncomfortable. He forced himself to concentrate on the track instead. Trees grew thick beside the path; the upland downs, when he saw them, were still a wilted brown. Caught from the corner of his eyes, however, a green aura hovered above the grass, and the nearby trees shimmered red with swelling leafbuds. The promise of spring was a force that could be tasted and smelled.

It was a bit early for the itinerant tradesmen, pilgrims, and crafters to begin their seasonal journeys, yet they were not alone on the Icknield. Twice during the long morning they exchanged greetings with other travelers.

"Where'd they be going?" Guy asked after a man leading a string of heavily laden donkeys disappeared behind them.

CONQUEST

"To London," Alison replied, "and beyond to where King Harold's called out the *fyrd* to defend the land."

The Normans grunted and spoke quickly among themselves, reminding their English companions that William the Bastard, their liege-lord, considered himself the rightful king here. A collective chill fell over the party. Harold Godwinson was a popular man in these parts and had done the king's work after Edward had retreated into an admirable but impractical asceticism. Harold was the only Englishman with the strength to rule. The commonfolk and the nobility alike trusted him; they certainly perferred him to any foreigner.

Springtime's gentle beauty was deceptive. By the time the hillsides were green and dotted by sheep, the campaigning season would be upon them. The Normans, who had the most to gain, radiated satisfaction; the English were silent.

The track curved southward and the forest thinned. Finally it descended from the ridge crest and brought them out of the forest for their first view of the great white chalk carving above the village of Uffington.

"Know you who set it there?" the Norman squire asked his English companions.

"It's always been there," Alison replied.

"The old gods left it," Wildecent corrected, "like they left so many other things."

The foreigners mumbled among themselves. Normandy, like England, was cluttered with mysterious derelicts from another time, but ancient monuments seemed more plentiful here, and more powerful as well, as if whatever had erected them still claimed the land. Ambrose made a thoughtful study of the enigmatic figure as they left the track and set out across the downs.

On a clear day the graceful abstract carving could be seen at the far end of the downs, almost a day's journey away. Close by, it dominated the landscape, a presence that was felt even when it was deliberately, carefully, not observed.

"What's it supposed to be?" the Norman squire asked.

"A warning."

"The bones of one of them old gods."

"A sign to the gods and all else that this land *belonged* to those who sacrificed for it," Alison explained.

There were no end of notions among the party, English and Norman alike, but Eodred got their attention when he made his charges bate and rattle their bell-crusted jesses.

" 'Tis where Saint George fought the dragon," the hawkmaster claimed. "He rode his horse into the sky and struck his spear in the devil's one vulnerable place. 'Twas a mortal wound and brought them all to the ground, with only the saint said to survive. 'Tis clear for all to see. Yonder's the mount where the dragon's blood first fell." He pointed to the bald crest of a nearby drumlin. "There'll be nothing growing there 'til Doomsday."

He said he'd grown up in sight of the carving and that he'd learned the truth from the parish priest, who'd read it from a book. Everyone knew that truth resided in the chained books of church and monastery libraries, but the carving did not seem to mark a saint's victory over evil. No one disputed Eodred, and no one believed him, either.

Ambrose guided his horse between the sisters' ponies. "So do you think we see the bones of a dragon or a horse?" he asked lightheartedly, though neither woman was deceived by his tone.

"The dragon," said Wildecent.

"No, his horse, a unicorn horse," Alison averred. "It protects this place, even in death."

Ambrose made a show of studying the creature. It might easily be a dragon, since no one alive had ever seen a dragon and it did not at all resemble a horse. Yet if it were a diabolic dragon, then men should be wary, for there was beauty, grace, and power in it.

"Perhaps a bit of each—if they died together," he suggested.

CONQUEST

Both young women gave him a sidelong glance.

"You'd like that," Alison accused after a moment's consideration. "Everything all jumbled together so you couldn't tell one part from the other. Good from evil or right from wrong. That would suit you, wouldn't it?"

Ambrose replied with a smile that was no less enigmatic than the carving. "I shouldn't think I desire anything that you would not yourself desire."

Alison was spared from responding when Stephen shouted and slapped his heels against Sulwyn's flanks. "Let's see it up close," he called over his shoulder as the chestnut thundered toward the lower slopes of the down. Alison turned away from the sorcerer and followed Stephen, leaving Wildecent alone beside him.

All attention focused on her, as if she could do something about the pair's impulsiveness. Wildecent glanced around, and found herself looking into Ambrose's black eyes. He was smiling as if to ask, *Well, young lady, will you follow the lovebirds or remain here with me?*

Wildecent concentrated on the meandering of the reins through her fingers, and felt her stomach contract. Alison and Stephen didn't need her—wouldn't want her now that Stephen had reined Sulwyn to a walk beside Alison's nut brown pony. They wouldn't likely send her away, but she'd be intruding, and red embarrassment spread from her back up her neck. The question became, was it worse to be the third in a pair or to bask in the discomfort of Ambrose's smile? If Ambrose were simply a sorcerer the decision would have been easier to make or justify. But there was more than sorcery in his smile.

"Join your friends, if you wish," he said as she made up her mind to do just that. He kept his mount at a steady pace a half stride in front of hers.

"I shall," she replied, looking once again at her hands.

Godfrey Hafwynder had loved his pleasure. He loved to hunt and had never let his lack of sons deprive him of companionship when he did. His girls were accomplished riders, and though their mounts were small by continen-

tal standards they were as good as Wessex grass had ever
produced. Wildecent took the reins in both hands, urged
the pony into a pivoting rear, and escaped behind Ambrose's larger horse before anyone saw the scarlet blush
on her cheeks.

The smile faded from Ambrose's face as she set out
after the others. Her sable plaits flew free of her cloak,
and her skirts blew back to reveal more of her legs than
a man was accustomed to seeing by daylight.

"I expect we'll be going no farther today," he told the
rest of them, annoyed by the tightness in his throat.
"We'll set our line over there, in the lee of the dragon's
blood, where that finger of trees comes down from the
forest."

"Rather be well out of sight of that thing," Hugh
muttered.

Ambrose turned around in his saddle. "A God-fearing
man like you, Hugh, afraid of a relic of Saint George?"
he asked drily, and all objections ceased.

Magic of considerable power lingered in the area, and
Ambrose was of a mind to explore it. He left them to set
the camp as they wished—and to mutter what they
wished—while he set off up the bald knob where the dragon's blood had fallen. Yet the bare patch of ground,
once he reached it, held no fascination. Instead he stared
at Stephen and the women playing a game of blind-man's
bluff around the white beast's head.

Ambrose had never truly belonged anywhere or to anyone—not to the magi who had rescued him in Byzantium, nor to Stephen, nor certainly to Stephen's ruthless
and uncouth uncle, Jean Beauleyas. He was nearly Guy's
age but he looked younger. His education had been of
the mind; he'd never developed the deep chest and broad
shoulders of a warrior. And he'd never spent a season or
six campaigning, gathering the scars and fractures that
made a warrior old before his time. He was seven years
older than Stephen, and those years had given him an
armor of cynicism that, along with his sorcery, served him

well enough against a world that found endless reasons to distrust him.

If there was a place for Ambrose, it was within the Church. Saint George was a magus and warrior before he'd become a saint. A churchman's career didn't begin until he was thirty—when a militant nobleman was beginning to think of passing the burden along to his sons, if he had them. Some of the magi in Byzantium had been European churchmen making their way eastward in search of a more perfect wisdom than could be found in the remains of the Western Empire. On their advice Ambrose had taken a deacon's vows before entering France—he had credentials as a scribe or tutor, but no binding commitment to the Church.

He had ambition, and pursued it carefully throughout Stephen's adolescence. The south of France, the ancient province of Aquitania, was rich enough to spark many men's ambition. Too many men. It languished in anarchy while upstart northerners, calling themselves kings of France and dukes of Normandy, stumbled into undeserved ascendance.

"We belong in Poitou," Ambrose whispered to the unheeding figures in the distance. "In Anjou, Cahors—anywhere but here."

This last year, since they'd taken service with Stephen's uncle, had been a disaster for the sorcerer. Beauleyas had no lands of his own in the south. He had been eager to lend his late sister's offspring a hand—but once he'd gotten Stephen in his grip he was loath to release him. And Ambrose found his own ambitions were nebulous beside the endemic Norman lust for land, wealth, and prestige.

But worst of all was England itself. Someday Ambrose would return to Byzantium, he promised himself. He'd alert the magi to the uncharted power and mystery of this island. The first thing he'd say would be *Beware the women.* The men here were like men everywhere, but the women who held the island's magic used it in a way a man could neither understand nor defend against.

He wanted to get Stephen back to France, back to the time when their goals had been the same: the recovery of Stephen's patrimony and the judicious expansion of it.

But mostly I want to get myself away from here before it's too late.

And he was not watching Alison or Stephen as the prayerful thought rolled through his mind.

The sun still stood some distance above the downs when everyone returned to the camp. A fire had been started, a lean-to erected for the sisters, the horses hobbled and set to grazing on the brown grass. Everything seemed settled until one of the hawks bated and screamed on her perch, drawing everyone's attention.

Alison had pulled on a heavy leather gauntlet and coaxed the hooded bird onto her wrist. She carefully stroked its breast with her free hand. "Hooded all day with the fresh air in your nostrils," she murmured, and it calmed. She carried it back to the campfire. "Can we fly them before dark?" she asked Eodred.

The old Saxon shook his head, a bit dismayed that she would even ask to release the valuable bird in a strange place without fresh bloody meat to lure it back.

Stephen saw the old man's disappointment. "Well, we can at least scare up some game. We'll fly them in the morning."

He took a bow down from the crook of one of the trees and headed into the low brush. Though the bow was a secondary weapon for a nobleman, who expected to confront his enemies face to face, it was not one which he ignored. When he wasn't fighting or training to fight, a wellborn man hunted for food and pleasure. The grimaces spreading from man to man around the fire had nothing to do with the young man's ability, but reflected that this was the second time in a single day he'd gone off on his own.

"Like as not there's nothing in range," Ambrose called without effect to his friend's back.

CONQUEST

No one was surprised when Alison took her hawk back to its perch, then scampered after Stephen.

"That one'll be the doom of us," Hugh protested, and for once Ambrose was in complete agreement with him.

he travelers gathered around the fire were quiet and minus two of their party. Stephen hadn't returned; neither had Alison. The men, who had settled on rocks, saddles, and fallen logs, watching the stewpot as the sun set, doubted they were lost. Stephen hadn't been blind to the beautiful heiress pursuing him.

"It be the best way," Hugh affirmed to no one in particular. " 'Specially when they're willing."

"An' when they're not, as well," the Gascon replied with a sly laugh.

Wildecent shrank under the lean-to. The afternoon's blue skies were gone, replaced by low, menacing storm clouds. She wanted to insist that the men go out to search for her sister, but they would only laugh lewdly if she did, and she couldn't face that. Not when they had the truth of the situation.

Courtship, here and everywhere, was chiefly concerned with land or dynasty rather than any notion of affection. It was conducted, especially among the wellborn, by the eldest and most powerful men of the family; the least of those consulted was the intended bride.

In better times Alison might have looked forward to all the proper rituals and a goodly measure of influence over Lord Godfrey's final choice. Now, with her father incapacitated, no brothers to stand for her rights, and a king whose reign was apt to plummet into war, she faced a future with no confidence that her wishes would count for anything at all.

Yet in all this bargaining for power and status there was one simple escape. The Holy Roman Church, always eager to extend its influence, held that marriage was a sacrament not lightly set aside—binding in this life and the next. As a sacrament it was subject to God's law, not the petty rules of men. The Church was pragmatic about this; there were enough uncertainties about God's law to keep

Rome's canon lawyers busy and rich. But the sum of the matter was that a promise of marriage, even in the absence of mortal witnesses, was a sufficient demonstration of the sacrament for an almighty, omnipresent God.

It was undoubtedly true that making off with the woman, willing or not, and keeping her in a place of some seclusion until an heir arrived was the clearest way for a pair to declare its marital intentions. But a promise in a woody grove as a chill rain began to fall was equally valid, albeit somewhat more difficult to prove.

Plight-troth, the Church called it, and it filled many a calculating dynast's heart with ice-cold dread. It could emerge from a man's youthful past: a moment's folly casting a pall of illegitimacy over an innocent generation. Invoked by rebellious sons or daughters, it could wreak havoc with a family's carefully nurtured alliances. Falsely sworn by a hot-blooded young knight, it was many a maiden's undoing. And yet, for all its weaknesses, it offered Stephen and Alison a slim chance to command their own destinies.

The men who pulled their cloaks around their faces to keep out the fine rain, and hunkered silently by the sputtering fire, saw an heiress such as Alison as the embodiment of land and legitimate children. They had little doubt that Stephen was bright enough to discern his best interests in the situation; it was a measure of their respect for his future power that they did not challenge his claim to her. Wildecent felt differently, of course, but of all those huddled in their cloaks, she was the most confident that the pair had shared just such a promise.

It was well past nightfall when the rain stopped. The camp was redolent with the smells of moisture on fresh, fertile earth. The horses whuffled as they dreamed of sweet grass; the men simply snored, and Wildecent rolled herself tighter in her cloak, ignoring the steady drips that fell from the crude roof of the lean-to.

Across the camp, hidden in the absence of firelight, Ambrose heard her turn away. He waited a while longer.

When she had remained silent for several moments he stretched himself upright. The clouds had thinned a bit, not to full moonlight but enough that a man might see his hand before his face or a tree in his path. Enough that a sorcerer might draw upon the power residing in his talisman and seek after his friend.

Stephen was with Alison, of course, and for that reason Ambrose was not unduly disturbed by the difficulty he had locating their path. Little as he liked the notion, he knew Alison had won. His hope now was to persuade them both to leave England quickly for the continent. Jean Beauleyas would not approve of their arrangement.

There was a special urgency to Ambrose's search. Lovers were notoriously unobservant, and there was something brewing in the dripping forest. He'd felt it rise as the rain ended. It was part of this magic-ridden land and none of Alison's making. He had studied it from the camp, but his careful, logical training could not penetrate its mysteries. It reminded him of the wind that blew around Ygurna's ghost and left him with a feeling that insects were marching relentlessly along his spine.

His cloak caught on unseen twigs; his passage was neither silent nor peaceful, but he had their trail now. The mark he'd placed on Stephen's thoughts so many years before clung to the bushes the younger man had pushed aside. Ambrose traced his friend no differently than a dog trailed its quarry, though the sorcerer followed a scent that was perceptible only in his arcanely trained mind.

Twice he found places where they'd sought shelter from the rain. The forest, though, was leafless, and the protection of its bare web of branches was not enough to satisfy the pair. They'd kept moving.

At least they moved away from the nexus. He wondered if Alison felt the power rising from the moist ground and had the sense to leave it alone.

She must, he thought, wiping the moisture from his face and pulling his cloak from the clutches of the nearby shrubs. *Surely she knows she's won now; she wouldn't risk what she's gained. She may even suspect it's my doing. As if I could. The magus who controlled this forest could control the world, and the gods as well.*

A humorless grin tightened Ambrose's face. His Byzantine mentors had enough trouble transmuting base metal into gold; they rarely attempted actual creation, and he was many years short of their skill.

The sky revealed the waning crescent moon and the brightest of the stars. There was more light, but it did him no good. The forest trapped the rain-mist beneath its branches. The air became translucent, and Ambrose was forced to move more cautiously.

It was only mist, he reminded himself. There were mists everywhere. Fogs rolled in off Byzantium's harbor, across the peninsulas of Normandy, and even in the pleasant lands of Aquitania. Mists of this English island should be no different from mists anywhere else, but they were, and the prickling irritation along Ambrose's spine became a subtle agony.

Because he was determined to avoid the branches around him, they became more numerous and tenacious. A cold, black twig lashed out of nowhere, striking him across the eyes. For a moment he was blind. He put his hand to his face, convinced that the moisture he felt was not rainwater but blood.

Let her *protect Stephen,* he swore, wiping his hand uselessly on his damp cloak. He could see, but his resolve had been shattered. *It's* her *damned forest.*

Ambrose thought again of the power manifest in these trees. There had always been rumors of barbaric fringelands where gods still moved among their worshippers and the arcane obeyed no laws, only a shaman's whim; but none of the Zoroastrians he'd known gave credence to them. The magi, his mentors, would want to know about this place. Ambrose could almost hear them counseling him to abandon Stephen and seek the source of the forest's power.

Friends can be found anywhere. The face of Masianos, first of the magi, swam before his mind's eye. *But true power's source is a rare thing.*

So they followed him, then—well, he'd always suspected they did. Why take an orphan from the gutters, educate him, mold him, provide him with life's advantages, if you didn't plan to collect the debt somewhere down the road? But they didn't compel him—not unless they already controlled the power of this forest. Ambrose did not choose to turn away from Stephen's trail until he felt the power tremble and begin to flow toward the center of the woods.

He moved toward the nexus, flowing with its summoned power and no longer plagued by brambles. He moved faster now, in rhythm with the pounding pulse of magic. The mist compacted, like wisps of carded fleece; it gave way as he pushed deeper, and upward to the crest of a drumlin invisible from the edge of the wood where they'd made camp.

Caught in the magical stream, buoyed by its energy and excitement, Ambrose shed his fears and cautions. He saw the luminescence hovering over the knob and hurried toward it. He inhaled deeply and felt its raw vitality sting through his lungs, then, as the mists parted for the final time, he collapsed to his knees.

There was an oak here at the top of the drumlin. A gnarled tree as old as the earth itself, shrouded with luminous mist. But it wasn't the oak that held the Byzantine sorcerer transfixed—or not only the oak. The mist had form—if one dared look into it. A face as big as the tree itself, fierce-eyed, grimacing, and with endless green-growing vines streaming from the corners of its mouth. It made no sound when it heard Ambrose's stifled scream, nor gave any indication it noticed him at all.

Ambrose clutched last year's grass and braced himself against the magic stream that flowed over him toward the leering giant. He closed his eyes and sought peace within himself and his crystal talisman, but the lifemaker was stronger. He was driven to open his eyes and glance again at its awesomeness.

The clearing was not silent. The oak groaned as the vines whirled through its branches and spread back into the mist. Everything the vines touched sighed and heaved as life was restored to it. Even the grass in Ambrose's hands quivered. He released it, but not before he felt it grow supple and green against his palms.

There was no mastering this power, no sequence of geometry or mnemonic that could circumscribe it. Not since his childhood in the gutters of the Imperial City had Ambrose known such abject helplessness and terror. He would have fled, if his body were not transfixed and beyond his mind's command.

So he stared and knew, in time, that he was not alone in the mist.

It was difficult to break the spell and look from the vine-spewing face to another part of the misty ring where a dark-cloaked figure stood. *Stood,* while he groveled like a whipped dog. Ambrose acknowledged only the barest abstraction of god, yet he offered up an impassioned prayer that his shame remain invisible when silver blond Alison came before the oak.

Alison had recognized the power throbbing atop the drumlin without knowing its name. She had not come to it until Stephen was asleep. Nothing in the rituals Lady Ygurna had taught her dealt explicitly with the green giant who breathed life and springtime back into the land, yet old knowledge rose within her and she approached him without fear.

He was the fourth king, of course: the nameless one, the most powerful one, the one who claimed the head of the strongest hero of the land. She'd seen the tree-high face much as Ambrose saw it while she stood in the mist, but within the clearing, she saw the king himself, the green man-shape of him, amid his court. She recognized the goddesses she'd met at Yuletide and made obeisance to them.

They gave her fairy-gentle smiles and welcomed her.

"We must dance," they said in one rich voice.

Leafy garlands materialized and twined through their arms, gathering Alison into their circle. She knew there had to be some risk in cavorting with immortals, but the growth pulse pushed fear from her, and she lifted her feet freely to its rhythm.

They sang, and she added her voice to theirs. They spun at a dizzying speed until the clearing, the mists, and the tree kings blurred together. Alison was aware of the untamed energy of springtime, and then, before she had an instant to become fearful, the earth opened and the dancers sank into a hollow hill.

Panicked, Alison released her hold on the garland—and felt the raw, moist earth surrounding her. She tried to breathe and found her nostrils filled with dirt; she tried to scream and found her jaw constricted by the real substance of the hill. Black terror engulfed her until the goddesses grasped her arms.

"Do not break the chain," they commanded, laying the garland again in her hands. "Only through its abundance of life are you here safely."

Alison gave a jerky nod, as if she still doubted her freedom to move. "Where am I?" she asked.

The goddesses laughed and the laughter changed them, allowing Alison to see them as individuals. One resembled her aunt, Ygurna; a second seemed to be a reflection of herself; the third was familiar in an aching way and might have been her mother. Three aspects: crone, maiden, and mother; then they stopped laughing and the individuality vanished.

"You were named to serve us, and your service has been chosen," they said sternly, drawing the garland tight and pulling her into their midst.

"I . . . I know that," Alison stammered, not quite frightened but suddenly cautious.

"You will choose the hero."

Alison nodded. This was the promise hidden in the *geas;* the task that was inescapable. "I will do what must be done."

They were harsh for a moment. Alison swallowed hard. She had indeed made a promise to these powers, and whatever tragedies she could imagine, she knew they could conjure circumstances far worse if she challenged them. They studied her and she wondered if they knew how reluctant her obedience might be. Then their features softened and the wild pulse of life penetrated the mystic hollow once more.

"Dance, little sister," they sang, relaxing their hold on the garland so they might all move more freely.

She danced with them, swirling and singing while the hollow shrank. They danced to the surface of the world and along the great green tracks through the trees and meadows in promise of what summer would be. She danced far longer than she'd thought possible, and clenched the garland in crabbed fingers, knowing that her body was still flesh, and exhausted.

As time wore on she wondered if she had already chosen and sacrificed. Perhaps this endless spiraling and chanting was her eternal doom for sins she had not known she had committed. Perhaps time itself was a circle and this was torment for sins she had not yet committed. Alison cried for help or pity, but her voice was caught in the song and her words blended seamlessly with those of the goddesses. She thought there could be nothing worse, and tried to pry her fingers free of the garland.

Only a faint glow along the horizon, which she took for dawn, dissuaded her. She held on and sang, though tears were flowing down her cheeks, but she did not pray. She was already with those who might have listened.

The mists lost their power as dawnlight touched them. Alison scarcely remembered sinking into the dewy grass, nor the last echoes of the spring-making song as it vanished for another year. She was dazed, drunk with exhaustion, as she heaved upright and stared without comprehension at ragged vines cluttered in her bloodless hands.

Alison willed her fists to open. The garland fell free, or vanished, she couldn't tell which. And she no longer cared. She took an unsteady step toward the scrub at the edge of the clearing made by the ancient oak's shade. There was something in the high grass . . . not a rock or a log . . . a cloak . . . a man . . . a creature of flesh and blood like herself.

She took another step, but the third was beyond her strength. She fell gently onto her side, arms outstretched, her fingers barely touching the thick, ordinary wool. Then she fell asleep.

They were still like that—Ambrose curled beneath his cloak and Alison reaching out to touch him—when, as the sun crested, Stephen pushed through the underbrush and found them.

tephen stopped outside the clearing. He recognized Ambrose's black cloak and Alison's deep green one. For a moment he thought they been set upon and slain, but he dismissed that thought quickly; no brigand would leave those heavy, valuable cloaks on a corpse. Yet it might have been easier if they had been killed. Then he could let his imagination concoct a benign explanation. As it was, he'd have to discover what had led Ambrose into the forest and taken Alison from his side. He'd learn what had brought them together under this huge and forbidding tree.

He did not want to know why Alison, to whom he'd promised his eternal life, was reaching out for his best and only friend as if her soul had depended upon it.

His palm wiped over the wrapped-leather pommel of his sword, an unconscious gesture that said much about his state of mind as he stepped out of the high grass. He knelt beside Alison, almost touching her shoulder, then reconsidered and went to lean against the tree.

Ambrose and his lady had made no secret of their dislike for each other; Alison hadn't, at any rate. They stood on opposite sides of everything, especially their precious notions of magic and sorcery. He was the only thing that held them together, and he felt them fighting over him like hounds over a bone.

Stephen caught himself rubbing the sword pommel again. Alison hadn't wanted to pledge her love. He'd had to plead and finally threaten before she consented—and even then she refused to consummate their love. She was quick enough to say she needed him, but Stephen was sadly certain her mind was not clouded with his image as his was with hers. All Alison's fire showed in her dislike—no, her hatred—for Ambrose. What was lacking in her declarations of love was altogether present when she denounced his friend.

He stared at them, convincing himself that only the arcane—not their professed affection for him or their often-voiced dislike for each other—could have brought them together like this. Common sense, if not concern for his immortal soul, advised Stephen to leave them to their just fate—but he was of an age where neither of those wise forces could sway him. He continued staring and was unsurprised when Alison rolled over and looked at him. He was not, however, prepared for the look of terror that passed over her face before she composed herself and greeted him with a shy smile.

"What a relief to see you standing there . . ."

Stephen let that lie pass, as Ambrose was stirring now and he was coolly eager to observe what passed between them. But Ambrose, paler than usual and shaking like he'd drunk the island dry, gave nothing away as he raked his fingers through his disheveled hair.

"Perhaps I shouldn't ask—" Stephen began.

"You shouldn't," Ambrose replied evenly as Alison muttered a heartfelt "Please, don't."

Stephen pounded his fist against the oak and let the effort push him upright. "Then let me guess. You heard some ancient music playing. You heard fairies dancing. You saw angels and a golden ladder to Heaven itself!" He'd spat out his hurt and his anger. His palm brushed the sword pommel again. He pulled his hand away from the weapon, but the agony remained. From early childhood he had been taught to be a knight, a noble man whose every emotion—every pain or twinge of anger—was channeled into his sword arm. He needed something in his hands: something to swing, something to break. He tore a low-hanging branch from the oak.

"Stephen," Ambrose said in a deliberately calm voice. He'd seen the cold rages that made these knights the most efficient warriors the world had seen in a thousand years—and made them damnably unpredictable friends as well. "Stephen," he repeated as the younger man swung the branch.

Alison took a tentative step forward and opened her mouth; Ambrose shot her a harsh, silencing glance, and for once she obeyed.

"Enough, Stephen!" He caught the branch when it next swung by and braced himself against his friend's greater strength. The wood bowed as Stephen trembled with uncontrolled emotion. Then, as suddenly as it had begun, the rage vanished. Stephen threw the branch down as if it, and not he, had been the cause of the outburst.

"You take too many risks," Stephen said to both of them, his voice still ragged.

The young knight watched as Alison glanced warily in Ambrose's direction. He'd frightened her—and the shame of that, the confusion and the pain, cut deeper than his anger. He lashed out, kicking the branch into the high grass, completely heedless that he'd done nothing to reassure her.

"Shouldn't we be joining the others?" Alison finally asked.

"Assuredly—once we figure out exactly where we might be." The words were out of his mouth before he'd considered their tone or impact. Even Ambrose seemed uneasy, and Ambrose was usually unperturbed by his moods. "No matter," Stephen said into their silence. "They can't be far, and that damned white beast won't be hard to find."

He sprang upward. His arms caught around a sturdy branch, and he wrestled himself higher until he could see over the tops of the nearby trees. The chalk carving dominated the horizon and a bit to its right was a thin plume of smoke that might well be his own men getting their breakfast. He was about to leap back to the ground when he caught Alison's voice and paused to listen.

"It's all your fault," she accused.

"*My* fault. However could it be my fault? They were *your* gods, *your* rituals; I assure you I had no power—"

"If you hadn't been here he wouldn't have gotten angry like that."

There was a pause; Stephen forced his fists to relax lest he break something before Ambrose had a chance to speak.

"Then you don't know his kind very well, do you? Or do you think you can train him to eat from your hand as you trained his horse?"

Stephen slumped back against the bole. He revolted against complexity; a warrior's life demanded a simple world—clear cases of right and wrong where battles were fought and the noblest knight emerged victorious. He loved Alison, that was simple enough, and in a different way he loved Ambrose as well, but they confounded everything. They compelled him to understand their arcane world, even if he would not embrace it, and they reduced the code of chivalry to swirling, angry confusion.

He let go of the branches and dropped free, savoring the shock as his feet slammed into the ground. Pain—real pain, the pain of muscles and bones—was something he could understand. Alison was at his side before he got to his feet.

"You fell! Are you hurt? Here, let me help you up."

Misunderstood again, Stephen got up without her help. He started to explain how he felt, but stopped when he saw the wounded, frightened look in her eyes. So he put his arms around her, feeling how much smaller she was, and weaker, and in need of his strength, not his anger. He found the taut muscles at the back of her neck and massaged them until they began to relax.

He thought she might be crying and held her closer against his tunic so he would not have to know for sure. There was a strange expression on Ambrose's face when their eyes met—not quite defiance, but a wariness. Perhaps it wasn't so complicated, perhaps it had nothing to do with the arcane, perhaps—despite his protestations—Ambrose had a simple hunger for Alison after all.

Stephen tensed. It would be a foolish friend who attempted to step between him and his chosen lady. It would be a man who was no longer his friend . . . Then the tension vanished, pushed aside by Alison's smiling image in his mind. He was reminded that she'd already pledged her love and her loyalty. There was no need to doubt her. Whatever was wrong was undoubtedly, and purely, the sorcerer's fault.

At the back of his mind Stephen recalled that he seldom thought of Ambrose as "the sorcerer." And although they'd argued over many things, they'd never once been attracted to the same woman. He could settle it with a few simple questions, but the urge passed and he buried his face in Alison's sun-touched hair.

He lost himself in her scent and presence, savoring the image of her running through a flower-strewn meadow. There was a pressure to remain in the reverie, but no amount of loveliness could completely seduce Stephen, or erase his uncle's stern visage from other portions of his mind.

"We'd best be going," he conceded, pushing her away.

Collecting his bow and quiver from the high grass, Stephen struck off in the general direction of the smoke plume he'd spotted from the oak's branches. He thrashed swiftly through the damp tangle, satisfied that his companions were pressed too hard for idle conversation.

Stephen's trailbreaking cut across a deer track, and he could no longer justify crashing violently through the brush, even though the track afforded everyone a chance to catch his breath. By then the tense silence was too well established for either Alison or Ambrose to consider breaking it until Stephen did himself.

He was grinding through the events of the last few hours, fitting them into his own memory and smoothing them into a tale that would satisfy not only the men waiting at the edge of the woods but his uncle, should word of this adventure reach those ears. The simple truth left too many gaps; he was tinkering with additional motivations when the track suddenly widened. Had he not been looking for excuses, Stephen would not have given the clearing a second thought, but as it was he paused.

Men had camped here sometime since the last leaves had fallen from the trees. Piles of decaying manure and broken twigs testified that a horse-line had been set between two trees. A fire pit had been dug against a rock. Two cheap earthenware jugs, cracked by frosts and half-buried in the leaves, lay at the edge of the clearing. Nothing extraordinary, but it bothered him, and he spread his arms to keep Ambrose and Alison from brushing past until he'd deciphered the rest.

Stephen considered the various types of travelers who might have stopped here during winter. Torworden men made such camps; so did pilgrims, outlaws, and other wanderers. There was no sign that the place had been occupied for long, yet some care had been taken in selecting it. It wasn't far from the Icknield, but hidden and inconvenient—unlike his own camp, which could be seen from the ridgeway. No wagon would have reached it; the heavy jugs had been brought here by donkey or on a man's own back. He could hardly guess its purpose until he spied a flash of blue amid the earth tones of the forest floor.

A feather, dyed and trimmed as fletching for an arrow, then apparently broken and discarded. Stephen sank down on the fire stone and studied the clearing again. He had a pattern now—a pattern that made his shoulder ache. All through winter the lands around here had been menaced by an outlaw band led by one who called himself the Black Wolf and who appropriated the blue-fletched arrows of Harold Godwinson's men for his own. It was such an arrow that had speared into his shoulder and still lay among his possessions at Torworden.

He twirled the broken feather against his lips.

"Any ideas?" Ambrose inquired, having recognized the feather, if not the other signs in the clearing.

Stephen paused before answering, prodding through the forest debris with his toe until he'd exposed a discolored length of wood: an arrow withy. He imagined himself sitting here on a cold winter day, replenishing his supplies from the well-hidden cache, warming himself by the fire and taking a few moments to sort through his arrows. He'd never believed that the outlaws who killed his companions and wounded him lived by their marauding alone. They received help from someone, and this was the clearest proof he'd yet seen. He shared it with Alison and Ambrose.

Alison had questions, but Stephen was moving again, plunging down the track at a slow run, putting greater distance between himself and his companions, who were less impervious to turned ankles and burdened with heavy cloaks.

"You'll leave us behind!" Ambrose shouted, and Stephen slowed without turning.

"Thank you," Alison murmured to him, though the discomfort at being grateful to the sorcerer almost stifled the good manners Lady Ygurna had labored long to teach her. "My boots aren't meant for these paths—"

"Why didn't you just *wish* him slower, then?"

The young woman came to attention, flicking her braids over her shoulders with a smooth toss of her head and glaring at the sorcerer with undisguised outrage. "I don't play games, sorcerer," she warned as she pushed past him. "And I won't have you standing between us."

Ambrose hesitated a moment, then followed her. There was no small folly in provoking her, not now that he'd witnessed the power that stood behind her, yet more than ever Ambrose was determined to break the English girl's hold over his friend, whatever the cost.

Stephen heard them talking, and resisted the temptation to turn around. He loved Alison best when she was alone in his arms or alone in his thoughts. There was peace at those times, which was far more than could be said when she was near Ambrose.

He expected better from his friend. Ambrose had read all the philosophers and knew that there was no rational way to deal with women. Stephen, who had never been in love before, considered it perfectly expectable that his thoughts were disordered because of her. There was nothing magical about it—or nothing but the magic that God, in his wisdom, had given to women anyway.

Ambrose never agreed. He claimed Alison didn't offer love but a twisted witch-talent that invaded a man's thoughts and left him without a will of his own. A weighty accusation, and one that Stephen was always determined to examine for himself the next time he and Alison were alone. But he never did; he never even thought about it until he saw Ambrose's disapproving face again.

More than once Stephen hoped that Ambrose would fall in love himself—perhaps with Alison's sister, which would be pleasantly convenient, or, failing that, with any available woman. Listening to them stomp along behind him, he considered that it might be time for action to replace idle thought. The bawdy songs of Aquitania were filled with helpful examples. He smiled as the choruses came back to him, and his mood lightened.

He felt more cheerful than he had since leaving Hafwynder Manor, and his mood survived the wary glances he got from the men and from Wildecent, who had become the keystone in his plans for dealing with Ambrose.

He fed the men the same tale he'd unravel for his uncle, focusing their attention on the camp he'd discovered rather than the absence that had led to its discovery. While his men talked of outlaws and Alison and Ambrose wolfed down their breakfasts, Stephen studied Wildecent, who sat alone and lonely by the lean-to.

It should be easy. Viewed by herself, Wildecent was pretty enough; her quiet reserve would suit Ambrose. The girl had to be aware that she'd lost Hafwynder's protection, and Stephen was certain he'd observed some hesitant attraction between the two already. Most importantly, his wit and manners rarely failed him with Wildecent as they so often did with Alison.

He had his tactics prepared and was about to approach the dark-haired girl when Alison slipped her arm beneath his.

"It would seem so lovely, wouldn't it—if my sister and your friend could find the love that we have," she said wistfully. "Too bad it can't be."

Once again everything that had seemed so simple was shaken. "Can't be . . ." Stephen repeated as his thoughts shifted and stretched and finally balked. "I think they'd be perfect for each other."

Alison slid around so she was looking straight into his eyes and there was no mistaking the unhappiness in hers. "Well," she explained, "I guess I can't speak for Ambrose, but I have spoken to my sister and she is much discomforted by your friend's foreign ways. She'd be too shy to say anything herself, but I'd take it very amiss if circumstances—any circumstances—forced them together."

Stephen blinked and let go of his love's wrists. It was unthinkable that he should deliberately make her unhappy, but, just this once, he simply couldn't agree with her. "We'll see," he said gently. "Perhaps once we get to Torworden, Ambrose will seem less strange to her . . . and to you." He tried to gather her into his arms, but she resisted and confronted him with undisguised anger.

"Never, Stephen. You'll have to learn to listen."

In a heartbeat Stephen's world was desolated by her scorn. He blinked back tears and let her go. Every thought and memory urged him to fall to his knees, but he knelt only to God and his lord. When he did not move, Alison turned and walked away from him. His anguish faded slowly.

hough the rain stopped, the blue skies that had brightened the first days of their journey did not return. The travelers rode northward for five days under bald clouds. There was a soft beauty in the pale colors of the new leaves and flowers against the colorless sky, but it could not compensate for the dampness that penetrated every layer of clothing on every back.

The journey had become sheer torment for the women. They were unaccustomed to riding day after day and they had never been schooled to ignore pain. Their muscles ached; their legs were chafed raw. Eodred flew the hawks alone, and if Stephen had wandered away from the campfire one of these later nights, Alison would not have followed him. She and Wildecent were content to move as little as possible once evening rest was called. They both longed for the deep wooden bathtub in the kitchen alcove back at Hafwynder Manor, but neither was so cruel as to mention it out loud.

Indeed, since that morning when Alison, Stephen, and Ambrose had returned from the forest together, the sisters had been estranged from each other. In such a small group it was impossible to be far apart or to avoid conversation altogether, but they spoke little. Alison began the estrangement by rebuffing Wildecent's innocent curiosity about the night she and Stephen had spent in the forest. But Wildecent had been easily and quickly dissuaded. The dark-haired woman passed her time with Eodred, helping with the hawks, or with Hugh de Lessay, who reluctantly helped her learn his language.

Just what, exactly, *had* happened that rainy night was not a complete mystery to Wildecent. There were no more powerful moments than those when the seasons changed; the burst of red buds and green leaves that had occurred the morning after Alison's disappearance was hardly coincidental. Nor was it coincidental that her sister's talents were more in evidence than ever. When they were together Wildecent felt an almost constant pressure against her thoughts and memories. The leanings that warned her away from Stephen were understandable, but the maelstrom that followed every time Ambrose's name was mentioned had a dangerous tenor, and Wildecent willingly kept her distance from all three of them.

She ate her lunch beside Eodred, trying not to listen too carefully to the old man's ramblings. He, like everyone else, had noticed the changes in Alison. He said she looked *serene* with Stephen sitting beside her, but many of his comments seemed to have second meanings. Wildecent would have preferred to eat with Hugh, if that hadn't meant standing on her aching legs.

Everyone at Hafwynder Manor had known what Lady Ygurna was and what Alison would become. Eodred's wife's family had dwelt on Hafwynder holdings as long as living memory could attest; he himself had taken care of the hawks since Lord Godfrey was a child. There was much genuine affection for the Hafwynders in the hearts of those who lived on their lands, but when Eodred stared at Alison, Wildecent wondered if affection would be enough.

The skies, which had darkened throughout their meal, opened. Not a driving rain that might be expected to run its course in an hour or less, but a gentler one that could easily last the rest of the day and into the night. Wildecent pushed herself to her feet, shook the crumbs from her clothes, and steeled herself for the afternoon's agony. She was startled when Alison approached her.

"Stephen says we could reach Torworden tonight if we ride hard and fast."

Wildecent rubbed her hand across her forehead—a reflexive gesture now that Alison could not ask a question or make a statement without putting some measure of magic behind it. As a matter of course Wildecent began to reject the notion, just to demonstrate her independence, then reconsidered. It would be better to ride a few additional hours than to sleep in the rain.

"Whatever it takes," she agreed wearily. "A roof over my head, a warm meal, and a dry bed—sounds like heaven to me."

Alison was no less bedraggled than her sister. Her hair had frizzed and surrounded her face like a mist. The rosy glow in her cheeks looked hectic, a reminder of how ill she had been at Christmastide. She was not the robust pillar of strength she had been before her aunt's death. A freezing night beneath the juniper—not to mention all that had happened since then—had left her a nervous shadow of her former self.

On impulse—her own impulse—Wildecent pulled her sister into a heartfelt embrace. "We'll be there soon, then we can rest . . ."

Alison returned the affectionate gesture. "I knew you'd agree," she whispered in her sister's ear.

The moment broke as quickly as it had arisen. Wildecent turned away lest she snarl that she had agreed of her own free will and not because of magic.

"You're so moody these days, Wili," Alison complained as she went to rejoin Stephen.

"*Just like you, Alison,*" Wildecent muttered as she took her pony's reins from the English squire. *Just like you to think that I'm the moody one when it's you making everything unpredictable.* She accepted the boy's help in mounting and settled into the saddle with a groan that covered her emotional pain under a physical one.

All that had been merely damp became thoroughly soaked. Clouds settled in the rolling valleys. They couldn't see the thick forests of the Wychwood until the trees closed in around them. It was hard riding, but not especially swift as the horses made their way along the uneven, muddy track. There was no conversation, only a string of grim-faced riders pushing homeward.

The final barrier was the river Windraes itself. Swollen

from snow-melt and spring rains, it was a dirty torrent. Stephen circled them within the trees.

"The only bridge is 'round on the other side of Torworden itself," he explained. "I know our horses can swim it, but what about your ponies . . . and you?"

"We were born here," Alison averred, not looking back to see if Wildecent agreed or even troubling to lean on her magically if she didn't. "Let's just get to the other side."

Stephen directed Sulwyn toward the bank. "I'll try it first, to test the footing—"

But Hugh would have none of that. The Windraes was treacherous, and neither he nor any of the other Torwordeners had any desire to tell Jean Beauleyas that his nephew had been swept away a few miles from the keep. They'd sooner drown themselves. So Hugh made the crossing first and pronounced the footing no worse than was to be expected. He tied his horse and stood on the bank ready to help the next half-drowned man up the steep, slippery slope.

Stephen and his companions needn't have worried. The sturdy English ponies had kept pace with their larger brethren from the start of the journey and weren't about to be bested by three lengths of churning water. Even burdened by swirling skirts, the ponies plunged in without complaint and scrambled to the high ground without any assistance. Their riders did no less. The one animal who balked was Sulwyn, who had had enough of rain and wanted nothing to do with water in a more concentrated form. His flanks were bloody from Stephen's spurs before he leaped to the middle of the stream and started swimming.

"Damned fool beast!" Stephen shouted, springing down from the saddle and threatening the stallion with his fist.

They were both showing white around the eyes when first Sulwyn, then Stephen, relaxed. For once Wildecent approved of the uses to which Alison could put her talents, and even shot a sly grin to her sister.

Water still streaming from their boots, the party made its way to the Torworden track. The dismal afternoon became a gloomy evening. There was no way they'd reach Torworden until well after dark, and no way they'd stop before they reached it.

Wildecent had passed the upper threshold of discomfort. Numb from neck to toes, she fell asleep until the track became steeper and the men congratulated themselves on a safe, if soggy, homecoming. Once she was awake, the fetid reek of the settlement ensured that she would remain that way. Only Stephen, at the front of their line, carried a torch. He could see a few feet of track; they followed him blindly. All the English knew was that Hafwynder Manor never smelled this bad.

At length torches wove down the hillside to join them at a leveled place partway up the slope. The greetings were all in Norman French, but some of the men carrying the torches were English and recognized Alison as one of their own.

"So you're the heiress from the southern manor?" came the overly familiar greeting from a man who put a firm grip on the pony's reins.

"I've come to Lord Beauleyas for protection in these troubled times. King Harold himself has given permission." That was a lie, of course, but Alison counted on the power of the king's name to protect her from Beauleyas and his men.

She was mistaken. No one who dwelt at Torworden would openly dispute Duke William's claim to the throne. The English king's name brought a snort of laughter that froze Alison's heart.

"Take your hands off my horse!" she commanded, pressing sore calves into the mare's sides and backing her away. The man let go, but the look he gave her was amused, not respectful. Alison was outraged and she reacted as she always reacted: impulsively and magically.

Her willfulness swirled out—and washed away without effect.

No one had been aware of her efforts. The renewed sense of power she had during the journey was gone. When the Normans had visited her father's manor and filled the hall with their foreign chatter she'd been indignant, and refused to learn any scraps of French conversation. She'd learned little more during the journey, though Stephen offered to practice with her. She didn't need to speak French with Stephen; her meddling with his fantasies had given him a superb command of English. Now, surrounded by voices she could not understand, she was frightened, and guided her pony to Wildecent's side.

"What are they talking about?" she whispered urgently.

Wildecent shrugged and shook the water from the edge of her hood. "It's so fast . . . I understand maybe two words in four, I think. Something's wrong, maybe. There's no place for us or—"

"Who's *that?*"

More torches had criss-crossed down the hill. They hissed and smoked in the rain but gradually they were turning the faceless mass of the Torworden garrison into individuals. One such individual, a latecomer who did not carry his own torch, caught Alison's eye. He was a heavyset man some few years older than Stephen. His features weren't unpleasant in themselves; it was the way his lips twisted back when he smiled, the way his eyes disappeared when he talked, and the scorn in his voice as he addressed the returning men that made him unattractive.

Neither young woman knew who he was, but he had to be someone of some importance, for the other Torworden men deferred to him, and Stephen gave him his full attention. Wildecent recalled her conversation with Ambrose and judged that this was Eudo, Jean Beauleyas's bastard and the one most directly diminished by Ste-

phen's accomplishments. She was about to share her ob-
servation with Alison when the conversation became
particularly strident. With a shout that could only be a
challenge, Stephen threw Sulwyn's reins to another man
and sprang to the ground, the sputtering torch before
him as a weapon.

The Torwordeners moved swiftly between the enraged
men, surrounding and separating them from each other.
Before the Englishwomen could sort through the ill-lit
faces, Stephen appeared at Alison's side.

"Go with Hugh," he ordered.

Alison reached out to touch his shoulder, then pulled
her hand back. She used her talents impulsively, and on
those rare occasions when she gave a situation any
thought, she knew when to stay out. This was such a
time, and she meekly consented as Hugh took her pony's
reins, leading her and Wildecent away from the excitement.

"It's nothing to worry about," Hugh said unconvinc-
ingly.

Torchlight fell on a series of wattle-and-daub huts that
were as slick and shiny as the churned-up mud beneath
their horses' feet. Alison regretted her meekness when
the Norman came to a halt beside one of them and wrestled the door open.

"You'll be more comfortable here."

He saw them across the threshold and shoved his torch
into a wall notch, where it seemed certain to ignite the
thatched roof. Then—before either woman protested—he
vanished into the rainy night with their ponies.

"More comfortable than what?" Alison complained.
"The pigs? The sheep? The goats?"

Wildecent removed her cloak and looked around for a
place to put it. She spun like a forlorn top. The hut's
furniture—if it could be dignified by the word—consisted
of a square box bed, a rickety stool, which might actually
be a rickety table, and, of course, the torch Hugh had
left stuck in the wall. At length she spied a chopped-off

crook in one of the upright timbers and hung the cloak on that.

"I'm glad our lord father didn't come with us," Alison murmured as water plinked into the straw covering the floor.

"It's a mistake. It's got to be a mistake."

Alison hung up her cloak on another crook and clutched her arms across her breast as she gave the hut another examination. These *were* Torworden's guesting rooms, and this wasn't likely to be a mistake. She tried the door. It refused to open and so, fearing they might be locked into these miserable quarters, she gave it a tremendous tug. It popped open and brought a gust of wet wind between them.

She thrust her head into the night and shouted, "Aren't we even going to get our supper?" No one answered, and after a moment, at Wildecent's insistence, she shoved the door closed again.

"I simply don't believe it," she continued, thumping down into the straw of the box bed. "I simply don't. It's all a horrible dream. I'll wake up and I'll be back at Hafwynder Manor where I belong."

Wildecent said nothing, but sat down, and they put their arms around each other for comfort and warmth. The torch fizzled out. Neither was close to sleep when the door thumped open.

"Stephen!" Alison called in hope more than belief.

"Sorry to disappoint . . ."

Ambrose stepped down into the straw, removed the spent torch from its notch, and shoved his own into its place. He stepped aside, shook the water from his hair, and allowed two men to enter the hut behind them. They deposited their burdens, then departed on the sorcerer's command.

"Stephen is with his uncle," Ambrose explained as he sorted through the parcels. "And the rest—well, the less said about that the better, I suppose."

He produced a thong from his sleeve and a lamp from

the parcels, and in short order light was flickering down from a crossbeam. His second feat of civilization was a trio of mugs and a flask of warm, spiced wine, which he shared before revealing his true marvels: a hearty supper; thick, dry blankets; and the leather sacks of clean linen each woman had left on the pack animals. It was almost too good to be true, and halfway through her wine Alison said so.

"Why you?" she began, emboldened by the wine and too tired to care how he might react. "Why're you being so generous? We're hardly friends, you know."

A faint smile formed on Ambrose's face as he carefully swept water from the cloak he'd hung beside the others. "I'd scarcely presume to argue with you, my lady," he said with exaggerated politeness. "But I do have my own sense of honor. I was part of your escort, and this hill is, for the moment, my home. I do not see guests sent to their beds with empty stomachs or dripping linen—

"Strange—I'd always thought you English set great store by hospitality."

Since Alison and Ambrose could not speak without sparring, it fell to Wildecent to effect a truce. "I don't think I've ever eaten a better stew," she interjected.

"If that were the case, Lord Beauleyas wouldn't want Hafwynder's cook almost as much as he wants its land and its daughters."

Alison nested her dishes in the straw beside her. "I won't stay here," she warned. "I won't live in a byre unfit for a whipped slave. I won't be held against my will . . . and so long as I or my father lives, no one will take Hafwynder Manor from us." Fire and determination ran through her words as she stood and glared at the man she considered her enemy.

But Ambrose did not respond directly to her challenge. He kept his voice soft and sincere. "My Lady Alison, if you have any hope at all of keeping your precious manor, you'll *do as you're told*. You might just as well be in another world—in Normandy itself—right now, and if you're half as clever as you think you are, you'll start thinking first and acting later.''

"I have my rights. Stephen—"

"Leave Stephen out of this!" His voice rose into an uncharacteristic shout; he paused, swallowed hard, and continued in a more normal tone. "Very well—we are *not* friends. But we share a friend, and if you love him as he loves you, don't tie yourself like a stone around his neck: you'll both drown."

Wildecent tried again. "Was that Eudo out there, the one you told me about? The one who was scornful and whom Stephen was about to fight?"

"You recognized him, then, the Beau-Bastard? You might take note: he doesn't think his rival should have the credit for bringing Hafwynder Manor and its treasure into the Beauleyas fold . . ."

Alison restrained the indignation she felt at the discovery that Wildecent knew something about Stephen she did not, and sought to correct the situation. "This Eudo, he's Jean Beauleyas's natural son, and he fears that Stephen threatens whatever inheritance he might receive?"

Ambrose nodded. "Not without reason."

"Well, he shall see he has nothing to fear . . ."

It became Ambrose's turn to issue a warning. "Don't even think about it. These are not the sort of men you can twist to your will—"

"Not my will alone," Alison shot back. "You know what I could call upon."

Wildecent shrank back; one didn't need to know the particulars to follow the general flow of this conversation. But Ambrose shook his head in mirthless laughter.

"Do that. These Normans will be impressed. They'll go to the top of your hill, cut down your oak tree, and put up a church with walls three feet thick. The world hasn't seen men like these for a long time, dear lady. Northmen with a taste for civilization; Vikings for the Church of Rome. Their own land isn't big enough for them. They fight, and feud, and murder endlessly; the only time they unite is to ravage someone else's lands. They have no art, no learning, no religion—but they usurp ruthlessly. And, by the mystic two, they rule as well as they conquer.

"Everybody wants a Norman or three in his pay—and fighting somewhere else. They'd crusade for the devil himself, if Satan had made them half as good an offer as the pope. They don't need your magic; they've got their own! You'll have no influence over them."

"Speak for yourself. Stephen's no Norman."

"Hah! Let me tell you about Rollo the Red—Bloody Rollo. Once, he boiled an abbot in holy water. He made war on all his neighbors, and when he finally died, poisoned by his children, they carved his flesh from his bones and fed it to the ravens. He had a child at every hearth in his domain, but the two you'd be most interested in are Jean Beauleyas and Mabelle . . . Stephen's mother. Shall I tell you *why* she feared to return to Normandy after her first husband's death?"

Alison shook her head. The violence in all of France, not just Normandy, was legendary. Murder was commonplace; if a man or woman happened to die unmarked by violence, poison was always suspected. Stephen could not have grown up ignorant or untainted, but Alison had no desire to know the extent of his education.

"Leave us," she said, with her back to Ambrose and a cautioning eye at her sister lest Wildecent object.

Ambrose threw his cloak over his shoulder and opened the door. "Be careful," he said as he vanished into the night.

here were no windows in the hut—no warning that dawn had come and long since gone when the young women finally opened their eyes and stumbled about the dark room.

"You must be wary of Ambrose," Alison admonished. "He has the power to tempt you."

"Umm . . ."

"No, I'm serious. Aside from Stephen, he's the only civil soul here. It will seem natural for you, my sister, to be paired with him, Stephen's friend. Even Stephen has almost succumbed to the idea. And the sorcerer's already shown how he intends to seduce us with kindness. You will have to be wary."

"Umm . . ."

"Wili! You're not listening to me!"

Wildecent paused in the braiding of her hair. "I *am* listening to you. What I'm *not* doing is arguing with you at this unholy hour of the morning. Alison, I simply don't agree with you."

"He's poison, don't you understand that? Think what he's done to Stephen! What he's done to the men of Torworden to make them brutes and animals!"

"What he's done *for* Stephen is spare him from becoming another Eudo. I'd think you owe him a debt of gratitude. Eudo made my skin crawl. Ambrose wasn't bragging about what he'd done here, you goose, he was saying what he couldn't do—and what you shouldn't try to do."

Alison had nothing left to offer but a dramatic sigh. She stomped through the straw and wrestled the door open, blinding them both with sunlight. *"Egede,* it must be midday," she groaned with her arm up to protect her eyes.

"We're off to an outstanding start," Wildecent agreed.

Nothing about Torworden was familiar or inviting. Already the disagreement they'd had in the hut seemed insignificant. In this strange place, they needed each other too much to argue over men or magic.

Torworden had sprung into existence two years before, when Jean Beauleyas secured permission from King Edward to dwell in English lands until such time as Duke William of Normandy claimed the English throne. Notwithstanding his agreements with Edward, Harold's sacred oath, and the betrothal between Harold and the duke's daughter Adele, William expected trouble gaining the English throne. He could scarcely expect otherwise: he had been fighting all his life. Wanting and fighting were inseparable in William's mind. He wanted England; he expected to fight for it.

His directions to Jean Beauleyas had been precise: find a defensible place away from English eyes, secure it, hold it, and wait. Beauleyas had followed the instructions scrupulously.

Torworden commanded a sweeping view of a clear route from the North into the English heartland. Duke William had expected to fight Scots and the various Scandinavian kings. He'd hoped Harold Godwinson, his prospective son-in-law, would be foremost among his English commanders. The earl's betrayal had hurt the duke deeply and personally, and made a shambles of his plans. Torworden would be nowhere near William's fighting when it came.

The motte was a huge earth mound constructed atop an already substantial hill. A bailey for the men and their horses had been created at the base of the motte following the lines of the original crest. Here were the lines of partially enclosed stalls that the women had smelled in the rain; here, too, were the long barracks where the men lived; and the sunken huts where guests spent the night. Other structures, smaller than the sunken huts, were filled with supplies.

Torworden had been preparing for a siege since its foundation. There was no life here, not in the same sense that there had been daily life at Hafwynder Manor. No common people dwelt behind the stout earthworks and their crowning stockades—only knights. There was a day-village at the foot of the hill, more squalid than anything the women had seen before, where Englishmen provided services to these foreigners who paid with money—when they paid at all—because they did not produce anything themselves.

"Where are the fields? The byres?" Alison asked an Englishman who'd just come through the stockade gate leading a donkey.

The man pointed at the arc of forest behind the crude buildings at the foot of the hill. "Yonder, my lady. At Lachebroc, the old village beyond the Windraes."

Alison was pleased to learn that there was at least a village nearby. Although villages were not closed, familial communities like Hafwynder Manor, they were respectable places. Tradesmen and artisans might congregate in a village and its men might work the land of several manors. "Is your village prosperous now that Torworden is nearby?"

"Prosperous?" The man repeated the question as if the notion had never occurred to him before. "Before we tilled fields for the Bishop of Winchester, what lived far away and cared nothing for us. Now our lord and his men're on the other side of our hill. We feel his eyes on our back and his foot on our neck every day."

Neither woman was so naive as to believe life everywhere was as pleasant as it was at Hafwynder Manor. There were slaves at Hafwynder Manor, and cottars, whose lot in life was little better. A woman like Bethanil might be a freewoman, but she was dependent on the goodwill of the Hafwynder lord, who could turn her out in the cold as he could not do with his slaves or cottars. And there were men of the local hundred who lived little better than their animals and were never more than few morsels ahead of starvation.

But the young women had never encountered the bleak spirit that marked the man before them.

"Your wives and children?" Wildecent asked hesitantly. "Do they suffer, too?"

"Those of us as could sent them away long ago. Begging your pardon, my lady, this is not a place for an honorable woman."

He tugged at his donkey's bridle. They plodded past, leaving the sisters with the unsettling notion that he either considered they were not honorable women or that their honor would not last for long.

"No wonder they need a woman to supervise their kitchen . . ." Wildecent murmured when he was gone.

"Bethanil won't stay. I wouldn't have her living here. It's bad enough we must be here. Our blood defends us."

Wildecent said nothing, though Alison's confidence hardly reassured her. Bethanil could trace her lineage in Wessex almost as far back as the Hafwynders could, while Wildecent knew the names or stations of neither of her own parents. She was suddenly—uncomfortably—aware that the rain had made her gown shrink. The cloth pulled tight across her breasts and hips. She tugged at it and wished she hadn't left her heavy cloak in the hut.

The Englishman and his donkey had come to the inner stockade that surrounded the base of the motte. He unloaded the baskets and jars from the beast's back. The track that led from the day-village to the bailey-yard where the women stood stopped at the inner gate. The only way up the steep motte was a spiral of split logs shoved into the mud. The Englishman balanced a heavy jar across his shoulders and became his own beast of burden. There were other men about, some Englishmen by their clothes, but no one offered to help.

"I don't think I'm going to like it here," Wildecent said.

They continued their explorations. There was little open space within the bailey. It was unlikely that domestic gardens had ever been planted here. Men as sullen as the one they had already met worked the stables, loading manure into waiting oxcarts.

The bailey wasn't a quiet place. A farrier was working among the horses, and some of the workmen sang or shouted as they went about their labors. Still, the greatest furor came from the other side of the motte, and it was toward those shouts that the women headed. What they found was not surprising. They'd already learned that Torworden was preeminently a stronghold; a lodging for knights. It was only natural that these men would need a place to practice their peculiar craft.

Not that a young Englishman didn't learn his martial arts, but there were no sons or fosterlings at Hafwynder Manor, and such seasonal practice as the grown men needed they got casually in the grass beyond the stockade. Here at Torworden the practice arena was the focus of daily life. The entrance of the donjon overlooked it; yet another wooden fence separated it from the rest of the yard. There were easily forty men, armored as suited their personal tastes, brandishing blunted weapons. They flailed away at each other, shouting encouragement or learning some refined method for separating an enemy from his life.

A row of tall shields rested along the fence, each in perfect condition. The looped guiges, which allowed the knight to sling the shield around his neck while he rode, were new leather. The enarmes had been freshly padded to ensure a firm grip in combat. The hides had been bleached then painted with a variety of bright designs. Neither Alison nor Wildecent could doubt that the owners of these shields were not merely ready for battle; they welcomed it.

Stephen was not there, nor were any of the men who had traveled from Hafwynder Manor, but Eudo was. The powerful young man had laid claim to the center of the arena and was calling for challengers. Despite the cool breeze he was naked to the waist, and swinging his sword slowly through arcs and feints. He proved to all who watched that he knew his craft, but he did not impress the women.

"Whatever else may be true of these Normans," Alison said after a moment watching him. "I think they're among the ugliest men on earth."

Wildecent nodded, though the allegation was not entirely true. Eudo's bearing made him distasteful, not his features. Still, there were aesthetic differences. English warriors marked their skins with scars and tattoos, like the Scandinavians; smooth, pale flesh was a telling sign of inexperience. The English found beauty in their hair; they cultivated it among both men and women. Unmarried women displayed their hip-length plaits proudly. Boys weren't men until their beards were full.

The Norman host was not immune to the allure of a woman's hair, but they considered their own a dangerous vanity. Their beards were cropped short lest they become tangled in their hauberks or offer a fatal handhold to an enemy. The ideal knight was clean-shaven, but even a Norman chin could not withstand daily rasping with pumice or the edge of his knife. Torworden faces were most often shawdowed with stubble. The same smooth-skin ideals applied to a Norman knight's neck, where hair could interfere with the fit of his conical helmet. His bare nape was as distinctive as a priest's tonsure.

Thus Eudo, who prided his martial prowess above all else, had a welter of cuts on his face and nape, and his reddish hair resembled a small wig sliding forward across a bald skull. A skilled observer might have guessed that, whatever the success of the English king, the English hairstyles would triumph over the Norman ones. Already about a third of the men were content to trim their beards and napes rather than submit to the rigors of shaving. Such compromise only accentuated Eudo's brutishness.

"He's like a rutting bull," Alison decided. "Come, let's see if we can find where they've sent Eodred and our hawks."

They headed back toward the stables and huts, wandering without success until their hunger overshadowed their curiosity.

"Do you think anyone would mind if we went down to the day-village below the gate?" Wildecent asked.

"No one's said we couldn't."

Alison led the way back to the gate which was, at this hour, standing open and unguarded. Skirts gathered up, they were picking their way through the mud when a hand fell heavily on Alison's shoulder.

"I go with you," Eudo announced, pushing between them without lifting his hand from Alison's shoulder. His English was slurred, but he did not need many words to make his meaning clear.

"Take your hand off me," Alison commanded, to no effect.

The mood become dangerous. Wildecent took a step backward and was caught from behind. Terror rose above all other feelings as she remembered how she had been similarly captured at Hafwynder Manor during the Black Wolf's attack. Her body went weak with the memory of the outlaw twisting her arm until it snapped. Whoever held her was not yet hurting her, but she had no will to resist him, and watched in bleak silence as the confrontation continued. Alison attempted to slap Eudo's hand away.

"You amuse me," Eudo said as he parried with a rock-hard forearm.

Alison was a head taller than her sister and strong for a woman, but she was no match for a knight. She winced as her arm struck his. Her eyes widened. Wildecent was certain her sister put all her will into a burst of magical thought—and equally certain that it had absolutely failed to affect the laughing Eudo.

"Lord Stephen—"

Eudo cut her off. "You are, I think, too much woman for my little cousin . . ."

Alison recalled that she had seen no other women at

Torworden since their arrival. She had compared Eudo to a rutting bull without realizing what truths the allusion might hide. In her mind she cursed Stephen for bringing her here, then she remembered the plight-troth. "We are plighted to each other," she announced, and saw she'd made a serious mistake.

Something akin to blind hatred narrowed Eudo's eyes and tightened his grip on her shoulder until it took all her strength not to shout with pain. He was brutal, but not stupid. He thought while he held her, and his face slowly relaxed into a satisfied grin.

"Stephen makes promises he cannot keep," he said, flinging her backward into the arms of another crony. Then he barked a command in French and the men all laughed. Wildecent was dragged farther away and Alison was given a shove toward the open gate. The women had a helpless heartbeat with which to look at each other before another man caught Alison and threw her over his shoulder. She screamed and hammered at his back with her fists, but he was running and almost through the gate when an arrow dropped one of the men and everyone froze.

Alison heard Jean Beauleyas's voice booming from the donjon just before she was dumped to the muddy ground. Eudo's men stood motionless, under the watchful eyes of Beauleyas's personal archers, as the lord left the tower roof. They stayed that way as he led a procession into the bailey-yard.

She was still sitting in the mud when Beauleyas ordered them to stand aside. Her unceremonious fall had addled her thoughts. She saw Stephen standing beside his uncle but she could not understand why he looked so grim.

Beauleyas had injured one leg many years before. Already bowlegged from a lifetime in the saddle, he habitually balanced on his good leg and did not, at first, seem a figure to command respect from his powerful son. But Eudo looked nervous when he was called forward.

The Beau-Bastard hesitated under rapid questioning,

and was rewarded with a blow that staggered him back two steps. He was a man, but Beauleyas was his lord and father, so he bore the insult in sullen silence. The question was repea*ed.

"She claims they promised to each other before God," he answered in English. "She was not to be promised. I had your word. Stephen disobeyed you."

The lord of Torworden was not pleased. He studied Alison with casual contempt and turned to glower at Stephen. "Is this true?" Beauleyas demanded of his nephew.

Conscious of the attention focused upon him, Stephen came forward. He gave no indication he was even aware of Alison, but he spoke clearly and in English for her benefit. "Yes, my lord, it is." Beauleyas struck him as he'd struck his son: a closed-fist blow that resounded through the yard. Stephen held his ground and did not stagger back. Blood streamed from his nose; he ignored it and faced his uncle with quiet dignity.

The simmering conflict between the two prospective heirs lay naked in the bailey. Eudo, who had embraced all the explosive virtues appropriate to his station, against Stephen, whose irregular education had taught him something of restraint and strategy. Jean Beauleyas did not know what to make of his sister's disenfranchised son, so he turned away and considered the cause of the outburst.

"You have been the death of a good man, lady of Hafwynder. What do you say for yourself?"

The blood had drained from Alison's face. Her whole body trembled as she picked herself up from the mud and shook her skirts straight. Then she steeled herself and faced him as a daughter of English nobility with a longer heritage than his own.

"His blood is not on me," she averred, speaking slowly to keep her voice from rising into a woman's hysteria.

"You behaved wantonly. You made a rash and foolish promise. You betray your freedom. I may punish those you led astray. How shall I punish you?"

CONQUEST

The world had constricted until it contained nothing but her pounding heart and the cold, calculating eyes of the Norman lord. "You have no right to punish me," she said, though she understood perfectly that the discussion was not about rights but power.

"I must know you will obey me. I must see this futile vow repudiated. You are not some base-born wench who may give her body as she pleases."

Alison blushed a violent crimson. "You have not the right!" she shouted. "Only my lord father may give my hand in marriage. I shall not be made to marry without my consent nor place Hafwynder lands in the custody of a man I do not chose!"

"Your lord father no longer knows your name."

She looked quickly through the crowd and saw that no one, not even Stephen, would intercede for her. They reminded her of wolves cowed by their leader—a man who had brought all his commanding energies to bear against her. Wisdom counseled to accept her defeat and acknowledge his power. But Alison Hafwynder had never been known for her admiration of wisdom.

"I appeal to my lord's lord—to Harold Godwinson, Earl of Wessex and rightful king of England," she proclaimed in a voice that was once again even and controlled.

Beauleyas was unperturbed; he even gave her a little smile. "Ah, yes—the rightful king of England, for the moment. I thought of him after I left Hafwynder Manor. He is a busy man, harried on every front, scarcely able to consider the fate of one heiress while his country prepares for war.

"I sent my messenger to Westminster offering myself as lord and guardian for all that belonged to your father. You need not doubt that my petition was swiftly granted."

Alison's head slumped forward. She stared at the ground, unable to say anything more.

But Jean Beauleyas was not quite finished. "I would

have you all remember," he proclaimed, "that I am myself without a wife. I'll have the life"—he paused to stare equally at his natural son and his nephew—"of any man who interferes with my ward."

Alison looked up. Despite her efforts, there were tears running down her cheeks, but they had no effect on Beauleyas, and she did not turn to look at Stephen.

"Take her up to the donjon," Beauleyas told the man standing nearest to him, and Hugh stepped forward to take Alison's arm and lead her limply to the gate. The men began to disperse. Wildecent was left alone. She stared blankly at Beauleyas. "That one, too. No sense having one of them locked up and the other running loose."

He spoke in French, but Wildecent understood him well enough and walked meekly toward the gate without assistance.

he full power of Torworden could only be appreciated from the motte. The donjon resembled the tower at Hafwynder Manor in style, but far exceeded it in size. Windowless stone foundations descended deep into the natural hillside. Each side of the square they created was the width of Hafwynder Hall. The upper stories of the donjon were wooden—the motte was too young to support a donjon built entirely of stone—and were reached by an external wooden stairway.

If it was difficult to imagine an enemy charging up the natural hill to the bailey, it was impossible to imagine a successful assault on the motte and its donjon. Siege was the only way to bring down a donjon, except for arson, which accounted for the dressed stone heaped at the base of the motte awaiting the conversion of another wooden wall to unburnable stone.

The heroic scale of the donjon was not translated to its interior. A timber wall divided the entrance level. The larger portion served as Torworden's great hall. Its floor was made of wooden planks that echoed when the heavy-footed knights trod across it, and its hearth was carved into the outer walls. Tables were nowhere to be seen, and the most sophisticated piece of furniture was a low-backed chair draped with animal hides. Neither frescoes nor tapestries relieved the blank walls. This part of donjon was, after all, only temporary. Nonetheless, it had a depressing effect on the two Englishwomen.

Unembroidered hangings, little more than blankets hung on hooks, concealed two passages through the interior wall. The sisters were escorted into the rear room, which took up no more than a third of the entrance level.

"I thought it couldn't get worse," Alison said when they were alone.

The room was shuttered and dim. Though nothing more substantial than the drapery separated them from

the outer room, the aura of a prison clung to the place. Alison no longer contained her sobs, and sank to the floor.

Wildecent said nothing, but unlatched the shutters for light and air. While Alison cried, her sister studied the room.

"Well, brace yourself," she said after a few moments. "I don't doubt that it's going to get worse."

Alison looked up slowly. The lord's bed dominated the far end of the room. It stood on a platform and was hung with heavy velvet and dressed with fine linen. No one had bothered to straighten the linen; Beauleyas's night shift trailed to the floor on one side. The remainder of the room was dominated by locked chests and boxes: Torworden's treasury kept safe by its lord.

"At least he considers us valuable," Wildecent said after a moment.

"How can this be happening? Where's Stephen? Eodred? Anyone who could take us from here? I'd rather run and hide in a convent than spend a night in this room!"

Wildecent laughed. Whorehouses had better reputations than England's convents. Then she looked closely at Alison's face and realized she was sweating feverishly.

"Why don't you curl up and get some sleep," she suggested, knowing Alison would never take more specific advice from someone who healed by memory rather than magic. "We'll survive this somehow."

"We must do more than survive," Alison replied, her voice turning shrill. She went to the foot of the huge bed and stared at the rumpled linen as if she could read her future in its folds. "There must be a purpose to this. A grand design that will point us to triumph; an unveiling of the Old Ways—"

Wildecent said nothing. She'd burned through a lifetime of outrage when she'd watched Jean Beauleyas assault his heirs and humiliate her sister. She'd looked inward and found neither the stoic courage that fueled

Alison and Stephen nor the sullen hatred that strengthened Eudo. She'd bend her knee if that was what it took
to maintain a facade of dignity. Wildecent admired her
sister, but could not imagine imitating her. She had no
interest in grand designs, and nothing but fear for the
bloody old gods of Britain.

"I'm not you. I've lost everything before," Wildecent
explained in a rare allusion to her shadowed infancy in
France. "I don't remember names or faces. Maybe in
time I can forget Hafwynder Manor . . ."

Of course not, Alison thought, more absorbed in her
own thoughts than Wildecent's confession. *I'm the one
they've called upon. The one they've chosen. The inheritance of
land from my father; the power from my mother . . .* Her
vision blurred as her thoughts plunged back to the moments she had spent with the ancient gods. *The hero must
be chosen. I must choose the hero.*

The *geas* was weaker now. Alison could see the masks
of the tree kings waiting for her to choose. Except there
were four masks now. The last hung upside down and
was drenched in blood.

Blood flowed across Alison's inner eye, staining the dis-
arrayed linen. She turned away from the horror and began to gasp for breath. The sky beyond the open windows
turned green, and she collapsed headlong across the bed.

Wildecent could not reach her before she fell. There
could not be a worse time for Alison's mysterious mala-
dies to return, and Wildecent cursed the ancient gods
Alison and Lady Ygurna venerated who had not prevented it. Alison's hands were icy, her eyes had rolled
back in her head, and all their herbs were in sacks at
Hafwynder Manor. She tugged and pushed until Alison
was swaddled in blankets.

The sense of outrage Wildecent had thought extinguished flickered back to life. It had no focus, as if she
could not choose among the many sources of her bleak
anger: Alison, whose magic would be their downfall? The
ancient gods, who inspired Alison's most reckless actions?

Lord Beauleyas, who had power in this world? For that matter, why not focus on Stephen, whose mishaps had begun the changes in their lives? Or Ambrose? Or Lady Ygurna?

There were so many targets, Wildecent had not selected one above the others before faint color had returned to Alison's cheeks and her skin felt normally warm to the touch. Wildecent freed the bed hangings so the light would not fall across her sister's eyes, then went to the window.

A slow-moving entourage made its way past the long stables. She could distinguish Beauleyas's distinctive walk at its center and the black-clad presence of Ambrose a step or two behind, but she saw no one who might be Stephen . . . or Eudo. Eudo! The Beau-Bastard might come bursting in and find Alison helpless in his father's bed! There'd be hell to pay afterward—but afterward would be too late for Alison.

Wildecent shut and bolted the door beneath the blanket draperies before she thought better of her independence. If Jean Beauleyas wanted the door locked, he'd have commanded it. And having seen the Norman lord's rage, Wildecent was not about to do what he had not commanded. *What will be, will be,* she decided and re-opened the door.

She paced the length of the room, rubbing her palms against her thighs. Of all the things she had dreaded about Torworden, she had never imagined its most insidious torture: boredom. At Hafwynder Manor there had been no time for idleness. A year's spinning and weaving was scarcely complete before the next year's began. Wildecent felt as naked without her spindle and sleeveful of carded fleece as she would have felt without her linen. A whirling spindle was soothing in its own way and required just enough attention to keep a mind from wandering where it ought not go. It was hopeless to expect that Beauleyas counted a spindle among his treasures, but Wildecent looked.

Alison had rolled onto her side and was sleeping peacefully. Jean Beauleyas had gone to the other side of the motte, where his men could be heard practicing. Wildecent realized she had a headache from hunger and remembered the leftovers back in the hut. She braved the outer hall in search of food and found nothing the dogs had not already investigated. Disgusted and still hungry, she returned to the bedroom and settled herself amid the boxes of Torworden's treasure. Many a slave had a less comfortable bed; she willed herself to sleep.

She awoke with the floor shaking and the walls echoing with the sounds of men's shouting in the outer hall. The shadows had moved to the other side of the room. Wildecent judged she'd slept until the late afternoon and, despite lingering hunger pangs, felt better for her rest.

"They'll be the death of me," Jean Beauleyas could be heard shouting.

Wildecent crept closer to the drapery to catch the flow of his conversation, grateful for the hours she'd spent listening to Hugh de Lessay talk about himself. Crouched on the floor, she could see Beauleyas striding around his chair, a piece of cold chicken in his hand. Her mouth began to water; it took a conscious effort to examine the other faces.

Ambrose leaned casually against the far wall, looking out the window past his goblet as if his thoughts had returned to whatever place he called home. Wildecent knew him well enough, though, to know his distraction was a sham and that he alone was following the debate carefully.

"So young Stephen found more blue fletching. What does that prove?" a man as grizzled as Beauleyas himself demanded. "What does that tell us we didn't already know—except that he was a damned lucky fool when he ran off with the English bitch."

Hugh rose to Stephen's defense. "It reminds us, if we'd forgotten, that we are not alone in coveting England. Tostig Godwinson plays his own games. He's made allies in the North. We do not know if that fletching lay on the leaves a night or a month. The peasants here look to us for protection. For William's sake—for our honor's sake we owe them our duty and our swords."

Beauleyas rasped his fingers along the scar on his cheek. "Indeed," he agreed cautiously.

"Tostig's not in the North—and he's not with Hardrada in Norway," the original doubter asserted. "Tostig's gone to his cousin in Flanders. If he invades this spring it will likely be from the south—just as Duke William will."

Hugh was distressed but not dissuaded. "His alliance with Hardrada holds. There is still danger in the North. They've made oaths to each other—"

"A Godwinson oath is worthless," Beauleyas interjected, using a lordly tone that brooked no disagreement. "Tostig's a kinslayer. No one trusts him."

Which was true enough. Tostig Godwinson's failings had precipitated the anarchy creeping across England. When the men of Northumbria had sought to have another man as their overlord—any man but the rapacious, unpredictable, and immature Tostig Godwinson—Tostig reacted with rage beyond the bounds of reason. He had attempted the murder of his own brother, Harold, and of his brother-in-law, King Edward. There were those who said it was Tostig's revolt that broke the king's health and sanity.

There was a new earl in Northumbria. Tostig had spent the fall and winter visiting his wife's kin and powerful men who, for their own reasons, encouraged his imagined grievance. What better way for Hardrada of Norway to sneak onto England's throne than to give Tostig an army and let the Godwinson brothers destroy each other? William of Normandy was among the few whom Tostig had not courted—but William did not need a madman to better *his* claim to the English throne.

"We ought to investigate," Hugh said, determined to save face.

"Shall I send a messenger to Hardrada?" Beauleyas snapped, his patience clearly at an end.

Ambrose pushed away from his wall. "Send out some of the men. They're restless. It's not a fool's errand if it keeps the peace. They may turn something up, they may not. It won't hurt to let the folk know we're the enemies of their enemies."

Beauleyas grinned. He kept his Greek around to have the benefit of his deviousness. He cared not a whit for the state of the sorcerer's soul, only that he provide clever advice—and, on occasion, invoke those powers an orthodox Christian might not. "I like that," he told his other men. "A hunting party."

The men fell into a heated discussion of who among the Torworden garrison should have the honor of plunging through the countryside. Wildecent took the opportunity to retreat from the curtained doorway. She itched in four places and dared not move while she was near the drapery. Hopefully she owed her discomfort to nothing worse than the aftereffects of holding still too long; if not, only a herbal bath would get rid of the fleas, and the saints alone knew where she'd find a bathtub at Torworden.

She was scratching her right calf when she realized Alison was awake and standing at the foot of Beauleyas's bed.

"What's going on?" Alison asked, stretching her arms over her head and giving a great yawn as she did.

"Our lord is meeting with his men. They've been talking politics—"

Alison wrinkled her nose. "He's not our lord, not yet he's not. I don't believe he's sent a messenger to our king. That was just talk for his men's benefit. Beauleyas hasn't won yet. Threats won't be enough."

Wildecent studied her sister in the fading light. Since Christmastide Alison's illness, if it were an illness, had evolved a particular pattern. She fainted in a thoroughly terrifying manner, then she fell asleep, and then she woke up unaware of either her collapse or the reasons for it. Wildecent watched another moment and reconsidered her judgment: Alison's behavior went beyond a simple loss of memory. It was as if she'd spent her dreams someplace where her strength was restored.

"I do not think we should do anything rash. We need more time to learn their ways. To learn what is possible and what is not—as Ambrose suggested," Wildecent said firmly.

A baleful look passed across Alison's face when the sorcerer's name was mentioned, but Wildecent had already crept back to the drapery and missed it.

"What are they saying?" Alison demanded in a loud whisper, unable to understand the conversation herself.

Wildecent countered with a slashing gesture for silence. "They're sending men out of the castle to search for outlaws," she whispered. "Keep quiet or they'll know we're listening!"

"Sending who? When? What outlaws?"

Wildecent's hand cut through the air again, this time with enough force to make her sleeve snap. Alison resigned herself to watching over her sister's shoulder.

"Twenty men-at-arms?" one of the older advisors asked with some dismay. "Who will lead that many? Will you travel with them yourself?"

There was only one chair in the hall that had both arms and a back: the lord's chair. Jean Beauleyas made good use of its superiority as he sprawled, raising his good leg up until it rested on the carved griffin of the armpiece. "Too early in the season for me," he averred. "But you're right, it's a goodly number of men. It will, I think, take both Eudo and young Stephen to keep things in hand."

That brought Ambrose back from his wall. His expression was dark and worried, but he was not the first among Beauleyas's men to speak.

"It will take more than twenty men to keep those two from killing each other this summer," Hugh said.

Beauleyas grinned again.

"What's going on?" Alison hissed; she'd heard the names and seen Ambrose's reaction. She and the sorcerer were enemies because they shared the same concerns; she knew to be worried.

"You don't want to know."

The Norman lord had swung his leg down and was sitting upright in his chair again. "I'll not have the one defying me and the other lying to me—"

"My lord, it is not in Stephen's nature to either defy or lie to you." That from Ambrose, who had joined the informal circle.

Now another side of Beauleyas's lordship asserted it-self—the side that feared the cleverness in the sorcerer's eyes, and feared the way both he and Stephen could stand calmly before his rages. "He would concoct this tale of outlaws in the woods to cover the fact he meant to have the heiress for his own! For all I know he may have lain her down in the forest and taken her there and then—but it won't do him any good, I'm telling you that. It's not her purity I'm interested in. It's her land and her loins: I'll have a son yet!"

Ambrose appeared to back down. Only a slight stiffness in his movements indicated he was not content to have his problems with Alison resolved in his lord's bedroom. Wildecent took note of his reticence and admired him. Her admiration was interrupted; Alison could no longer contain her curiosity.

"What's going on? They're angry. Is Stephen in some sort of trouble? Is he in danger?"

Jean Beauleyas glanced over his shoulder. Wildecent bit back a harsh reply and whispered, instead, "I don't know."

"Her father is not dead yet." That from one of the younger men of the council.

"Her father is an idiot! A man without a brain—why else did I tell my nephew to leave him behind? I've got what matters now, and if the damned wench will use her head she'll realize she's got the best of it. She'll be better off than the rest of her English sisters!"

Ambrose ventured a soft question. "And what about her sister, my lord?"

"Hafwynder told me himself the dark-haired one was his ward. An orphan he'd taken in for charity with no family or fortune. She doesn't figure in my plans at all. She can join a convent for all I care."

"I had wondered if, perhaps, since you see fit to marry Alison yourself—"

"Waters run deep, eh?" The scar on Beauleyas's face twisted his broad grin into a sneer. Wildecent was trembling and clutched Alison's hand without thinking. "You want her for yourself?"

The merest trace of redness marred Ambrose's pale complexion. "No, my lord, for Stephen . . . or Eudo, whichever of them survives—"

"She's an orphan, man! A common whore for a mother and God Almighty knows who for a father—Hafwynder swore she wasn't his get."

"She's French—"

"So much the worse."

"My lord, I think—"

"I don't care what you think, man. She's no different from a wench from the village. I don't care who wants her. God's blood, if you decide you *want* her—she's no part of my honor. But even my bastard's blood is too good for her to marry!"

There was nothing more for anyone to say. Ambrose retreated and Wildecent hid her face behind her free hand. Alison pulled her sister away from the curtain, into the dusk-lit room.

"What did they say? What's wrong? I heard them mention my name. What did he say? Is he going to keep Stephen and me apart? Does he think he can force me to his bed?"

For a moment Wildecent was frozen between rage and

horror. She opened her mouth, but no sound came out—
no angry words for Alison's insensitivity or pleas for compassion. Then she ran sobbing to the treasure boxes, and
did not care who in the outer hall heard her cries.

CHAPTER FOURTEEN

f Wildecent had hoped for comfort while she cried, she was doubly hurt. Alison had recognized no name but her own, and worried for no fate but her own or Stephen's. She left her sister huddled amid the treasure boxes and went to the outer hall, determined to wring some explanation from the man who claimed to be her lord.

A small troop of day-laborers had come up to the donjon from the bailey and were erecting tables for the lord's supper. There was a well in the bailey, and a bread oven, but all other food was prepared at the foot of the hill and carried each evening to the griffin chair where Jean Beauleyas chose to eat.

Alison was noticed, but no one spoke with her—not even Stephen, whose face was swollen and bruised from the blow he'd taken on her behalf. She caught his eye, but his expression was unreadable. She took a step toward him, but an Englishman was at her side, telling her it was time to go to the stool beside Lord Jean Beauleyas. She cast another glance in Stephen's direction, but he had already taken a place near Hugh de Lessay.

The food was cooling—as it could not help but be, considering its journey—but it had a pleasant aroma. Wildecent inhaled the last of her tears. She was hungry enough to face Jean Beauleyas and the rest of his men. Shaking her plaits behind her shoulders, smoothing the folds of her skirt, and withdrawing her hands demurely in her sleeves, she pushed through the drapery.

And came to a stunned halt.

Alison was already at the high table, sitting on Lord Beauleyas's left side. No stool was set to Alison's left, nor was there any other empty place at the linen-covered table. Wildecent dug her fingernails into her palms and tried to swallow the lump in her throat. Did they expect her to serve her sister? No, they expected her to serve the lord's intended wife.

CONQUEST

A common woman of no particular parentage might be grateful for the opportunity to pour a noble lady's wine, to fetch her dainties from a distant platter and offer her own sleeves as a napkin. But Wildecent was not a common woman, regardless of her parentage. Had she been naked she could not have felt more shame; had the Church not forbidden it, she would have plunged her dagger into her heart.

"My lady?"

She turned. Ambrose. *Ambrose,* her mind's voice repeated but her tongue could not recognize him.

"You were listening earlier, weren't you?"

Numbly, willing muscles to move but not feeling when they did, Wildecent nodded. There was concern in his face, but precious little compassion. Still, when he extended his hand, she unknotted her own and placed her fingers across his.

"Will you share my plate?"

Again she nodded. The lump fell from her throat to her stomach; she wished she and it could fall through the floor. He led her to the far right end of the high table and, in a voice every bit as commanding as the Norman lord's, demanded another stool be brought to his side.

It was a subtle thing to share a person's plate—not the same as sitting to one side or the other, sharing only common platters and a water bowl. She and Alison often shared a single, bread-covered plate. Sharing was a mark of closeness. It was an honor between equals . . . or lovers, though some fed their dogs in just such a manner. Wildecent did not know if sharing Ambrose's plate was an honor for her.

Of course, they had to sit close together. She could smell the scent of him—rather spicy, as if he masked himself behind musky perfumes. Certainly he was fastidious at the table—using a little gilt fork while everyone else, including herself, was quite comfortable using the left hand to fish food from the common platters and the right to bring it from the shared plate to the mouth. English society was considered quite civilized, even overcivilized, but Wildecent felt coarse beside him.

They shared the same wine cup. Wildecent was careful to reach for it only while he was chewing, lest he reached for it as well and the wine cup become a love cup. She was careful where she looked as well—never to her left, where she might meet Ambrose's eyes; nor further left, where Alison could be heard engaging Lord Beauleyas in artless conversation; nor out to the center of the hall, where she was certain she'd meet a dozen pairs of condescending eyes.

Then she was careless and reached for the wine cup when she might better have reached for her bread. His fingers closed over hers and she had no choice but to look at him.

"I thought you, of all people, knew not to be afraid of me."

Her hand went limp beneath the mild accusation. "I . . . I'm not afraid . . . of you. But I have no *place* here. I can be cast aside without a moment's hesitation. In his eyes I'm no different than anyone who warms his bed at night."

"You could be raised up just as easily."

She shook her head. "Alison perhaps, but not me. I'm no fool, *Lord* Ambrose." She put her bitterness in the honorary title. "It does not take land or noble blood to give me wisdom."

He had the courtesy to release the wine cup. "I have never thought you a fool. But you would be a fool if you surrendered easily. Someone went to considerable trouble to see you safely into England. Surely it would have been easier to put you in a convent someplace in France—"

The wine burned in her mouth and throat. "I do not think of such things," she insisted weakly.

"You should. Jean Beauleyas will."

"You'll put ideas in his mind?"

Ambrose managed a laugh. "Like your foster sister, Alison? Let us agree that neither of us is a fool, nor is the lord of this donjon. What you heard notwithstanding, Lord Beauleyas gives nothing away but that he gets its value back. It won't take sorcery to get him thinking about you."

"He may take too long, then. I learned today it will be no easy thing to live at Torworden."

The sorcerer took the cup from her hand. It was empty; he called for an English boy to refill it. "I have," he assured Wildecent, "defended myself in the most ordinary of ways. I do not encumber myself with a sword because I do not need to—not because I cannot use one to good effect. My shadow is long enough to protect you—and Stephen."

The boy came back with the wine. Wildecent stared past Ambrose and for a moment found herself looking straight into Alison's eyes.

"It was one thing," Ambrose whispered in her ear, "to plunge into Stephen's private thoughts while he lay injured. But it is something else that she does now. She has bound him so close that I cannot see between them. I think even she knows it is beyond her control. You may tell her I will help break this binding if she cannot. All she need do is ask."

"She will never do that," Wildecent whispered as Alison glowered. "She would sooner die, and take Stephen with her, than turn to your sorcery. Besides, they love each other. How it began doesn't matter now."

Ambrose frowned. "Stephen loves her because he has no choice. I cannot be certain about Alison. Your sister is not the woman she was. Her mind is no more her own than her father's is."

"Alison has been ill. She is weak, and tires easily; the journey exhausted her more than she will admit. She feels the changes in our life, and grows melancholy. She thinks of Stephen because he is the sun of her life." Wildecent tried to sway the sorcerer with her eloquence, but his frown deepened.

"She has nightmares, does she not? And fainting spells? No—don't deny it. I can read the truth on your face."

Wildecent shredded the embroidered hem of her sleeve. "Alison would never hurt anyone. She loves Stephen. She's promised herself to him. You heard her—"

"Lying does not become you, Wildecent."

She flushed scarlet and gulped the wine.

For her part, Alison saw Wildecent's whispered conversation with the sorcerer, and her final radiant blush, as nothing short of betrayal. She had not forgotten her foster sister, or abandoned her. Indeed, Alison had never been more aware of her obligation to the girl her father had brought to Hafwynder Manor. She would see Wildecent well-settled—once she had her own situation in order.

Beauleyas was courting her; she'd been courted often enough in the past to recognize the signs. But the Norman's politeness was facile. It would be so much more convenient if she agreed to marriage. His pleasantries—phrased in English, of course—served only to make his true goal easier to see. Why else ask how many men had sworn to her father and how many of those could bear arms? She replied politely, and truthfully, for he might have sources of his own, but she kept her emotions close about her.

From time to time Alison cast a discreet glance at Stephen. Discreet because Eudo was watching, and she knew that Eudo would move swiftly against Stephen where he did not dare to move against his father. It was a dangerous game she played: dissembling with Beauleyas to keep his son at a distance, while seeking a clear avenue to Stephen. Even with her magic, Alison's ingenuity would have been taxed, but she faced these Frenchmen with nothing more than the ordinary feminine wiles any head-blind woman possessed.

And, in light of that, Alison had short temper for Wildecent's blundering. She was preparing an oration calculated to reduce her sister to obedience, when Lord

Beauleyas pounded his fist on the table. The hall quieted. He got up and shoved his chair aside.

Jean Beauleyas held the oaths of a half-dozen Englishmen. Even among the men who had followed him from Normandy, there were a handful of dialects and regional loyalties. When he addressed his entire company, he spoke slowly and in a mercenary argot Alison could comprehend. Thus she learned that twenty men would leave Torworden in search of outlaws and minions of the Norse king, Harald Hardrada.

She approved, in a cautious way, until Beauleyas proclaimed that two men would lead the party: his nephew and his son. Then Alison, like everyone else, gasped inwardly. She threw caution to the winds and confronted the cat-smiling nobleman as soon as he settled in his chair again.

"Murderer!"

His smile never wavered. "You must share the blame, my lady. I controlled their rivalry until you set yourself between them."

"Set myself between them! I never laid eyes on your bastard until this morning!"

"You see what you cause by meddling in men's affairs?" His voice grew harsh and his eyes flinty. "It is not a mistake you will make again—now that you are *my* ward and will become *my* wife."

Alison's acid curse was lost as Eudo, drunk on wine and his father's favor, shoved platters, plates, and cups to the floor. He bestrode the table and bellowed his father's war cry. Men who had no love for the Beau-Bastard took up the cheer. A sense of fellowship spread through the hall. Perhaps it infected Eudo; perhaps he was simply smarter than most believed. He opened his arms to his cousin.

"Let us be brothers," he invited.

All eyes turned toward Stephen; the hall was quiet again, but none was quieter than Alison and Ambrose. Alison felt her thoughts twist into a plea for Stephen to reject those outflung arms. Everyone blinked as thunder crashed against Torworden's donjon; when their eyes opened again, Stephen had vaulted atop his own table. He assayed the distance separating him from his cousin: too far for a standing leap, so he took a falling step to the floor and bounded up to accept his cousin's embrace.

Close beside each other—Stephen a bit taller, Eudo somewhat broader in the shoulders—the family resemblance was strong. A warlord would be proud to make either his heir. Yet it was equally clear, despite the fraternal support they proclaimed, that they could not stand for long on the same mountain. In some eyes, Stephen was the superior leader: subtler, deeper, polished with a fine charisma.

Yet others detected the softness of the Mediterranean: an indolence, an appetite for unmanly loves of women, cleanliness, and luxury. These preferred Eudo, whose appetites matched their own.

The young men shrugged off each other's arms. While the hall still echoed with unwon praises, they exchanged looks that promised their next embrace would not be empty-handed.

"Wine and ale for our men!" Stephen proclaimed, lest anyone dwell too long on the falseness of his affection for his cousin.

Alison pulled her lips into a thin, pale line as the English servants assembled at the outer door. Another peal of thunder had rocked the donjon; the open shutters showed dark stains where the first raindrops had struck them. Yet the English, solid freemen who had, perhaps, farmed this land before Beauleyas made it his own, were sent back into the night to haul casks and skins for their patrons' pleasure.

She sent another thought winging across the hall to Stephen, chastising him for mistreating her people, but— like her earlier pleas and commands—it did not touch his conscious soul. When Stephen was among his peers he was as impervious to her magic as Beauleyas himself. And Beauleyas, though he kept a sorcerer near his right hand, was utterly untouched by anything arcane.

The English heiress made a show of turning her wine cup upside down and realized, belatedly, that only Beauleyas had watched her.

"Do you refuse to wish them godspeed?" he challenged.

Alison shook her head but refused to right the cup. "I would not be served by men who labor like beasts."

"Torworden is served by freemen; did *I* object when you sent *slaves* to serve me at Hafwynder? I do not ask them to like me, and they do not need to ask me to protect them. How well did you protect your people? Can you protect them from Harald Hardrada, much less Duke William?"

He did not talk down to her—she was grateful for that—but his confidence was unassailable. So long as he and his kind dwelt in England, neither she nor her father nor all the Hafwynder Manors with their full larders and tidy stock pens could promise protection to anyone.

"King Harold will drive you back across the Channel," she replied with more hope than conviction.

Beauleyas ran his finger along his scar as another man might absently scratch behind his ear while he sought the best answer to an annoying question.

"It was over long ago," he began, speaking as softly as the raucous bragging in the hall would allow. "Before you were born; before *I* was born. Our Normandy was held by the first Duke Richard. We still spoke like Danes, and our rivalries were not with the French but our Viking grandparents. Your England had a king—Ethelred . . ."

Alison grimaced: Aethelred Unraed, Ethelred Bad Counsel, whose mismanagement had plunged England into civil war a half century before.

"Everyone had an enemy in the Danish kings Svein Forkbeard and Cnut. Duke Richard had a daughter, Emma. When Ethelred married Emma, alliance was made between the English kings and the Norman dukes. The Danes got nervous and the damned Capetians in Paris got greedy; there was war. But the English king had no stomach and the Norman dukes could not win alone. Ethelred was killed; Emma sent his children to Normandy, then married Cnut. Both Normandy and England fought for their lives."

The saga was sung differently in Hafwynder Hall, but Beauleyas's version was not wrong.

"Kings are annointed by the Church; so is a Norman duke. He carries the souls of his people on his shoulders like a priest. Between her two husbands Emma of Normandy got a handful of children. The English dynasty should have been strong for generations—but it wasn't. Twenty years, my lady, for twenty years your English nobles tried to make grist of your Norman-Danish meal, as we Normans made grist of our French neighbors.

"We came through the fire as tempered steel. You— your greatest families were dust by the time King Edward reached the throne. For English advisors Edward turned to Godwin of Mercia—who revealed his lineage to no man, not even his king! Duke William may not have the blood of Alfred or Cerdic in his veins, but, *Deus aie,* who IS this man you call your king?"

Alison bit off the reply that William was a bastard. It was irrelevant. William knew his parents; he honored his common-blood mother and ennobled his half brothers, but no one, not even King Harold himself, knew the names of Godwin's parents. Bastardy was an inconvenience easily overcome by a man of strength, but unknown ancestry—hidden, concealed ancestry—implied a shameful ancestry, and that was a fatal flaw.

"He was a good earl to my father. A strong warlord for Edward."

Beauleyas closed in for the kill. "These things and more he would have been had he kept his oath to William and not taken the throne for himself. Together, England and Normandy would push Hardrada back to Norway and then deal with the Capetian fools in Paris! He broke a sacred oath, Alison Hafwynder; by your own laws he should have been executed, but you crowned him king!"

To Alison's surprise there were tears in his eyes. She

had no interest in politics, yet she felt a poignant empathy with Harold.

"What was he to do?" she asked, not caring that her voice strained and broke. "Where was William of Normandy? Where is he now? England must have a king, and Edward had no sons. Harold Godwinson did what was best for England. What more can a *king* do?"

Beauleyas traced his scar again in silent agreement. "The tragedy must be played out," he conceded. "Sacrifices must be made."

Alison swallowed her tears in a hard lump. Haloes grew around the torch flames, and her stomach churned in rhythm with the thunder.

Sacrifice!

For a moment the Norman lord's face blurred. It became the face she'd seen in her dreams and in the forest, his scar mimicking the tendrils of life flowing from the Green King's mouth. It became her father's face and the face of King Edward—whom she'd glimpsed just once in her life. Then it became King Harold's face—or perhaps just an Englishman's face, for she'd never seen an image of their new king. Alison closed her eyes hard.

"Are you unwell?" Beauleyas inquired.

She opened them again and stared into the Norman's eyes. The light had lost its radiance, but she felt as if she'd fallen from a great height. "I am . . . tired. I would retire, if I could."

"I shall have a chamber prepared for you."

He called two men and pointed to a frayed tapestry beside the outer door. Numbly Alison realized the donjon contained more than the two rooms she and her sister had seen, but she was still too stunned by her visions to feel at all grateful or relieved.

CHAPTER FIFTEEN

f you please, Lady Alison . . ." Hugh held the tapestry back with his left arm—and opened the door to the outer stairway with his right.

Alison looked up at him, aware that, as he and Guy stood, no one in the hall would realize she had not climbed the interior stairs but had descended the exterior ones.

"If you please . . . ?" Hugh repeated.

She had a satisfying image of Jean Beauleyas's rage when he discovered she was missing, and gathered her skirts under her arm.

"Why?" she asked when Guy threw his cloak around her for protection from the weather.

The men held their peace. Though they laid only the gentlest of guiding and supporting hands on her as they negotiated the slick, muddy log path from the donjon to the bailey, it was apparent they were following orders, and explanations had not been included.

Lightning struck so close Alison could smell it. The thunder was so loud she felt it. Despite herself, she cowered in Guy's arms. He held her steady. She could feel his body trembling—though he did not seem the sort to fear the elements.

"Quickly now," Hugh called, as if either of them needed any urging.

Then they were in the bailey-yard, splashing through the puddles past the stable lines. Alison moved too cautiously for Hugh, so he swooped her up and carried her to the sunken hut where she'd spent the previous night. Guy pulled the door open, and Hugh thrust her across the threshold before swiftly shutting the door.

If this was Lord Beauleyas's idea . . .

"Alison?"

Stephen's voice. Alison cast back her borrowed cloak as he stepped into the lamplight. They embraced, kissed until he winced, and she pulled back to study the dark shadow that spread beside his nose. Feather-light, she drew her fingertips across his injuries, appraising them as any healer might, until he caught her wrist and pulled her hand away.

"I hate him," she proclaimed. "I'll run away. I'll jump from the roof of the donjon—"

"It won't come to that," Stephen assured her.

"He's sending you to your death!"

He caught her other hand and gathered them both between his own: the symbol of fealty and protection from lord to vassal. "He's sending my cousin and me out to do what must be done. I am not blind to Eudo, but we will not take our quarrels beyond Torworden's gate. That would be both dangerous and dishonorable—"

"Don't be foolish, Stephen. He told me he did not expect you both to return—and he did not seem to care which of you killed the other."

Stephen's face grew hard with thoughts that led away from this moment, but he had taken some risk to be alone with his beloved and did not intend to waste precious time arguing about Eudo. Releasing her hands, he pulled her close and rested his unswollen cheek against her damp hair.

"I'm sure if I were going to die beneath Eudo's hand, Ambrose would take great pains to warn me. I'll hear no more of it tonight."

His fingers moved beneath her braids, loosening the laces at the neck of her tunic. His lips followed the curve of her cheekbone and chin until they rested against hers. When Alison was relaxed and no longer protesting he carried her through the straw to the box-bed and lay down beside her.

As bastardy was a Churchly sin of no great import to folk of either high or low birth, so virginity was a Churchly virtue and already nullified by the plight-troth they had sworn in the forest. Yet Alison could not give herself to any man—not even Stephen, who loved her.

Plight-troth or no, she captured his roving hand and let hot tears fall onto his neck.

With a sigh that shook his whole body, Stephen levered himself onto one elbow. "There is nothing to fear. No one shall come between us, I have sworn that," he said, smoothing her plaits against her ears. "I doubt, sometimes, that I am as firmly fixed in your heart as you are in mine."

Alison's tears turned to shame. She could be sure of Stephen; she had—as he said—fixed herself in his heart. Before Stephen had stumbled into Hafwynder Manor, all injured and mysterious, Alison had given few thoughts to love. She had trusted her father to sort through the shire swains who paid court in the great hall. She would say yea or nay, of course, but a man was the best judge of other men.

Since the plight-troth, Alison had seen that there was more to the bond between herself and Stephen than either her own meddling or love. She didn't love Stephen; she needed his love. The thought of him lying dead somewhere filled her with horror and sent cold tremors down her back.

The Cymric gods had accepted Stephen as her lover. They appeared in her dreams to praise him—then, invariably, the dreams became black nightmares. He was her hero, and she built a wall around her heart. Alison held Stephen's love—the love she had brought into being—at arm's length, knowing she must surrender it.

Stephen knew nothing of old gods or dreams. He only knew that he had hurt her with his words. Women were, after all, not like men. He caught her tears on his sleeve and directed dire thoughts toward the Englishmen who were so callous with their daughters that they were not taught to trust the men who cared for them. All of England would be better off when William got the island in hand. If he could make a good show of himself in the coming campaign, Stephen was certain the duke would

overrule his uncle in the matter of Alison Hafwynder and
her land.

They rested side by side, lost in their own thoughts,
while the storm passed beyond Torworden. There was
still thunder. They did not hear Hugh's knocking, and
he had to push the door open.

"It's time."

Stephen grumbled something unpleasant in Greek he
had learned from Ambrose, and pushed himself free of
the straw.

"Do not worry about me," he commanded, giving her
one last kiss before sending her to the donjon and his
uncle.

"I must. Nothing must happen to you," Alison insisted, wresting herself free of his grasp.

He had not really expected her to say anything else. "I
am no soft English lord to sit quiet on my lands counting
my sheep," he warned her as he searched within his tunic
for a pouch. "Still, if you must worry, hold this as a
token of my love."

He put a small object in her hand. An earring—only
one; the other had been sold during the journey to Torworden—that had long been in his father's family. The
stone was not large, but it glowed with a rich, emerald
fire in Alison's palm.

Green, she thought, unwilling to wrap her fingers
around it as he expected her to do. "Dear God, Stephen—by all that you hold holy—"

Folding her fingers over the gemstone, Stephen tried
unsuccessfully to hide his disappointment. Most men of
his station, especially at his age, were not wealthy in possessions. A good sword, good armor, and a strong horse
were more important than gold. He had not yet begun
the campaigning that would lead to land and treasure.
Yet the emerald was beautiful, and Alison had stared at
it as if it might sprout legs like an insect.

He resented the way she spurned his gift, hooking it
casually into her linen undertunic before taking up a sack

of her clothes that lay in the straw. He remembered the warnings he'd had from Ambrose and thought to turn Alison out of his heart. Then she looked up at him, and he realized the pain of loving her was far less than the pain of losing her.

Hugh came into the hut and picked up another of the bundles. "We'll see her safely to the upper room," he said quickly.

Stephen said nothing as his men escorted his ladylove away. The thunderstorm had left a gentler rain in its waked. Gentle, but still winter-cold. He pulled his tunic high around his ears and scrambled toward the long barracks. It had been less than a week since he had pledged his love to Alison, barely a season since he had first met her, and though he would admit it to no one—not even admit it fully to himself—he welcomed the chance to leave Torworden.

Alison held her head high through the rain as they climbed the log path to the tower. She knew what the men with her must be thinking. They'd think less of her if they knew how the emerald burned against her skin.

The hall still echoed with raucous shouts and slurred proclamations. They ascended the interior stairs without attracting attention. Pleasant incense hung in the air; light outlined a wooden door at the top of the stairs. Alison clutched her sack tight as Hugh rapped on the door.

It swung open, revealing the first comfortable room Alison had seen since leaving Hafwynder Manor. Wool tapestries shrouded the walls; a hot brazier sat in a stout, sand-filled box; a washbasin sat on the sideboard, with steam rising from its depths.

"Saints and angels be praised," she whispered, taking a long stride into the room and letting her sack fall to the floor beside her.

"Good evening, Lady Alison."

She spun around to the feared and hated voice. Ambrose knelt amid an assortment of scrolls and manuscripts, some of which had already been placed in the chest at his side. Wildecent, looking guilty, sat on a stool beyond the chest. The finer details of the room—the images woven into the tapestry, the strange objects beside the washbasin—now caught Alison's attention.

"Lord Beauleyas suggested you might be more comfortable here," Ambrose said, rising to his feet.

"I . . . I don't want . . ." Alison remembered Hugh and Guy standing behind her. She didn't discuss magic in front of the head-blind, not at Hafwynder Manor and certainly not in a sorcerer's chamber.

Wildecent stood up and took the bundle Guy had carried from the hut. "Thank you for remembering my clothes," she interjected gracefully. "I'm sure, Alison, there is no better place in all Torworden for us to stay."

None of the men missed the duel between the sisters. Ambrose gathered his papers and shoved them into the chest, letting its lid slam shut as he joined the other two men beside the door. "I'm sure you'll rest comfortably here," he said, leading the masculine retreat.

"How could you!" Alison swore once the stairway was quiet.

"How could I what?"

"How could you agree to spend the night in *this* room?"

The smile on Wildecent's face was not a pleasant one. She scattered the contents of her sack across the bed with one violent shake, then turned to face her sister.

"Would you like the truth, dear sister? Shall I remind you that no one is fighting for *my* inheritance? No one makes rash promises to *me* in the greenwood. Shall I be my common, coarse, bastard self and remind you that I cannot choose much of anything, but must grab what passes my way like a drowning man? Or perhaps I should ask you how you came to be with Hugh and Guy. Why is your tunic so wet? Why is there straw sticking in your hair?"

Mortified, Alison reached for her plaits and removed

an offending bit of yellow grass. Then, satisfied that she had humbled her sister sufficiently, Wildecent purged the anger from her voice.

"Actually, it was much as Ambrose said, though he did not mention the village girls who joined us in the hall after you left. I think Lord Beauleyas finally realized he could not seat wenches beside us if he was to keep control over his men. Most of the men he has here have neither family nor fortune—and they are all a long way from home. I don't think he regrets bringing us here, but I suspect we'll see a lot of this room."

"It reeks of sorcery!"

"It reeks of sandalwood—I put the incense in the brazier myself."

"You know what I mean. It grieves me, Wili, to see you enrapt with a sorcerer. The Cymric gods do not abandon you merely because you cannot speak with them. They'll protect you—"

"They'll have their hands full protecting you from your three men, Alison. They won't have time for me. I've seen how we're watched. If I'm to be thrown to the wolves, I'm grateful to be caught by a wolf with clean hands."

Alison considered her sister's words, then knelt down to warm her hands over the brazier. "I am stretched and bent until I feel as though I will break. I wish you truly were my sister, Wili. I wish we truly shared everything. I feel so terribly alone."

"It would be different, but no better," Wildecent said coldly. "And I wonder, now, if any of our dreams could ever come true. I do not think even Lord Godfrey knew who my parents were or why they sent me away. Sooner or later it would have come to this, I think. I'm glad you have Stephen—but I must find my own course."

Wildecent meant to be firm, but not to show her bitterness. She meant to break the false bond of sisterhood between them but leave the threads of friendship intact. She couldn't begin to guess how Alison would feel, but she certainly hadn't expected her to burst into tears.

"I'd gladly give you Stephen," Alison sobbed, producing the emerald earring and holding it above the brazier.

Wildecent hid her hands in the folds of her skirt. "Stephen loves you, and you love him. Between the two of you, I expect you'll have your way in the end."

That brought more and louder tears. "He can't love anyone but me. And I don't want to love him—not anymore. I'll be the death of him."

Head-blind she might be, but Wildecent could tell when something was said for effect and when it contained a grain of unnatural truth. "Alison, what have you seen? Since Christmastide you've talked of blood and sacrifice. Until a week ago it was our lord fa— Lord Godfrey's death, now you're talking about Stephen the same way. What do you see when the madness comes over you?"

Childlike and guilty, Alison shuffled her feet and twisted her shoulders. She wanted to confess, but the images grew misty. The *geas* clamped down on her thoughts. Her eyes and limbs grew heavy. The emerald winked with seductive warmth; she clasped it onto her tunic again and went to the bed as if Wildecent had vanished from her world.

The dark-haired woman watched her go. If this were magic, she'd choose sorcery. Ambrose's eyes were never so unfocused. She pulled the muddy boots from Alison's feet and tucked the bedclothes around her. Her sister began to speak in a sleeper's voice, but Wildecent did not try to understand. She lowered the bedcurtains and left Alison to her strange, dreaming world.

Alone beside the brazier, Wildecent was drawn to the chest Ambrose had left unlocked. She had gotten a glimpse of the scrolls and manuscripts as they were tucked away. Most were in languages she did not recognize, much less understand; a few were in Latin, with which she had a halting familiarity, but none had been in English. Still, she lifted the lid and stirred through the scraps of parchment.

But while kneeling beside it she felt a draft and then, seeking its source, discovered a low passage behind the tapestry. She lit an oil-lamp from the brazier and crawled into Ambrose's inner sanctum; he had not, after all, forbidden them to explore his quarters. The sanctum was about the size of the bedroom, but austere and cold. A spider's-web dome of shining wire was suspended from the beams; a pattern of mind-addling complexity was drawn on the floor beneath it. Scattered along the walls were sacks of dirt, stones, scraps of cloth, miniatures of buildings, and machines whose purposes Wildecent could not guess. She remembered the *micros* Ambrose had constructed in the tower room at Hafwynder Manor and knew this was where he worked his major sorceries.

The wire web was elongated, dropping toward the floor at the northern limit of the circle. A cushion rested outside the complex pattern, showing where Ambrose knelt during his sorcery.

This is how Alison got into trouble, Wildecent reminded herself as she approached the cushion. *Tampering with Ambrose's sorcery. Leave it alone. If anything could be done, Ambrose should do it. I could ask him—he said he'd teach me . . .*

Her wisdom vanished in the drafts that pervaded the room and kept the wire basket in constant, shimmering motion. Wildecent touched an exposed wire, and got a lightninglike spark for her effrontery.

Get out of here, she told herself as she knelt down on the cushion. *You'll get hurt. But I didn't get hurt before. I saved Alison's life.* She recalled Alison's listless body lying in Ambrose's bed. *I should just ask him. He won't turn his back on Alison. He said he'd help her . . . if she wanted to set Stephen free. I think she wants to set him free now, but she can't.*

He'll know how to stop the Cymric gods. He could set them both free.

Wildecent stared at the floor. Her eyes followed the maze of lines, pausing at the symbols inscribed at some of its junctions. Alison and Lady Ygurna used herbs to achieve an ecstatic union with nature; Ambrose followed the paths he'd drawn with colored chalks and the shadows from the wires that hung over them. He also used a talisman and, remembering that she had no such object, Wildecent relaxed. Without a talisman she could work no sorcery.

The sanctum was peaceful in a way that churches or the bolt-hole at Hafwynder Manor were not. There was an emptiness here that allowed Wildecent to spread her worries and concerns over a larger area. She used the pattern on the floor to guide her. She imagined the bolt-hole at one juncture, with Alison and her aunt beside it. Those three intersections in the south—were they the three wood kings . . . or were they Stephen, Eudo, and Lord Beauleyas . . . or Lord Godfrey, Stephen, and . . . who? In the center, where the powder was thick, and glinted in the lamplight, was that Ambrose . . . or was that she?

Wildecent shook her head. She didn't want to think about Ambrose, at least not while she was thinking of Alison and blood sacrifices. A powerful gust of wind drove rain against the outside walls and set the wire trembling. The shadows moved, and Wildecent rocked back on her heels.

But it was too late. The hypnotic movements of the wire-cast shadows had her. Even her prayers and curses fell into its rhythms. She looked past the patterns, past the donjon into a dark, cramped hut where someone slept restlessly.

"Ambrose? Ambrose? Ambrose, I've made a terrible mistake. I didn't think anything could happen—"

Light came. Wildecent was not surprised to see the sorcerer sprawled on his back, his bare shoulders visible above the blankets.

"I'm sorry, Ambrose. I'll get this undone . . . somehow."

His lips parted. He seemed about to wake up when—
to Wildecent's utter horror and amazement—a ghostly
Ambrose separated from the sleeping figure. He held his
arms before him and made slow passes through the air.
He seemed to be reaching for her—and it seemed he could
not reach her.

"Ambrose, it's me—Wildecent. I'm sorry—"

"Wildecent?"

His eyes opened—very much his eyes, just as it was very
much his naked body. Wildecent averted her eyes, and
noticed as she did that she was also ghostly: faintly glowing, definitely naked. The glow turned pink.

"What haunts me?" Ambrose's eyes grew wider. He
made warding gestures with both hands. "Alison?
Ygurna? The green power of the forests?"

"No, me—*me,* Wildecent," she protested before realizing that he could not see and hear her. There was some
small comfort in that. "I'll leave. I'm trying to leave."

She thought it might actually be possible. She had tried
and found she could move, then she hit something—his
wardings—and now when Ambrose looked at her, Wildecent knew she was visible. She expected anger but what
was in his eyes was hardly anger.

"How did you come here?"

Suddenly he was no longer naked but clothed in rich
garments of black and silver. Wildecent felt her naked
image glow crimson. She did not have the power to clothe
herself, and Ambrose did not look away. She tried to
explain the tangle of thoughts that had brought the web
to life. At last he turned away from her.

"I should have known from the first," he said, more
to himself than to her. "You are too much like me. I
found the magi in much the same way." He shook his
head, remembering some private joke. "They had to take
me in . . . make me part of their brotherhood. I was too
much of a nuisance to leave outside. In that you are not
enough like me—I dare not bring you close."

Wildecent reached out for him. She felt, rather than heard, his scream.

"Gods! Dear lady—have you no mercy?"

But Wildecent had felt it—a spark that shot through her insubstantial body: a sense of life, of ecstasy. She knew what he meant. Men and women could be sorcerers; they could live in the outer world—have lovers as they wished. But they were advised not to look to each other for such pleasures, for when sorcery wove through passion, the lovers might well lose their separate souls.

Ambrose threw up a barrier between them. The last thing Wildecent felt before a wind swept her back to her own body was his anguished denial: the triumph of the mind over the heart.

CHAPTER SIXTEEN

t was still raining the next morning. A capricious wind drove cold needles of moisture against Ambrose's face. He hurried up the log steps of the motte.

The great hall was deserted except for a hound, feasting on the dregs of dinner, and two ragged Englishmen scrounging in advance of the hound. None of the three noticed the fluttering drapery that marked Ambrose's passing. He paused outside his room to remove his cloak and boots before pulling the latch-string.

Putting the women in the upper chamber of the donjon had not been Ambrose's idea—no matter what Alison chose to believe. When he had sworn his services to Beauleyas, the Norman lord had, in turn, promised Ambrose privacy. The sorcerer wouldn't complain—not aloud, anyway—but he meant to secure his possessions, if it was not already way too late.

He expected the sisters would sleep late. His bed was as comfortable as anything Hafwynder Manor had to offer, the tapestries kept the room quiet, and his sandalwood incense was not without its soporific qualities. He put a lock on his manuscript chest, then raised the tapestry Wildecent had discovered the previous night. Once inside his sanctum, Ambrose lowered behind him a panel Wildecent had not discovered. Then he opened a high clerestory shutter and checked the room for damage.

A pool of oil stained the floor where Wildecent had dropped the lamp in her escape after their midnight encounter, but otherwise the room was undisturbed. Ambrose sighed; he had hoped for chaos. He studied his basket of light: the wire and silk web suspended from the ceiling. It had not even swung out of alignment with the geometria inscribed on the floor. All was as he'd feared, and he marveled that he had not suspected anything before.

The girl had used his talisman at Christmastide without

destroying either it or herself. His master in Byzantium might have been capable of such a feat; or his twin, if he'd had one—or the woman who fit snugly into all the hidden places of his heart.

He unknotted a length of red silk, removed a silver wire from the basket of light, and twisted the wire around his finger. The dome wouldn't work for him until he replaced it—and shouldn't work for Wildecent. Then he closed the shutter. Unless they were very observant they'd never know he'd come back to his chamber—and if they did notice, he hoped they'd take it as a warning.

The practice arena was deserted. Not even the most dedicated Norman chose to improve his skill in such miserable weather. A few men congregated in the stableyard tending their horses, a few more could be heard laughing and swearing in the long barracks. Most of them, including Beauleyas and all those who would ride out with Stephen and Eudo, had gone down to the village to be shriven.

The Normans and their companions gave only passing thought to their souls. The wealthier among them bought salvation when they endowed a church, but the rest attended to their sins only at the start of the campaigning season or other holy days. The men of Torworden had caroused until dawn, then staggered off in search of a priest.

Ambrose had never confessed his sins. It did not seem likely that a man who raised the spirits of the dead could only be absolved by a superstitious parish priest. If he needed to be absolved at all.

He headed for the jumble of huts and stalls outside the bailey gate. Torworden was an enigma on the English landscape. Jean Beauleyas had wrought changes all along this stretch of the Windraes, but he had not induced the families of the nearby village of Lachebroc to settle within sight of his walls.

Artisans, farmers, and tradesmen had been drawn by the needs of forty-odd men. They came each day to the gate to offer their services and vanished each night to live with their own kind. The Torworden men had to go outside for everything they could not, or would not, do for themselves. Ambrose got his bread at a ramshackle hut and would have stopped at a fuller's stall to have the dirt brushed from his cloak if it had not been raining.

Pondering the twists of fate that had brought him from the magi of Byzantium to the rain-slick cartways of England, Ambrose left the nameless day-village behind. Asia Minor was not immune to bad weather, but it was not a place where rainy, overcast skies were the norm. Good weather was God's weather here in England. Nothing grew in the Mediterranean world that could compare to the greens of England's forests and fields, but by Ambrose's careful calculations there were four miserable days for every clear one.

With the world constricted to a circular patch seen through his cloak's hood, Ambrose wondered—and not for the first time—why his masters had pointed him westward to complete his education. A stone turned under his heel, and he skidded to one knee before regaining his balance. He stopped dreaming of sunshine and watched his footing more carefully.

Ambrose left the cartway for a steep footpath a bit before the river-straddling village of Lachebroc. A staff would have been useful, this final leg of his journey, but he reached the ruins of a hermit's rectangular cell without falling. He and Stephen had discovered the stone cell shortly after their arrival at Torworden the past August. They each had other retreats now, but the hermitage was still their favorite whenever life at Torworden became unbearable.

Huddled into a corner, Ambrose let his mind escape into contemplation of alchemic transformations—specifically the one producing dry heat. Stephen would find him eventually.

"You look absolutely miserable, my friend," Stephen

began sometime later when, fresh from the Lachebroc church, he stumbled into the hermitage.

Ambrose hadn't expected to be discovered until much later in the day; he suspected his friend had been looking to get away by himself also. As always, Stephen disdained a cloak's protection. His hair was plastered against his face; his cheeks were red and his words made wispy clouds between them. Ambrose, by contrast, had managed to dry the inner layers of his clothing and was almost comfortable. "Not so miserable as you," he retorted.

"Ah, you should have seen me earlier this morning. The wine had flowed freely since sunset—"

"Spare me."

"Make room on the bench?"

Ambrose shifted around so they both could sit in the shelter, though his legs were once again exposed to the cold rain.

"Don't suppose you could start a fire for us?"

The sorcerer cast a withering look. "If I could start a fire, you don't think I'd need you to suggest it, do you?"

"You said you never stop learning."

"For a man who's been on his knees baring his sins and soul to his God, you're in extraordinarily good spirits. I don't suppose you could be persuaded to take them elsewhere?"

Stephen shrugged, but his smile faded. "I'd been shriven before I left for Pevensey at Christmastide. I haven't had much opportunity for sinning since then."

"Opportunity or desire?"

The young knight sighed, a steamy exhalation that left him hunched over and morose. "God knows what's happened to me since then," he conceded, "but not any priest. She loves me, Ambrose, I swear it. She's given me her troth—" The sorcerer raised his eyebrows and Stephen looked down at his feet before continuing. "But not as I love her," he admitted.

"You don't really love her." Ambrose paused. "Not freely."

Stephen hid his face in his left hand and parried Ambrose's words with his right. "You don't understand. You're right—but you don't understand. It is because I *do* love her. What's done is done. I realized that last night. She's run rampant through my memories; I see her in places she's never been, doing things she will not do— does it please you to hear me admit that?—but I can't bear the thought of losing her."

"We should leave this place, Stephen; leave England altogether. There're other places to win a name and fortune. We could go to Sicily. Surely there's a place there for two sell-swords . . ."

"Two?" Stephen asked, lowering his hand.

Ambrose nodded.

"You'd set aside your sorcery?"

Ambrose nodded again, wondering if Stephen would ask why; wondering how he would answer if Stephen did. But there was only silence, and silence made him uneasy. "I can," he said defensively.

"Set aside sorcery or take up a sword?"

"Both—if necessary."

Stephen leaned back. "Hmm, you're fast enough with your damned Greek sword, and you ride well enough. You're as good an archer as I am—we've proved that often enough—but you can't ride and fight at the same time—and you don't know the first thing about a lance—"

"I'll learn!"

Stephen shook his head. "Too late. I learned to fight; you learned to read—"

"And you could learn to read if you wanted to."

"You're serious, aren't you?" the younger man said, as much to himself as to his friend. "You want out of here that bad, and you want to be done with sorcery?" He looked into the rain, piecing things together before he looked back at Ambrose's face. "What's happened to *you?*"

Ambrose recalled what Wildecent had awakened within him. He sought words to describe it, but there were none in any of his languages. When he finally spoke he touched only the very edges of his turmoil. "If I do not leave soon, I fear I may never leave. I have no defense against the magic of this land."

"Of the land or of the woman? I *did* notice Wildecent last night."

"They are not sisters, you know. At first I felt sorry for her—"

"At first?"

"She grew up with Allison . . . and Ygurna. They told her of magic but denied her the practice. Of course there is some attraction—"

Stephen laughed and shoved Ambrose's shoulder. *"Deus aie!* I grew up around you and I never felt the least attraction! So, you've finally found yourself a woman. It's about time." Then, more confidentially, "You're not breaking any vows, are you?"

The sorcerer could not suppress a grim smile. "No, no vows. But a man like myself must be very careful. And I was not careful at all."

"No one's going to stop you from marrying her, like you said—they aren't sisters. You aren't going to have to fight your kin for her."

"I could become obsessed by her. There would be nothing else in my world except her. I could starve and not care so long as she was with me."

Stephen understood that feeling; it gnawed in his gut even as they talked. "Do you think leaving England would solve our problems?" he asked.

"I cannot see how leaving would make them worse."

For several moments Stephen stared at the trees. He felt the grief of leaving Alison—the empty places in his memories—and knew in time the grieving and mourning would fade, as it always did when the living kept on living. Then he shook his head. "Not now," he whispered. "It's more than Alison, Ambrose. It's my honor, my name. I'd be leaving her to Eudo or my lord uncle himself. I can't leave until I know I won't be abandoning her."

"She is what they call *witegestre,* Stephen, a priestess of these forests—a witch. You might abandon her, but I do not think she will be abandoned."

Now Ambrose had pushed the matter too hard. Stubbornness and pride hardened Stephen's face. "You can go; I give you leave to go back to France, or Sicily, or Byzantium if that's what you want, but I will stay until Alison and her lands are safe."

"You have forgotten your homeland."

"Haven't you?"

They sat listening to the rain. Ambrose was wet to the skin, cold to the bone; he had not forgotten Byzantium, but he could conjure none of its warmth in his mind. He willed himself to ignore the coldness in his hands and feet. His will broke, and a shiver ran along his spine. "I gave my word to your father that I would help you so long as we both lived—"

"Cheer up, then," Stephen said, punching Ambrose's shoulder again. "If my cousin has his way, you'll be on a ship for France before the trees are full green." It had been a jest; men always laughed when they could not feel heroic, but the humor was lost on the sorcerer. Stephen stared at Ambrose's sodden hood, unable to see his friend's face. "I'm not going to die, am I, Ambrose?" he asked in a tight, boyish voice. "You'd know if I were going to die, wouldn't you?"

Ambrose shook his head. The hood fell back and they looked into each other's eyes. "So long as I remain here I will not look into the future, Stephen—not even to see tonight's supper. But I will know if you are ever in danger, and I will do what I can to help you."

"*Deus aie,* how did it come to this?" Stephen asked, not expecting an answer, and not getting one either. He waited until a frigid trickle of water slid past his collar before jumping to his feet. "If there are no answers, my friend, then there's no use in sitting out here in the rain . . ."

Ambrose managed a weak smile as he got to his feet and pulled his hood around his face again.

"And, if you're not peeking at the future, then you don't know which of us will get to Lachebroc first. But I say the one who gets to the millrace last buys ale enough for both of us!"

Stephen was off, whooping and shouting as he crashed through the trees. Ambrose hesitated; the gap between them felt far wider than seven years. He grabbed a winter-killed sapling, thinking he'd best have a staff to negotiate the steep path. He felt weary, exhausted . . . *old*. And suddenly he could not let Stephen beat him to the millrace. Sweeping the heavy cloak under one arm, he plunged recklessly down the slope after his friend.

"He's been here," Wildecent said. It was almost mid-day and the sisters were just getting dressed.

"How do you know?" Alison looked around the chamber, unable to see that anything had changed until Wildecent pointed out the lock on the manuscript chest and the tapestry, which, when she turned it up, revealed a solid panel rather than the crawlway she remembered. "Why should he care about a piece of cloth?" Alison asked.

"I don't know," Wildecent lied.

"Well, it must mean something. He came seeking in here while we were still sleeping. We'll have to check if he's set some sort of trap for us—"

"He wouldn't do that, Alison," the dark-haired girl insisted. "He's not petty."

Alison let the laces drop from her fingers. "Don't get involved with him, Wildecent. No matter what good you think might come from it, don't meddle with sorcery," she said in a voice that was more pleading than angry. "It may be that we can no longer be as sisters but, please, don't meddle with him. The price is way too high . . ."

Wildecent turned away. *Little do you know, dear sister. Little do you know.*

he weather had cleared by the next morning. Alison and Wildecent stood at Ambrose's window and watched the men ride north from Torworden. It did not promise to be a dangerous journey; they wore mail hauberks, but they laughed and rode easy in their saddles. They'd be gone about a fortnight, following the Windraes until it met the Roman road they called the Foss Way, then northeast into the old Danelaw where Hardrada and Tostig would have spies if they had spies at all.

Alison remained at the window, fumbling with the neck edge of her linen tunic, after Wildecent had gone back to mending a tear in her sleeve.

The garrison had been reduced by half. Torworden was rarely quiet but it became more relaxed as the fair weather held. Men tended their horses and lazed in the sun, enjoying their rest at the start of what promised to be a long campaigning season. A message had arrived from William of Normandy; Lord Beauleyas had Ambrose read it aloud in the hall. The duke was gathering men, hiring ships, and buying supplies, but he would not land in England before he had secured the pope's blessing. The men rolled their eyes—few things were as slow as the Papal Curia.

They took more care with their armor and their swords after that. Harald Hardrada wouldn't wait for the pope. And if Harald swept down from the North, Torworden would muster with the English. Harold Godwinson might have two enemies in William of Normandy and Harald Hardrada of Denmark—but that didn't make Harald and William allies. But if Beauleyas led his men with Godwinson against Hardrada, what would he do when William finally set sail for England?

The dilemma made Torworden's lord irritable and he shared his ire with everyone. Norman honor would best be served by heroic death in a battle vanquishing Harald of Denmark and critically weakening Harold of England—but no man wanted to die.

Alison felt the ambient nervousness. Her command of Norman French improved each night as she sat on her stool beside Jean Beauleyas. He explained his dilemma, but she had no thought for honor, only for the peaceful life at Hafwynder Manor that seemed inexorably doomed. She fretted about everything: her father, Stephen, the manorfolk, her own fate, and the nightmares that were becoming worse, until everything was one thing and it gave her no peace.

She did not confide in Wildecent. Her foster sister was firmly in the sorcerer's shadow, though Alison watched them closely and noted they derived no pleasure from each other's company. They ate little from their shared plates and looked past each other when they conversed. In other times she might have sought her sister and comforted her—even though she loved a sorcerer—but in these times Alison had no strength for anyone but herself.

The two women were together constantly, however. Jean Beauleyas wanted it that way. They did their sewing under watchful, masculine eyes and were confined to the donjon and bailey. For nine interminable days the young women dwelt in their separate, anguished worlds. At dawn of the tenth day the walls between them shattered.

Alison burst from her nightmare. The *geas* had weakened; images lingered after her eyes were open. In her right hand she held a sickle, in her left, a man's head. There was warm blood running down her arms, and nothing within the dark confines of the bed could convince her otherwise. With a guttural wail, Alison thrashed through the curtains and shook the nonexistent blood onto the floor.

Wildecent looked up from the far side of the brazier.

Each was disheveled and vulnerable in the ruddy light. Each retreated behind defensive, empty masks that revealed nothing. Then slowly each realized she had not been caught by the other.

"I had a dream," Alison admitted.

"I couldn't sleep."

"I keep having the same nightmare over and over again. Each time it lasts a little longer; I get a little closer to the end."

Wildecent pulled a stool closer to the brazier so Alison might sit, if she chose. "I'd guessed as much," she said slowly.

"I make the hero's sacrifice to fertilize the land."

"I'd guessed that, too."

"With my own hands. I can feel the blood, but I can't see his face . . . yet."

"Maybe once you do, you'll know how to stop it."

"Maybe." Alison came closer to the brazier, then wearily sat down on the manuscript box. "Why couldn't you sleep?" she asked, more to fill the silence between them than from any curiosity.

"I guess I don't want to dream either."

"The hero's sacrifice?" the blond woman asked, feeling her heart start to pound, but Wildecent shook her head. "Ambrose? I—I have noticed you together. I should have . . . I didn't."

Wildecent looked up from the brazier. "Oh, Alison, can't you put that out of your mind?" But her voice was flat and her eyes were empty. "Ambrose isn't stealing my soul any more than he ever stole Stephen's."

"But—I *felt* sorcery. I did, Wili. There was something dark and heavy . . ."

"Stephen was seven years old—and he had a habit of running away from his tutor. Who got in trouble when *we* weren't where we were supposed to be, Alison? How often did Edwina get a beating instead of us? Ambrose marked Stephen so he could find him when he went hiding. Tell me you wouldn't do the same."

Alison plucked at the loose stitching of her sleeve and chewed her lip before answering. "You believe him?"

Wildecent nodded. "And you? Has he marked you so you won't get lost?"

"No, he hasn't. He couldn't—even if he wanted to."

"Our magic—the pure, wild magic of the forests and of the moon protects you?" Alison asked almost eagerly, unable to surrender her distrust of sorcery.

Wildecent got to her feet and strode to the other side of the brazier's pool of light. "I don't know why I even talk to you, Alison. You never listen. You're the one who goes around leaning on a person's thoughts; twisting their memories around. Ambrose can't do things with a *thought* the way you do. He has to plan; he has to have a reason. There's almost nothing wild about sorcery."

"Almost?"

Almost—but that *almost* lay like a sword between Wildecent and Ambrose. It kept Wildecent awake at night with the ache of knowing he, too, couldn't sleep. "We, Ambrose and I, are too much alike," Wildecent explained, choosing her words carefully. "We cannot be near the unrevealed world together. There would be too much . . . passion. We would lose ourselves in each other and"—she brought her hands together with a loud clap—"it would be over. I would not care for myself, I think, but he has so much to lose. We dare not even touch each other, for fear of what the spark might ignite. Sorcerers, it seems, may not love."

Alison recognized in Wildecent's voice the same morbid certainty she heard in her own thoughts. For the first time, she also heard the absurdity. "Don't be such a goose," she spat quickly. "Love and passion are the heart of magic—"

"Not magic, sorcery. Sorcery is order and reason. It stands opposed to nature."

"Then sorcery is a blind fool!"

Alison marveled at her own conclusion. With the *geas* exposed, it no longer mattered whether sorcery and magic were fundamentally opposed or fundamentally the same. All that mattered was that sorcery might free her from the obligations of her promise to the gods. Not that she would ever use sorcery, of course—there were still some thoughts that were simply unthinkable—but Wildecent might be induced to help.

"I believe I have been wrong," Alison began, catching Wildecent's attention immediately. "Magic and sorcery are different, but they do not need to be opposed to each other."

Wildecent considered Alison's sudden change of heart with evident distrust—but she considered it all the same.

"Now we know you have no aptitude for magic," Alison continued. "Yet you cannot learn sorcery because magic's passion stands between you and Ambrose. And because I did not understand the cold nature of sorcery, I overreacted to its presence in Stephen's thoughts."

Wildecent was not lulled by Alison's facile logic, and told her so with a dark glance.

Alison abandoned subtlety. "I can help you, Wili. I can give you a charm that will hold you and him safe from passion, but I'll need something in return."

"What?" Wildecent replied suspiciously.

"I need your help to protect Stephen from my dreams." Alison removed the emerald earring from her sleeve.

"Why turn to me? If you want to protect Stephen, talk to Ambrose."

Alison shook her head; she could not tell the sorcerer that this had all begun as a moment's jealousy. Her motives had been pure enough when she'd begun her quest through Stephen's memories, determined to free him from sorcerous domination—pure, even if incorrect. But Alison had been piqued to see that the women of the young knight's fantasies all looked more like Wildecent than her . . . and so she'd changed them. Not for love of Stephen, or for his love, but because he fancied small-boned, dark-haired women.

And if Ambrose would get angry because of her original motives, Alison knew he'd be justly furious when he learned that even now she wanted to set him free not to spare him—she did not, in her heart of hearts, believe he could escape her *geas*—but because she did not want his blood on *her* hands.

"You're the one I trust, Wili," she said finally.

"I'm no sorcerer, Alison. Ambrose and I—we've talked about sorcery, but he hasn't taught me anything."

Alison surged to her feet. "I trust you; I know you can do it. We're helping each other, just like we always used to." She put her heart into her words, but she followed them with a twist of her magic. *I'm sorry, Wili, I truly am—but I need your help.*

Magic rushed around Wildecent like a flooding stream. She could have fought it, but this time it was easier to move with it. "And, in turn, you'll give me what I need?"

Alison nodded.

They were sisters again. Laughter radiated from Ambrose's chamber, but it was shrill and born of a need to trust rather than any recapturing of trust. Ambrose had told Wildecent many of his secrets and, though he had not shown her how to work the panel to his sanctum, she knew where the lever was. She poked, prodded, pinched, and wriggled until the panel slid back, and she led Alison through the low door.

"What is that?" Alison asked as Wildecent cranked the ceiling open and light fell onto the web of wire.

"He calls it a 'basket of light'; it concentrates the power of sorcery."

Some similarity existed between magic and sorcery, Alison realized. She also cast a circle to concentrate magic's power, marking its perimeter with salt, water, and ashes before inviting the Cymric gods to share it with her. She had no need of wires, chalk, or silk, but she understood why Wildecent would take a position at the northern edge and instruct her to take the emerald to the center.

"I don't think this will work—" Wildecent settled under the point of the web but did not complete her thought.

"I have power within me," Alison reminded her. "Surely that is better than any cold crystal."

Wildecent gave a tentative nod. "To begin: concentrate on the image." Her hands began to shake and sweat. "Bring Stephen's face into the emerald . . . No. No, Alison. I cannot; I don't know what words to use. Something's missing. I don't want to go on." She began to rise.

"It's all right, Wili," Alison commanded. "You are the anchor; I will be the seeker."

"No. No, Alison—" But Wildecent did not have the strength to resist her sister's suggestions.

Alison knelt beneath the high arc of the basket of light. Her eyes were closed and the emerald caught the dawning sun in her cupped hands. Wildecent felt something shimmer through the wire tracery above and between them. Sparks and streaks of lambent green shot from the earring to the wire matrix. First Alison, then Wildecent, were swallowed in an emerald aura that sang against the basket of light.

Stephen rode on Eudo's left. A lance was balanced in his right stirrup although the surrounding forest was quiet. Too quiet. He was not alone in his unease as he rolled his gloved fingers across the rough haft of the lance. They all felt it, even Eudo, whose face glistened with sweat beneath his helm and coif.

"I feel eyes on our back," Eudo muttered, glancing away from the road.

"If there are, I wish they'd show themselves."

"I wish we could see more than a man's length into those damned trees."

Stephen bit his lip. It went against his grain to agree with Eudo, but he did agree. The English forests were forbidding in ways he could not describe. They were darker and wilder than they should be; they dominated the deteriorating Roman road. *Hwiccawudu* this forest was called; in English, Wychwood, the Wise Forest or the Witch's Forest.

He thought of Alison, and told himself there was no need for worry. They'd be at Torworden the day after tomorrow. They'd found no spies in the Danelaw. The worst of the journey was over.

They crested a hill and were confronted by a fallen tree blocking the road. They guided their horses into the stump-side of the forest.

Stephen heard a war cry and turned around to see a heavy net descend over the middle men of their column. He had a moment to wonder who had ambushed them; then he was surrounded and fighting for his life. Reflexes that had been hammered into his limbs took command. His shoulder dropped as he lifted the lance. His shield swung forward on its guige and his left hand grasped its enarmes before the lance was couched beneath his right arm. He took note of the weapons he faced: axes, single and double; the armor: inferior to his own; and his first target: a footman about to put his double-bit ax in a man still trapped by the net.

He came in from the side, ramming a man-width of iron-sheathed wood between the enemy's ribs; he let the falling corpse twist the lance free, and, with a shout of encouragement to his comrades, spurred Sulwyn about to face another assault. He couldn't count the men they faced or realize that there were, perhaps, too many for them to overcome, but his heart was pounding and he was praying as he lowered the bloody lance.

This one wore a hauberk similar in style to his own but constructed of leather scales and metal rings rather than dense chain links. He fairly ran onto the lance, but his scaled hauberk fouled the barbs, and the lance-head could not be withdrawn. Stephen thrust the useless weapon away, drew his sword, and kept Sulwyn pivoting.

The English battle-ax was a formidable weapon against the sword—even if the swordsman was mounted and the axman was on foot. Stephen gasped for breath and waited for someone to close with him.

He heard Eudo cry out, and the scream of his horse as it went down. He tried to get closer to his cousin, and they closed on him with a rush.

The sword's advantage was its mobility, its thrust, and its long, deadly edges; its disadvantage—against the ax— was a lack of power. A solid cut from an ax could do more damage than a similar cut from a sword, though a single sword-stroke in the right place would kill a man. Stephen kept his sword arm moving, deterring the axmen from committing their heavy weapons, waiting for the right moment.

It came. He brought the sword down and felt the shock as it bit deep into the enemy's unprotected neck. The bearded man dropped, and Stephen wrenched his sword free.

Eudo was swinging his sword double-handed and using the death throes of his horse to keep his back clear. Three men lay in the dirt around him; one writhed in agony; the other two were motionless.

The Normans acquitted themselves with the cold ferocity for which they were justly feared. All but three of the trapped men had cut their way loose. More than a dozen of the ambushers were dead or dying. It wasn't enough; the ambushers had archers with them as well. Arrows skidded off the chain mail or snagged in the felted padding beneath it.

The men of Torworden kept their vulnerable faces down and were slowly, individually pushed deeper into the forest. Here branches grabbed at the swirling swords; hidden roots tripped the war-horses. Stephen's style grew desperate; he and Sulwyn bled from a half-dozen minor wounds.

He backhanded the sword across an enemy's face and was, for a heartbeat, revolted by his own brutality. He lost awareness for an instant—when he regained it, he was looking at death. He couldn't parry the downward arc of the ax; it was going to hit something.

Stephen was not aware of driving his spurs into Sulwyn's flanks.

The horse reared. The ax came down in its shoulder and rose out of the axman's hands. Stephen dropped his feet from the stirrups and kicked free of the collapsing horse.

Reflex. Reflex and training. He couldn't hear himself screaming or feel the tears streaming down his cheeks. He charged the disarmed enemy, impaling him. That was a mistake: in the moments it took him to pull the sword free, pain shot across his back.

His shield was useless. He tried to shake it loose but his arm was slow. When his enemy grabbed it, it came free. The inside was brilliant with blood.

It's over, Stephen thought as he scrabbled backward, as pain gave way to a numbness no amount of discipline or will could overcome. *I'm dead.*

The green aura within the basket of light flashed crimson and began to churn malevolently. The women were caught in the sorcerous and magical wind. Wildecent tucked her head to her knees and Alison cried out.

Stephen!

Deep in the Wychwood, Stephen heard his name; heard Alison's voice. The sword was heavy in his hands, its point wobbled as he drew himself up for a final defense. The enemy was careless, already gloating. The young man had the satisfaction of knowing he would not die alone as the ax crashed through the ribs.

Stephen!

Alison fell to her knees beside him. Blood flowed from the corners of his mouth; his breath came in horrible gasps that rattled through the gaping wound. Alison's healer's reflexes were as deeply ingrained as any warrior's. She would watch him die. It wouldn't take long. She pushed his helmet back; there was no recognition in his eyes. He was already past any awareness of pain. He'd be dead before she'd begun to cry.

"What are you waiting for?"

Alison looked up into her sister's merciless eyes.

"Shall England survive? Shall we have a new king?"

It wasn't Wildecent, though Morrigan with her tangled black hair and her bloodstained robes resembled Wildecent. The only bright aspect of the goddess was the delicate silver sickle, which she placed in Alison's hand.

"What you have nurtured in love must be reaped in blood!"

Morrigan's fingers wove through air; Alison's fingers moved in harmony, reaching beneath Stephen's coif. Another figure joined them, a man as green as Morrigan was crimson. He had no head, but his gaping neck did not bleed.

"Give the king life!"

Alison pulled Stephen's head across her thigh, exposing the pale flesh of his neck. He was already dying—nothing worse could be done to him, and something of the England she loved would survive. She brought the edge of the sickle against his neck. Beads of blood seeped up where the supernaturally sharp silver touched his flesh. The necessary stroke would be gentle, like cutting water, and clean.

A shudder wracked his body. Dark blood flowed from his lips.

"Now!"

"No!"

She flung the sickle at the goddess and shoved Stephen's mangled corpse to the ground. The headless green man flailed the air before him. He dropped to his knees; his hands smeared across Stephen's face. But the sacrifice had not been made, and an ominous wailing filled the forest.

Alison crawled past Sulwyn and began to run.

he forest sounds pursued Alison. They changed as she ran, becoming the clang of an assembly gong. She embraced the noise, expecting it to pull her back to Hafwynder Manor. Instead she found herself in an unfamiliar room.

When she saw Wildecent, curled up at the edge of a sorcerer's circle, she recalled Torworden, and then everything came back. She had succumbed to sorcery. Images of Stephen's death in her arms, of crimson-streaked Morrigan, and the headless Green King hovered in her mind's eye. At least Alison hoped they were merely images placed there by the Cymric gods to chasten a rebellious priestess. She prayed they were not real memories of real events—but she did not know where to direct her prayers.

Alison reached out. There were crimson smears on her hands and tunic. Fresh blood. Stephen's blood. She stared at the marks, willing them to vanish, but they were very real.

"Wili!" she croaked. "Wildecent!"

Dark braids brushed over the chalk; hazel eyes looked up. Wildecent's hands and clothes were unstained, but she remembered everything. They groped toward each other; a sprig of holly fell to the planking between them.

"It was a dream," Wildecent whispered, stroking Alison's blond hair. "A nightmare. It didn't happen."

"Stephen's dead!"

"No. No he's not. It wasn't real. It didn't happen."

"Look at me, Wili. *Look at me!*" Alison pushed away from her sister and spread her arms. The blood had not, would not, disappear.

The gong still clanged. Men were running up the stairway to assemble on the guard-porch that surrounded Ambrose's chambers. It did not seem possible to either horror-struck woman that their misadventure could endanger Torworden itself. But then, it did not seem possible that it had happened at all.

"We've got to get out of here," Wildecent hissed.

Alison obeyed silently, crawling back to the bedroom. Wildecent cast a glance around the room. Nothing was amiss or out of place except the holly. She refused to speculate where it had come from, but she snatched it up before she blew out the lamp. By the time Wildecent returned to the bedroom, Alison had stripped to her linen shift, and was rasping at the bloodstains on her hands.

"I killed him," she repeated in rhythm with her rubbing. "I killed him."

"You didn't kill Stephen," Wildecent assured her, taking the coarse wool away.

The ruckus outside grew louder, but nothing intelligible penetrated the walls. Whatever was going on had everyone's attention. Wildecent allowed herself the hope that it was Stephen himself returning to give the lie to all she and Alison had witnessed.

"Get dressed," she urged Alison, thrusting a clean tunic into her hands.

Alison opened her mouth to argue just as someone put a fist to their door. She wasn't hysterical enough to greet someone in her linen, and hastily wriggled into the tunic. It slid down past her shoulders as Ambrose pushed the door open.

"Alison, Wildecent—you'd best . . ."

Wildecent pulled her sister's laces tight, but the sorcerer wasn't looking at them. The tapestry concealing the door to his sanctum had been left askew, but even that didn't hold his attention for long. Alison's clothes lay where she'd left them; the red stains were plainly visible.

"What have you done?" he demanded. Both women stood mute, and he repeated the question as he grabbed Alison's discarded tunic and touched the stain. He put his finger to his lips, then threw the cloth to the floor.

"You damned, abominable fools!"

His rage was more controlled than most men's, and all

the more frightening because he did not shout. He glared at Wildecent; she felt her heart sink. Alison looked away but he grasped her jaw and forced her to look at him.

Alison had never met anyone who was stronger than she was—not in an arcane sense. Until the coming of the Normans she'd never met anyone whose mind she couldn't manipulate. She never gave a thought to mental defenses because she'd never needed them. Ambrose's cold fingers, and the willpower marshaled behind his eyes, revealed a new dimension of fear to her.

"Tell me!" he commanded.

The whole misadventure, from the very beginning to the disaster in the grove, poured out of Alison's memory. He released her, but she had relived it all in a few heartbeats and leaned against the bed.

"Priestess? Do not flatter yourself. You're a spoiled child, a conniving pawn. You don't know yet that you've been used. A common murderer has more conscience than you!"

Alison slumped forward, and Wildecent rushed to catch her. "She didn't kill him, Ambrose. It was a dream," the dark-haired girl insisted despite her sister's stained tunic.

He was unmoved. "I'll deal with both of you later. For now I'm to escort you to the bailey-yard, where you'll welcome the caravan from Hafwynder Manor. And you'll act as if none of this has happened—do you understand?"

It was an impossible request, but both women nodded obediently.

"And let me assure you"—Ambrose took Alison's face between his hands again—"dear lady, it is not finished. Your blundering witcheries will not succeed. I will fight your damned bloody gods and your headless green kings if I must. But know this right now: your sacrifice failed; your king has no face and Stephen is *not* dead!"

His tone was as cruel as he could make it—and that was cruel indeed. It brought a flood of tears from Alison's eyes, and wracking sobs from her throat. She tried to get her arms around him, but he eluded her.

"The bailey-yard!" he commanded, giving them both a shove toward the door.

Wildecent stayed at her sister's side, still supporting her. They made their way down the steep stairs with the outraged sorcerer at their heels.

"He's alive!" Alison gasped, relying entirely on Wildecent to guide her. She missed a step, and both women lurched against the inner wall. "It can be undone."

Alison was pale and came down the log pathway slowly, but knowing that Stephen's death was not irrevocable was a powerful tonic. Bright sunlight and fresh air restored her strength. She was smiling when they reached the bailey.

There were only three carts, each pulled slowly by a team of oxen. Bethanil sat in the first, her pots and pans piled high behind her and her drudges walking stolidly beside the oxen. The second cart was covered and held the manor's treasure. The third carried personal possessions, including the baskets from the bolt-hole. Each cart was driven by a Hafwynder man. Greetings had been exchanged and the carts had passed under the stockade lintel before either sister realized something was terribly wrong.

All three Torworden men—Alan FitzAlan, Serlo, and Gauche-Robert—rode behind the carts. FitzAlan had the reins of a fourth horse tied to his saddle. The man on the fourth horse was not Godfrey Hafwynder but Thorkel Longsword, and he rode backward with his legs tied together beneath the horse's belly. Alison surged forward to demand an explanation, but FitzAlan would speak only with his lord.

"I bear witness to a crime," FitzAlan proclaimed once Beauleyas approached.

"He murdered our lord!" Bethanil shouted in plainer language that was echoed among the other English.

"Had you a reason?" Beauleyas demanded, while Alison struggled to get closer to the conversation.

"Not I, my lord, but the Viking. He struck Lord Godfrey's head from his shoulders not three days after his daughters had left." FitzAlan spoke clearly so all in the yard could hear him.

"Cut the Viking free and bring him forward," Beauleyas commanded.

A pathway was cleared and Alison was able to push her way to the edge of the crowd. She looked into Thorkel's face and knew the accusation was true. Hissing like a cat, fingers hooked and teeth showing, Alison launched herself at the murderer, but Ambrose caught her before anyone else was aware of her attack. His fingers probed the hollows beneath her ears and Alison found herself unable to move.

"There'll be no more bloodshed from you, my lady, not for any reason." He relaxed his grip somewhat—she could breathe and swallow normally—but a light pressure remained, and she dared not move against his wishes.

"Do you admit your crime?" Jean Beauleyas inquired in English. "Do you admit the murder of Godfrey Hafwynder, lord of Hafwynder Manor?"

The tall, blond Viking had suffered during the journey. His clothes were torn. A purple contusion swelled the right side of his face. He must have lost a few teeth as well, for he spoke with difficulty. But he spoke defiantly.

"I served my lord as he would be served. He was felled when Edward died, and should have accompanied his king into the next world. The gods cried out for the blood they had been denied, and I gave it to them."

Pagan practices persisted everywhere, but they were never mentioned aloud. The gathering in the bailey at Torworden drew its collective breath. For Alison the shock struck more slowly. Thorkel Longsword might cast his prayers to Thor, Odin, and that ilk, but his prayers had been *heard* by the ancient Cymric gods.

Alison kicked Ambrose in the shin and broke free, only

to find Wildecent holding her back. "They took my lord father," she cried, her words lost in the general tumult as Jean Beauleyas pondered justice in the matter. "It's my fault. I would not give them Stephen so they took my lord father instead!"

"Thorkel Longsword murdered our lord father," Wildecent insisted. "Murdered!"

"Because I refused to give them Stephen!"

"Didn't you understand FitzAlan? Our lord father was slain weeks ago. It has nothing to do with us or with Stephen. It's not our fault."

Alison quivered and stared coldly at her foster sister. Head-blind; even though she had witnessed all that had happened in the grove, Wildecent was still head-blind. The gods were not constrained by mortal notions of time. They could make a heartbeat last forever or age a man in a single night. They could fold time back on itself so all days were endlessly alike. Or they could rip time apart until no one could say what truly had happened or when.

Taking Godfrey Hafwynder instead of Stephen was a simple trick for the gods—but head-blind Wildecent would never understand that. The only one who would understand would be Ambrose—and he was worse than no one at all. So Alison surrendered to Wildecent, as much a prisoner as the Viking.

Jean Beauleyas had scratched the scruffy beard around his scar, he'd hitched the leather belt of his tunic, and he was ready to pronounce judgment.

"By English law—" he began.

"Riste blodorn paa rygen!" Longsword's voice rang out, and he straightened his beaten limbs to tower over the Norman lord. "No coward's English law! I claim the Blood Eagle!"

Beauleyas's brows knit together; he consulted with his men, none of whom knew what dignity the condemned man claimed. The Normans had been Vikings themselves not five generations ago, but they'd kept only the vigor of the North, none of the rituals. It remained for the

English, who'd been surrounded by Scandinavian customs since King Alfred's day, to explain Longsword's demand.

Eodred stood between Beauleyas and the criminal. "He claims his crime is against man's law only. He wants a hero's death: the Blood Eagle. He wants his ribs hacked through on either side of his spine and his living lungs lifted onto his shoulders. He would fly to Valhalla with his dying breath."

Jean Beauleyas paled. "Is this his right by law?" he asked quietly.

"I'll send him to his gods," Bethanil proclaimed, standing up in the oxcart and brandishing her cleaver for all to see. "For my lord and my ladies."

FitzAlan and Serlo wrestled the cook to the ground.

The Norman lord was astounded by the events in his bailey—and next to rage, astonishment was his most dangerous emotion. "Enough!" he shouted. "He is not a hero, and a cook does not dispense justice. All of you—stop gaping and go back to your tasks. A Viking's execution is none of your concern!" Then he told Serlo and Gauche-Robert to lock Longsword beneath the great hall.

Alison pushed past Wildecent, scarcely aware that she'd drawn her knife. "He has taken my father's life. His own is forfeit and mine to claim!"

The look in Beauleyas's eyes was more deadly than the look in her own. Torworden and Hafwynder men reached out to restrain her. Eodred himself pried the blade from her hand. She struggled until Beauleyas struck her; then she went limp.

"Take her up to the donjon. I'll have peace in my bailey!"

The little crowd dispersed as men carried Alison up the log path. Only Beauleyas, FitzAlan, Wildecent, and Ambrose remained by the gate. Wildecent came forward to reclaim the keys they had left with FitzAlan. The knight unhooked his belt and allowed them to slide toward her hand. The iron scarcely touched Wildecent's fingers before Jean Beauleyas took her wrist in a grip that made her cry out in pain.

"What do you think you're doing?" he demanded, squeezing until the keys fell to the dirt between them.

"Since our lady aunt's death we have held Hafwynder's keys—"

"Do you learn nothing from what I tell you? You are a nameless bastard and you have nothing whatsoever!"

FitzAlan looked away. He knew how the lord's temper always found a target every time he was discomfited. He knew what it was like to be that target—but that was no comfort to Wildecent, who staggered backward. Her mouth opened but no sound came out.

"Take her to my chamber. She'll learn this time! I'll put the proper look in her eyes."

Ambrose came from nowhere to pick up the keys and hand them to his lord. "As you wish, Lord Beauleyas." He put an arm around Wildecent's shoulders and guided her away. "He'll forget by tonight. I'll see to that."

Events had moved too swiftly for Wildecent. She tried to understand what had happened, tried to shake free of his arm. The layers of memory parted slowly. "You're touching me. You said we couldn't touch each other . . . mustn't touch—"

"I said I loved you. I was wrong."

"But, tonight . . . Why help me?"

"Because I'll need you and your damned sister tonight. After that I don't care who takes an interest in you—or for what."

They were on the far side of the motte, out of Jean Beauleyas's sight. Thorkel Longsword had already been taken into the donjon; the man carrying Alison had paused to get a better grip on her before climbing the stairs to Ambrose's chamber. Wildecent surprised even herself with the vigor she put into the slap that resounded on Ambrose's cheek. His hand went to his face and Wildecent backed slowly away.

He raised his fist at her, then caught himself. "She was

covered in his blood, Wildecent. Perhaps she didn't sacrifice him before, but now she'll do anything to get her father back. Do you dare deny it?

"And you helped her. Dear God, Wildecent, you helped her do it! Is this the magic, the sorcery you freely choose? Is this what love, and loyalty, and honor mean to you?"

Wildecent preferred his anger to the anguish she now heard in Ambrose's voice. "Is Stephen truly alive?" she asked softly.

The sorcerer turned away and put his hand over his eyes. "I don't know. I always thought I'd know . . . I touch the place where he is in my mind, and he's still there, still safe. I touch his blood . . ." Ambrose's chest heaved and it was some moments before he could continue. "I think—no, I *believe* Stephen is alive, but I don't know where . . . and I don't know when." His arm dropped to his side.

Wildecent took his hand. There was none of the ecstasy they had feared these last two weeks. Only an ordinary hand, moistened with tears. He would not look at her.

"I'll do whatever I can do to get Stephen back. Alison, too. Whatever must be done, I promise it, my lord."

He still would not look at her as they started climbing again, but neither did he pull his hand away.

lison heard a bar drop into place outside the door. She was locked in, confined as she had never been confined—and she didn't care. For four months, since she and her aunt had tried to protect Haf-wynder Manor from its fate, her nerves had been rasped by the conflict between the magical and the mundane. Now that, too, was over. Every sense had been reduced to numbness; every emotion had burned itself to a cold cinder.

The man who dropped her on Ambrose's bed had not even realized she was conscious. Alison could summon no anger toward him. Even the grief she summoned for her father was a distant thing. She was aware of no specific feeling, only a weariness that seduced her into sleep. She retreated within herself.

The bed rippled like a pond in a gentle summer breeze. She imagined drifting beneath warm sunlight—and slipped between the threads of reality. The sun disappeared behind wispy black clouds, and the wind carried a discordant chorus. Alison arose from a silk-draped barge, and stepped onto dry land.

This was a strange twilight world with no shadows or brilliance. It was autumn here, with flame-colored leaves and crisp grass beneath her feet. The wailing drew closer. Alison climbed the riverbank and scanned the dull gray horizon. A flock of black birds circled in the distance, moving slowly toward her. Hitching her skirts through her belt, she ran toward them.

A procession approached. Women, several dozen of them, rode mares the color of dried blood, and carried ravens on their outstretched arms. Hundreds more of the black birds wheeled overhead. The women wore stern, identical expressions. They hid their hair beneath black veils and their hands in leather gloves. They wore robes of deepest crimson, embroidered in gold and adorned with garnets that flashed blood-red in the strange light.

None looked toward the blond woman standing before them.

The first rider reined her mare to a halt. "Who are you to block our path?" she demanded.

"I am Alison Hafwynder, of England." She paused, and saw that neither her name nor her homeland brought a glimmer of recognition. "From the land of the living."

The woman turned to one of her companions and exchanged an enigmatic glance. "This too is the land of the living," she said with a touch of irony, a touch of malice. "But I do not think it is your land."

The procession split in half and flowed around her. As they rode by, Alison noticed that each of them had a silver sickle suspended from her belt, a sickle such as she had cast at Morrigan in the grove. She called out to them, demanding explanations, but they ignored her.

"You have used me!" Alison shouted. "You have tricked me. You have seduced me into betraying those who love me and you have made me an instrument of sacrifice. You owe me answers!"

They were unmoved by her protests; not even the horses or birds looked her way. Alison stared into each face, bringing her talent to bear in the hope that she could wring words from one of them. Most of the procession had passed by when one rider looked down.

"Ygurna! My lady aunt!" Alison exalted, weaving through the blood-bay mares to walk beside her aunt's stirrup. She tried to embrace her aunt, but the raven opened its beak and drove her back. "Lady Ygurna, help me—please . . ."

"You have failed us," Ygurna said, her jaw tight and her lips scarcely moving.

"It was not supposed to be like this. You knew what I had done. I did not mean for anything to go this far. He was never supposed to die! I couldn't take his life. I couldn't. It's not fair! How can anything be made whole with blood?"

Lady Ygurna's hands trembled; the raven bated with a grating cry. In the front of the procession the first rider turned around. Then they all turned and their eyes made Alison's skin crawl.

"You opened doors, created possibilities. Perhaps you did not intend anything, but you are dedicated to the gods. All that you do is done in their name. All that you have is theirs as well. The best sacrifice is made by the innocent and the holy. Nothing excuses you."

Alison took a step backward, dazed by her aunt's coldness. She had to run to catch up again. "Where are you going? What are you doing?"

"We go to complete the winnowing of the land. We have winnowed one battlefield; we ride to the last. All will be decided there."

"I must do something. I must make it right again."

"Join us."

Alison saw a riderless mare beyond Ygurna—where she would have sworn there was nothing at all a heartbeat before. She approached it. A vision engulfed her when she touched the mare's flank.

These women rode invisibly among the men during battle. They sought the mortally wounded men, and with their sickles made ritual incisions across their chests. The dying men's lifeblood was squeezed onto the land. It was the final vision beneath the *geas*.

Once she mounted she would be one of them. With all the rest of the long-dead Cymric priestesses, she'd reap the battlefields, renewing the land with warm, dripping blood. Alison could see the final battle toward which they rode. Normans would be there, and the English. She recognized Eudo's face and reached for her sickle—but it wasn't in its place at her waist.

The tableau shattered. The ravens surrounded her in violent chorus. Alison realized the procession had circled back, and the first rider stood before her. The sharp edge of a silver sickle glinted in Alison's face; she dropped the mare's reins and backed away.

"You have no gathering knife," the woman said in a beautiful voice that belied the harshness of her expression. "You cannot become one of us without your gathering knife. And if you cannot ride with us, then you must be sacrificed."

The other women began an antiphon: Not one of us, *sacrifice!* Not one of us, *sacrifice!* Alison looked for her aunt, but Ygurna had submerged into the chant. All the women had their sickles raised. The ravens were diving toward her, reaching for her eyes. She batted one of the birds away, then turned and ran.

She saved herself only because the women were unaccustomed to the unexpected. They were startled by a sacrifice who shouted and waved like a lunatic. The two women toward whom Alison ran lost control of their mares, and she was able to break out of the circle. The ravens pursued her to the river, where she found her barge had been replaced by a cup-shaped white hide coracle. The birds whirled around her head but they did not prevent her from leaping onto it.

"Take me home!" Alison shouted, as the round-bottomed craft bobbled into the current. "Take me home!"

The hide boat was steadied and began to move downstream.

It was late afternoon before Jean Beauleyas returned to his bedroom. He led a procession of knights and peasants, Normans and English carrying the Hafwynder treasure. He seemed genuinely surprised, and more than slightly displeased, to find Wildecent sitting by his hearth.

"My lord," she said, pushing the cat she held onto the floor.

"Get me some wine!"

She started for the door but halted when Ambrose called her. Another man ducked out.

"I hardly think Lady Wildecent knows where to find wine in the day-village," Ambrose explained.

"It's time the *lady* learned to do something useful!"

Wildecent took another step toward the door and again the sorcerer caught her eyes. "There'll be time enough for that later, my lord. She might be useful to us now."

Beauleyas spoke in French. "Why should I believe what any damned Englishwoman tells me? They're all devious. Devious witches." He walked to where Wildecent stood and grabbed her by the shoulder. He twisted her around until she faced him. "You and your sister, witches—both of you. Why should I take a witch into my bed where you'll work your curses on me?" He shook her as a cat shakes a mouse. "I should burn that damned manor to the ground!"

He thrust her aside. The English from Hafwynder Manor were gaping at him in horror and disbelief. When Beauleyas spoke again it was in a dialect they could understand.

"You're all peasants—and I'm your lord. Alison Hafwynder is my ward—not your mistress. And that one." He gestured where Wildecent cowered. "That one is simply mine."

Ambrose frowned, but before he could attempt to mollify his lord, Bethanil shoved her way to the forefront.

"You'll not be eating from my pots," she began, disdaining all honors and formalities. "I'm a freewoman and I'm not beholden to the likes of you."

"Then you, goodwife, may take the wench with you when you leave—but do not go back to Hafwynder Manor, for that is mine and I do not tolerate your insolence."

Bethanil propped her beefy hands on her hips. "Lady Wildecent is no kitchen drudge," she said with ringing finality, but she did not say she'd risk leaving.

"What is she then? Your dead lord's bastard? An orphan he found in the city and took in for Christian charity? She'd be dead but for him, and she'll be grateful to me if she knows what's best for her—"

The cook hesitated, then retrieved a velvet-wrapped treasure box from another of the Hafwynder men before advancing closer to the red-faced Norman. "My lord," she began in a more respectful tone. "It's true we don't know who her mother was, and that our lord was willing that she be considered his bastard. But Lady Wildecent's neither foundling nor orphan." Beauleyas opened his mouth to object, but she kept talking. "This box came to the manor when she did." She offered Beauleyas the box.

"FitzAlan!" Beauleyas raged in French, "what's the meaning of this? Do these peasants think to offer me what is already mine?"

The soldier shrugged and looked away from his lord's wrath. Beauleyas tore the velvet loose, but his anger evaporated when he considered the object the cloth had concealed. The ivory box glowed with age. The gilding on the carved stags that covered the top and sides was still intact. It was too delicate for a metal lock; three ivory pegs held it shut. And it had no place in the treasure of a rural English nobleman—or a rural Norman nobleman for that matter.

Beauleyas set it on the table and carefully removed the pegs. A silk scarf was folded within it. He unfolded it and stared at six huge coins sewn carefully onto the cloth. The coins were of a style he had never seen before, but were most obviously solid gold. They so captured his attention that he almost missed the pieces of vellum that remained in the box. These were covered with writing, and he thrust them at Ambrose.

"Here, read them to me!"

Ambrose stared at the largest of the three pieces. "It's in Hebrew, my lord."

"*Deus aie!* What have the Jews got to do with her? What does it say?"

"I don't know, my lord, there're some languages I can recognize but cannot read. Perhaps in Leicester—"

"Don't tell me I'm harboring a Jewess! Never mind Leicester. What about the other pieces?" he shouted.

Ambrose studied the other two scraps. "My lord, I think we should be alone."

The bedroom was cleared of everyone except Ambrose and Jean Beauleyas. Even Wildecent was sent into the hall, and FitzAlan was told to keep everyone—including himself—from the drapery.

"So, what are they?"

"They're receipts my lord, written in two columns, then torn apart. Lord Godfrey kept one half, the other remained with a Nathan of Winchester—"

"More Jews!"

"Yes, my lord. But Wildecent is no Jewess. Listen: 'By this I swear, before God and my kind, that the child Melisande, daughter of Count Arnulf and his wife, Phillipa—' "

"*Count* Arnulf? Who by the holy saints is *Count* Arnulf?"

" '—is alive and thriving in my care. I attest this with a lock of her hair and a drop of her blood to be sent back to her mother. In return I accept these two gold *mancuses* for her upkeep until Easter next, when I shall come again and her family may reclaim her.' It's sworn and sealed. The other is much the same except . . ." Ambrose paused to recheck his Latin. "It mentions returning milk-teeth and the name Saint Suzanne."

"*Deus aie,*" God help me, Beauleyas swore in a more respectful tone. "I know Arnulfs and Phillipas by the handful; even a Melisande or two—but one family, and a count?"

"It is not impossible, my lord. And these coins. Hafwynder could have run his whole manor for a year on two of these coins—"

"Not if he were trying to keep the child hidden," the ever-pragmatic Beauleyas averred. "They'd have to be melted down. By all the relics, man, look at them—look at the profiles. Have you ever seen people dressed like that?

"By their marks they commemorate the baptism of King Clothar—"

"Clothar? There hasn't been a King Clothar in three hundred years. And six of them; the family still had six of them . . . at least six of them after three hundred years. Rich bastards . . . Saint Suzanne—I know a town of that name, and a dozen churches . . . a priory . . . Bring the girl and the cook back in. Maybe they remember something."

Wildecent stared in awe at the gold discs. She admitted what little she could remember of her childhood. Yes, she thought she might have lived in a stonework donjon once before and, yes, she remembered men with mail and swords, but she remembered no names. Beauleyas turned to Bethanil.

"You were there, weren't you? You folk see everything. What did you see?"

Bethanil knew little that was not already revealed in the scraps of parchment. The little girl was about six when Lord Godfrey brought her to the manor. She spoke nothing but French then, easily frightened and wary of everyone, though Alison eventually won her friendship. They called her Wildecent because she recognized it as her name beneath their accents.

When she had been with them a year, the Lady Ygurna had pricked the child's finger onto a white cloth and clipped a lock of her sable hair for Lord Godfrey to take with him to Winchester. The ritual was repeated the next year and the year after that, but when Hafwynder returned from Winchester the third time he still had the cloth and the tiny braid. The Jew was gone, and Wildecent's family was known to Almighty God alone.

Beauleyas grumbled his thanks and sent Bethanil away so only he, Ambrose, and Wildecent remained. It was beginning to get dark, and men could be heard erecting tables in the great hall.

"You're saved," Jean Beauleyas admitted, holding the gold-crusted velvet in his hands. "Someone tried very hard to protect you; someone had powerful enemies and something that was worth protecting. I don't know your people, but the south is riddled with counts—and feuds. The gold stopped. You may be as out of luck as my nephew, Stephen, but you might be worth more than your foster sister. And, just like her, you're my ward; your gold is mine and your future is mine."

Wildecent nodded, not that she equated herself with Alison, but that she understood she had become a valued pawn rather than a common one.

"Go now, make yourself ready for dinner. You shall continue to sit with us at the high table."

She nodded again and headed for the door. Ambrose was there first to open it for her. "Do we still have an agreement?" he asked softly, since it wasn't through his efforts that she had been reprieved.

She glanced up at him and nodded with her eyes alone before running through the doorway.

here had not been enough time for Bethanil to unload her pots, pans, and knives.
Supper at Torworden that night was no
different than it had ever been—at least as
regarded the food. The men knew their
lord was a richer man now and that a murderer languished in the locked storerooms beneath the hall. Jean
Beauleyas had made no proclamation regarding his second ward, the dark-haired woman, who continued to
share a plate with his sorcerer.

Still, there were few secrets in a donjon, and most of
the men showed Wildecent some greater courtesy than
they'd showed her on other nights. Likewise, they made
no mention of the empty stool beside Lord Beauleyas.
Alison had not come down for the evening meal, nor had
a plate been taken upstairs to her. Wildecent explained
that Alison remained in seclusion out of respect for their
father. No one argued, but no one completely believed
her. There were no secrets in a donjon.

"Has Alison agreed?" Ambrose asked Wildecent casually while they sat beside each other.

Wildecent swirled the wine in her cup then set it down
without drinking. "She is lost in her own world. I had to
bind her with sheets lest she harm herself while I ate supper
with you. There will be no talking with her tonight."

"We do not have time, Wildecent. She left Stephen
someplace where only she can reach him. You and she
knotted the fabric of time itself. It was an act against
reason *and* an act against nature. One of you must untan-
gle it."

Wildecent shook her head. "I don't know. I don't
know how to get there. I have no magic of my own. I
know nothing of sorcery. Both of you seem to expect me
to help, when I have no power of my own."

Ambrose lifted the teardrop crystal from around his
neck and placed it in her unwilling hand. "What do you

feel?" he demanded, closing his fist over hers. She cringed and wriggled her fingers beneath his. "Try! Don't give up so easily!"

The sharp edges of the stone cut into her skin. She squirmed; he squeezed tighter. Then warmth spread from Ambrose's hands and the crystal no longer hurt. Wildecent had never held the talisman before, never felt the sorcerous beacon that connected Ambrose to his younger friend, yet even without that experience, she could tell something was not right. Stephen was there—whatever, wherever "there" was—but he was trapped like a fly in amber. Barring the arcane, the magical, or the sorcerous, his only way out was death.

Wildecent looked up into Ambrose's eyes. "There's nothing I can do."

"You were there, weren't you? You were beneath my basket of light. Perhaps if you sat at the center and I along the circumference?"

She wrested her hand free as her whole being recoiled against that idea. "I can't," she insisted. "I won't try. I won't go there again."

Ambrose's eyes cursed her silently and he left the table. Wildecent stared at the plate without eating. In one day she had learned more about her ancestry than she had ever imagined. The stigma of bastardy had been removed. She had a new name, but she felt more at the mercy of those around her than ever. The dinner was endless; so was the climb from the great hall to the upper room she shared with Alison.

Wildecent sat on the edge of the bed and offered her sister slices of apple soaked in wine. To her surprise, Alison ate them eagerly. The wine brought color to her cheeks, and she gained enough strength to sit up.

"They have not finished with me," Alison explained as she took another slice of apple from the dish. "I have escaped them once, but they are not satisfied. It is not enough that they've taken our lord father; they would have both my heroes."

Wildecent shuddered, spilling wine across her skirts. "Our lord father is dead. Stephen is going to die," she said, hoping to convince herself if not Alison. "There is nothing that can be done except make matters worse!"

Alison gripped her sister's hand with a wild strength. The little plate went flying across the room. "I will make fools of them all. Every last one of them. They tried to use me, but I am more than they are. I have danced with the goddesses, while they have only gathered blood from the dead—"

Wildecent shoved Alison back onto the pillows. She wanted to believe that Alison was maddened by grief and fever, but there was no madness in her sister's eyes. Alison spoke of goddesses, and Wildecent began to suspect devils. She wanted to run down to the bailey-yard and search for Ambrose. But Alison had enthralled her and she could not move.

"All I need is the silver sickle," Alison whispered. "The silver sickle, and they shall have sacrifice and blood enough for the end of time."

With great difficulty Wildecent shook her head and took a step backward. "It's wrong. You must not shed a man's blood, Alison—no man's blood." She had not expected her words to affect Alison, but they did, and the blond woman slumped forward, her face hidden by her tangled braids.

Wildecent put her hands on her sister's shoulders. "What will be, will be, Alison. There will be life without our lord father; he was dying anyway, Alison, we both knew that. And there will be life without Stephen; you, yourself, said you never really loved him. But we can't make time flow backward, and we mustn't shed more blood."

Alison looked up. The wineglow was gone from her cheeks; her eyes were red-rimmed and hollow. "They tricked me, you know—used me—even our lady aunt. When they saw what I'd done, they came to me in my dreams. They said if Stephen died loving me, if he died by my hand, England would be safe and the Normans would never come." She leaned her head against her sister's breast. "It is so hard. I'm sworn to the land, Wili. My mother, my grandmother, all of us—all sworn to the land. I was born to do this. I can be the hero. If I can find the sickle, I can go back to the grove. Everything will be all right . . ."

She tugged at the binding sheet Wildecent had twisted around her waist, but her strength was fading and she couldn't pull the linen free from the bedframe. She said something more about the grove and the sickle, then fell back onto the pillows.

Wildecent tucked the blankets under Alison's chin and lowered the curtains. She was appalled by the idea of blood sacrifices, but even more determined that Alison would no longer be used by anyone or anything. She stared, not seeing anything until her sight fell upon the holly.

Two of the deep green leaves had fallen to the floor; several more were bruised. Wildecent lifted the branch carefully, afraid it might crumble—or slice through her fingers. She went to the wall, grabbed a corner of the tapestry, and whipped the branch across it. She'd hoped the cloth would come apart, proving that the holly was the silver sickle that Alison had cast at Morrigan's breast. But the tapestry remained intact. She opened the panel and took the holly into the sanctum.

She intended to demand the transformation of the holly into the sickle, as she had once demanded knowledge of where Alison lay beneath the junipers. She hadn't understood the *micros* when she'd made that construct work; she was not concerned that she did not understand the basket of light or its underlying *geometria*. She knelt on the northern pillow and concentrated her thoughts until the veins of her forehead throbbed and sweat ran down her back.

The branch remained resolutely holly beneath the center of the inverted wire and silk basket.

She crept to the center of the geometria, clutching her skirts tightly under her arm and careful not to disturb any of Ambrose's marks. With the branch pressed between her palms she tried again. Her heart pounded; her breath grew ragged and her palms became sticky.

The holly thorns pierced her skin, but the branch had not become a sickle.

Frustrated and overwrought from her exertions, Wildecent crept back to the bedroom. Those bundles from the oxcarts that had not been taken to Beauleyas's treasury or kept with Bethanil had been brought upstairs. After checking that Alison still slept, Wildecent ransacked the baskets until she found the masks of the three kings—one of whom was the Holly King—and carried them into the sanctum.

The outer circumference of the geometria was quartered. Wildecent arranged the kings at the outer quarters, sat in the north, and tried again. Five more times she tried, changing the positions of the kings before each trial. Finally she set them as they had been when she'd first laid them out—Lady Ygurna had said that chance held the greatest measure of truth—and crawled back to the center where the holly lay.

She spared nothing. Waves of heat flowed down her arms into the branch. The branch grew warm between her hands, but it would not change.

"You're going about it wrong."

Wildecent shrieked and flung the branch across the room. Her eyes recognized Ambrose long before her mind or heart. He was dressed in black and midnight blue, as was his custom, but these were not the austere clothes he wore in the sunlight. His velvets were as dark as winter, his silks shone like moonlit summer sky, and across both fabrics metal threads glinted in the lamplight, elaborating the patterns of the geometria. Wildecent was still panting and unable to speak when he gathered up the holly and laid it on the pillow.

His hands were elegant, moving with mystifying competence to bend a wire here, straighten one there, and unwind a fine one from the index finger of his right hand.

"Come here," he requested, extending a hand toward her. His voice was honey coating her fears. She reached for him and he grabbed her wrist. He pressed the sharp tip of the wire against a vein; her blood spiraled along the metal. "Now, where do you want to go?"

The bloodletting was more shocking than painful. Wildecent was transfixed by the dark beads clinging to the wire as Ambrose wove it into the basket of light. Then he took his talisman and suspended it from the same bit of wire. Wildecent's blood flowed downward, coating the crystal.

"Please don't tell me you don't know where you're going." There was pure and human pleading in his voice as he knelt down to stare at her.

"I wished to change the holly into a sickle," Wildecent said, snatching the branch from the pillow and retreating back to the center of the geometria. She felt the wires changing above her. Her heart trusted the sorcerer, although her mind did not.

"What would you do with the sickle?"

"I don't know—" She watched his face fall. "I don't . . . I can't put it into words, Ambrose. I'll know once I have the sickle."

He gave a weary smile and extended his arms crosswise from his shoulders. The wires of the basket of light began to glow, and the talisman shuddered and slipped to the first nexus of silk and copper.

"It must be a silver sickle," Wildecent added quickly.

His eyes opened once, then closed, and he began to chant. Wildecent tried to listen to his words—if they were words—but sorcery flowed beneath the chant, not within it. The talisman moved from joining to joining, sometimes rising against the curve of the basket, sometimes skittering along the circumference, making the entire web sway in the lamplight.

Wildecent felt nothing at first—less than she'd felt when

she'd struggled to focus her thoughts beneath the incomplete basket. Then the holly grew heavy in her hands and began to pull her downward. She was startled.

Don't drop it! Ambrose's exasperated voice boomed directly into her mind.

Wildecent clutched the silver sickle as it bore her downward through the donjon tower to the storerooms where Thorkel Longsword awaited the Blood Eagle. The air shimmered. Wildecent was in the condemned Viking's cell but they were not alone.

The three green kings stood vigil at the quarter marks—grim, disembodied faces. Wildecent remained at the center, standing rather than kneeling, and facing the pallet where Thorkel slept.

Get on with it.

She looked around, but Ambrose had not made the descent in any physical sense. Wildecent's courage balked. She stared from the sickle to the sleeping man and knew, beyond any doubt, that she could not hack apart his ribs or lift his fluttering lungs onto his shoulders. She couldn't even take a step forward.

By whatever you deem holy, woman—do something! I cannot hold this forever!

Wildecent whimpered and took a step forward. Thorkel opened his eyes. He saw something—but not Wildecent, for the names he whispered were strange to her. He was shackled; heavy chains grated across the stone as he ripped his shirt open. His bruised and beaten back was exposed to her, awaiting the ritual that would transport him to the gods of his people.

"I cannot. Forgive me." Wildecent whispered apologetically as she came around to stand at his head. "It must be our hero's sacrifice. For the land. As you gave our lord father—"

Her fingers obeyed her thoughts without feeling. She yanked his four braids upward and slashed across his naked neck. She held a goddess's sickle in her right hand;

it cut easily through bone and sinew. And—more miraculously—it seared the wound. There was very little blood.

If there had been blood, Wildecent would have fainted, sorcery or no sorcery. Without blood, she clung to consciousness—a tight grip on the sickle, a tighter grip on Longsword's grinning head—trying to breathe and vomit at the same time.

Get back to the center!

Wildecent heard Ambrose. She felt the apprehension in his voice and understood it. The green kings were beginning to move. She was more aware of her danger than was the sorcerer beside the geometria above her, but she made no move toward the center.

I can't hold you!

She hoped, as the green men surrounded her and bore her off, that Ambrose understood that whatever happened would not be his fault—any more than it was going to be hers. Then, as the world became a black maelstrom, Wildecent didn't think of anything at all.

She was back in the grove. Stephen was dead. His corpse lay at her feet. Blood still oozed from his wounds and his flesh was still warm to the touch, but the timeless moment had ended. Stephen was dead.

Alison should have been there but was not, and Wildecent began to fear everything had been for naught, for the green kings were gone as well. She felt a thinning of the magic and sorcery that insulated her from the passage of time. She could become stranded *here* and left outside the flow of events as Stephen had been. It was unlikely Ambrose would be able to find her if he had not been able to find Stephen.

Wildecent's only hope was that Alison would eventually arrive—though eventually and eternity might well mean the same thing. Gingerly, she set her burdens on the ground and shoved her wind-blown plaits behind her ears. Then she picked up the sickle and the head, and settled down to wait beside Stephen.

CONQUEST

Time had little meaning in the grove. The shadows didn't move; Stephen's wounds didn't harden, and it was only with the greatest of difficulty that she could feel her heart beating. Perhaps her emotions were frozen as well, since she grew no more apprehensive as she waited.

"They'll come—eventually," she told herself, and Stephen, and Longsword's head.

And eventually they did.

Alison came first, in a white coracle sailing a stream that shimmered in some other world. They could see each other but they could not hear.

"I've got the hero's sacrifice," Wildecent shouted, raising the head. She made each word clear and distinct, hoping Alison would see their meaning.

Alison was startled by Wildecent's gesture. Her hide boat bobbed and rocked as she fell back against its rail.

"Take Stephen away. I've promised that you'll set him *free.*" Wildecent enunciated the last words as broadly as possible, but there was no gesture she could make with a severed head in one hand and a sickle in the other that would make meaning clear.

Alison said something in reply. Wildecent tried to shape her lips in imitation, hoping to learn the words by their physical shapes, but she had no knack for it. There was a breeze across the treetops now, blowing counter to the stream. She set the head down again and placed the sickle beside it; then she reached into the stream and grabbed the rail of Alison's boat.

The physical force of the wind roaring between their worlds deafened her. "You must take Stephen away!" she shouted, but mostly she braced herself and slowly tugged Alison, the boat, the stream, and the other world across the grove.

She needed another hand, or six, but Alison was fully occupied bailing water out of the hide boat, so Wildecent took the sickle, stabbed through the hide, and anchored the two worlds one to the other. Alison roared a curse that cowed the wind; then she noticed Stephen. She dared not leave her boat any more than Wildecent dared leave the grove, but together, as gently as possible, they moved Stephen's body past the sickle.

"Set him free," Wildecent admonished, touching Alison's arm. "Whatever the cost—set him free. I'll see to this place."

Alison nodded and pushed free of the grove—taking the sickle with her.

Wildecent did not have time to be angry with her foster sister. The sun had moved across the open sky above the grove with gut-wrenching speed. It was night, and the winds descended to the forest floor. Shadowy figures emerged from the dark trees: gods and goddesses, some of whom she knew from before. She recognized Ygurna among a group of dark-robed women, but there was no affection in her foster aunt's face. Wildecent had a moment to marvel at her own audacity before a green man strode into the grove wearing Godfrey Hafwynder's head. She lifted Thorkel Longsword's head and greeted him.

"I have your sacrifice," she said in a voice that did not reveal her terror.

"It is too late," the giant said with her foster father's voice.

Wildecent swallowed hard. Her arm shook and Longsword's teeth clashed together with a sound that set her stomach reeling. "This is the man we give you," she said uncertainly. "We didn't give you the other ones. You can't have them. Not Stephen, and not my lord father."

"Who are you who says what the gods themselves may or may not possess?" A stately woman, looking very much like Wildecent herself, separated from the darkness and came to stand between the green man and Wildecent.

Before Wildecent could answer, a goddess who looked like Alison as Morrigan resembled Wildecent entered the argument. "We needed a conqueror, a hero who loved the land of the Cymry. We marked the one from over the water, but the living priestess betrayed us. So we took this one, whose conquering blood is many generations weak though his love was strong. This I understand, but what is *that?*" She pointed at Thorkel Longsword's grinning head.

Wildecent saw her chance. "He is also a man from across the waters; a man from a conquering race." So far she'd told the truth and gotten their attention, but Thorkel Longsword had never loved anyone but himself. "I do not know if he loved the Cymry," she hedged, "but he asked for a hero's death. He is the one who killed my foster father."

The sister goddesses looked to the green king. Communication passed among them without words and made Wildecent nervous. She gripped Longsword's hair tighter. Time was passing quickly now, or at least her heart was pounding. Then the man, the fourth green king, who had no image of his own, placed his hands against Godfrey Hafwynder's temples and lifted the head from his shoulders. The Alison-goddess took the now-white head lovingly in her arms, and the headless king reached out to Wildecent.

Her hands trembled; she feared the touch of his miscolored flesh, but his fingers were strong and warm when they brushed against hers. She released her burden and began to breathe easily again.

Longsword's face was green now, as were his braids and eyes. "It is good," the king said with Thorkel's voice. He began to smile before he left the grove. Wildecent said nothing as first the goddesses, then the others slowly left the grove. Finally only Ygurna remained.

"You," the old woman said, shaking her head slowly. "I would never have believed it would be you."

"I did what I could, Aunt."

"You have not done enough, you know. It's no good to give him Thorkel Longsword's head; Vikings are almost as useless as Saxons. Our king needed new vitality—and you didn't give him that. Oh, England may not be destroyed, but it will bleed, and it won't bleed any less because of what you've done in this grove."

"You're just bitter because Alison didn't do what you wanted her to do."

Ygurna lowered her eyes in defeat. "Maybe so, maybe so. I never had the gift of vision. But then again, neither have you—or you'd never have come to a grove set apart from all other places and all other times. I do not believe you'll find your way home so easily."

With that she was gone, and Wildecent, who now felt time moving around her, considered the truth in the dead woman's words. For the first time she realized that she was not the only living thing in the grove. Sulwyn was cropping tender grass at the edge of the trees.

She approached the stallion warily, but he seemed undisturbed by her presence. The Torworden men claimed no woman could ride one of their horses but, in the circumstances, Wildecent thought it was worth a try. She gathered the reins in one hand and heaved herself up into the high saddle. He felt her weight land on his back, and reared. Wildecent pressed in with her knees, clutched the reins and the pommel in a death grip, and closed her eyes.

Sulwyn plunged and kicked, then stood still. Wildecent opened her eyes and found herself seated on a milk white horse. By then, after everything else that had happened, very little could surprise or unsettle her.

"I don't suppose you know the way home?" she inquired.

"Of course I do," replied the horse goddess, Epona, and she began moving down the path.

he white hide coracle spun back into the current. It drifted low in the water under the weight of both Stephen's armored body and Alison. She bailed continuously. There was no time to think about the fast-running stream or the corpse braced against her legs.

Alison had escaped the coracle once before; she'd dived into the stream and returned to Torworden. She'd come back hoping to find Stephen's grove, and to steal him away from the Cymric gods. She tried not to think about Wildecent and scooped another handful of water over the side.

The coracle tipped precariously as the stream descended into another stretch of rock-strewn white water. Alison shrieked, clung to the rail like a half-drowned animal, and prayed Stephen's weight wouldn't drag them under. Then it spun out into water that was calm by comparison. She cupped her hands and began, once again, to bail.

The water wasn't cold, but Alison's arms were like lead. She slid down until her neck rested against the rail, and closed her eyes. The stream flowed out of twilight and into moonlit darkness.

Most streams flow eventually to the sea, but this one, Alison suspected, would dive beneath the earth. She could ride until it descended, or she could let the coracle sink in the next rapids. Either way she'd have taken Stephen to the world beneath the hills; the summer land where he would await rebirth.

She'd have set him free, as everyone asked her to do, and she could return to her own life. If she was lucky she'd never have to deal with gods or magic again. Then it began to rain—and the rain was cold.

"It's not fair!" she yelled at the clouds.

Faint luminescence rose from the stream itself. The

banks were not more than a dozen feet away. Alison tore strips from her linen, knotted them together, and attached the makeshift rope to the sickle. It was pitch dark beyond the banks, with nothing to recommend one side over the other. She cast the sickle to the right. On the third try it caught, and she was able to pull her ungainly craft toward land.

She was luckier than she'd dared hope. Though she rattled her teeth bouncing over several boulders, those same boulders created a calm pool beside the steep bank. She clambered safely onto land.

Alison's legs ached when she tried to stand up straight after being hunched over for so long. The weight of her water-logged clothing was more noticeable on land and, after a few moments, she began shivering as well. She wanted nothing more than to crawl under the nearest tree. Instead she lay down at the stream's edge and reached into the hide boat.

Moving Stephen's body into the coracle had taken all the strength and desperation she and Wildecent could muster. Lifting it straight up was more than Alison alone could manage. She gave up and began to cough. As a healer she knew to fear the sounds rasping from her chest more than anything else the gods chose to heap on her shoulders.

"I tried," she croaked to the darkness when the coughing subsided. She pushed herself upright and stumbled along the knotted rope to the sickle. "I was wrong. I made a lot of mistakes. I'm ashamed of myself, but I'm going home. I'll set Stephen free right here. Do what you will with me; I don't care anymore."

Alison pulled the sickle out of the ground and raised it over her head, but before she could fling it into the stream, the rope jerked forward. She was dragged along the bank. She cursed the rain, the rope, the darkness, and the gods themselves before she got herself untangled.

She got slowly to her feet and uselessly shook out her skirts. "That's it. I'm done. I'm going home," she shouted at the stream. It didn't answer, of course; it didn't need to. The coracle rested only a few yards away on a small shelf of rock that glowed insolently though the rain.

It did not take long for Alison to turn the white hide boat over and create a cramped, but dry, shelter for herself and Stephen. He was cold now. He certainly didn't care whether he was wet or dry, but Alison would not leave him alone in the darkness. She cradled him in her lap and rocked him gently.

She warmed herself the same way Ambrose did. It wasn't an arcane talent. Once everyone had known how to raise his body temperature, to melt snow, or to dry his clothes. It was a simple exercise of imagination, and beneath the oxhide it was quite effective.

Sheltered in a world where the ordinary was not what it seemed to be, with the rain drumming on the white hide, and her own flesh radiating a comfortable warmth, Alison eased into a trance. She forgot her aching muscles and the tight bands across her chest. She remembered the times she had never spent with Stephen—the moments she had stolen from his fantasies.

Alison touched each image lightly as it passed, returning it to its original form. She wondered if all men concealed such desires in their hearts. He had never known her, much less loved *her*. She was not the gentle, yielding woman of his dreams.

Nor was he the man she had tried to make of him.

They were both impulsive. They both preferred to move swiftly across the surface rather than explore beneath it. Beyond that, they were different. Alison thought she might have come to love him anyway, if they'd met in a more ordinary manner. Now all she could do was mourn while the rain beat furiously against the white ox hide.

Morning came. The rain had ended, and bright sunlight poured through the stretched seams of the coracle.

The blood and sweat had washed away from Stephen's face. Alison smoothed his hair over his forehead, noting that his skin was no longer cold. But then, it was almost hot beneath the boat; even the rock on which they rested was warm. For sentiment's sake Alison traced the line of his cheek and chin with her fingertip and thought of keeping a lock of his hair.

He opened his eyes.

They stared at each other—then sprang apart in an explosion of disbelief. The coracle bounced over the rocks. The white hide had lost its luster; the wood was brittle. The coracle collapsed when it came to a stop in the sunlight.

In the oldest of the sagas it was said that a hero might be brought back to life in a sacred cauldron or wrapped in the hide of a white bull. The sagas were sung by bards, not handed down through the Cymric myths Alison had learned from Ygurna, but she thought she understood what had happened. She thought she'd been forgiven and opened her arms to him.

Stephen reeled away. "Who are you?" he demanded. "What have you done with me? Where am I?"

"Stephen, it's me, Alison! I've brought you back." She came another step closer, but no further.

"Stay away, old woman," he warned, raising his fists before him. "Don't come any closer."

"Stephen, it's *me* . . ." But as she spoke Alison looked at her hands and saw spotted, leathery skin stretched over gnarled bones. Horrified, she touched her face. She didn't feel old, not inside, but she was not tempted to glance down at the pools beside her feet.

She reached out to him with her mind, then drew the thought back. Better to let him go than to pile new tragedy atop the old.

"Crone. Witch. Stay away from me," Stephen shouted. He was still shouting when he escaped into the trees.

He's free, Alison thought, staring at her crabbed hands.

CONQUEST

It's over. Everything's over. She didn't doubt he'd find his way. There were layers of magic all through the deep green forests of England. The unwary might take one step off the track and enter an ancient, timeless world, but Stephen wouldn't—not this day.

Magic lingered faintly beside the stream. Alison could see the luminous water of the other world out of the corner of her eye, just as she could see her own hands beneath the twisted ones. The silver sickle lay where she'd left it, but the hide boat had already vanished. When sunlight struck the sickle it began to shimmer.

Alison knew she didn't have much time, or timelessness, left. She took the sickle into the shade, where the magic remained. She did not know what she'd find when she returned to Torworden, but she had to return there now, or never.

Wildecent yawned. She wasn't in bed; she knew that before she opened her eyes, but she was comfortable and, as always, in no great hurry to begin the day. It was warm and spicy-smelling where she was, which, as the night's memories came back to her, was a considerable improvement.

She opened her eyes and looked up at the basket of light. She looked down and saw black velvet—and a man's hand resting lightly over her own.

Ambrose! It was all she could do to keep from leaping to her feet, but she held her breath and stayed still. It was not that surprising, she told herself as she carefully wriggled free. She didn't quite remember returning to the sanctum, but it seemed likely that he'd been waiting for her. She thought she might even have chosen to sleep beside him herself. He might have been asleep and might never have noticed her at all.

He was still asleep when she sat up. He'd slept soundly at Hafwynder Manor after working sorcery, and Wildecent began to hope she'd escape her compromised position without waking him.

"The men return! The men return!" Someone was on the guard-porch. Someone was beating the assembly gong with all his heart and strength.

That was it. Ambrose was blinking, and Wildecent was mortified. She scuttled to the opposite wall, and he made matters infinitely worse by laughing.

Wildecent's hose had clumped around her ankles, and the laces of her tunic dangled down past her waist. He seemed completely clothed and unrumpled—but then, he always did. Wildecent yanked the laces tight and secured them with a knot. She turned around and tried to rewrap her hose without revealing her legs.

"The far side of the vale! They return . . . with wounded!"

The gong clanged again and Wildecent lost her balance. She caught herself, but the strip of dark cloth had fallen to the floor, and her skirts were bunched up. Even her thigh was blushing.

Ambrose laughed all the harder. "Gods' eyes, woman—you're hardly in any danger *now,*" he explained between laughs.

That was true enough—with the men mustering on the other side of the wall—but it was hardly reassuring. "Oh, dear God, the angels and all the saints—what have I done?" she whispered, snatching up her stocking.

"From the beginning? You began by cutting off a man's head. He was condemned and waiting to die, but you got to him before Lord Beauleyas did. I checked. Longsword's lying in a storeroom, not a mark on him, but very dead. Then, you let yourself be carried off by three large green kings. After that you found your sister, I think, and together you moved Stephen. What else you did, I cannot imagine, but I was hardly about to take advantage of you when you crawled into my arms."

Wildecent shook her skirts down. There was no mistaking the good humor in Ambrose's voice. She dreaded what he'd do or say when she told him the truth. "Stephen's dead," she said softly. "He was dead when I got to the

214

grove. I gave his body to Alison and told her to set him free. He wasn't sacrificed, but he wasn't alive—"

She was nearsighted, but she could see Ambrose clearly enough. The exuberance dropped from his face; Wildecent didn't know how to interpret what remained. It wasn't rage, and she was grateful enough for that. She was relieved that they were not enemies, and did not press her luck. Greed was a cardinal sin.

"I must see about Alison," she said quickly, darting from the room before he had a chance to say anything.

Alison sat on the edge of the bed. Her hair was loose and there were tears on her cheeks. She met Wildecent's eyes, then hid behind her hands.

Wildecent's only hope had been that her sister had been able to get Stephen's body away from the interference of Cymric magic. She'd seen the young man's seeping wounds. He was better off dead. Alison's quavering announcement that Stephen was alive and well took her completely by surprise—but no more so than the wail of tears that accompanied it.

"You've wrought a miracle!" Wildecent took Alison's hands and pulled them away from her face. "For heaven's sake—why are you crying about it?" She brushed her sister's hair to one side.

"He took one look at me and called me a witch. He ran away from me. He didn't even thank me—he just ran like I was the most loathsome creature in all England."

Wildecent had nothing to say. She'd ridden away from the grove on a goddess's back; she wasn't head-blind anymore. The Alison who leaned on her shoulder was the Alison she had always known—blue-eyed, golden-haired, and beautiful despite her tearstained face. But the Alison whom Stephen beheld after his resurrection?

They weren't going to get out of this without paying a price, Wildecent knew. There was nothing between her and Ambrose now. Why shouldn't Alison seem like a

crone to Stephen? Any why shouldn't she realize she loved him only when it was too late?

"All that matters," Wildecent said, wiping Alison's tears away, "is that you're here. You'll have other suitors. We both will." She did not add that no love would be like the love they had each felt slip through their hands.

"I don't care. He doesn't love me; he doesn't even *like* me, Wili. I set everything to right, and *now* he thinks I'm a witch."

Alison's lamentations were interrupted by a cough. Wildecent stiffened and tried to block Alison from seeing Ambrose.

"I think it would be more seemly if the two of you descended first. I can appear a little later, and no one will likely notice. But they *do* expect to see the two of you leave this room."

Alison took a deep breath and wiped her face on her sleeve. "Stephen is with them."

"I know," Ambrose replied softly.

"No—Stephen is with them . . . riding . . . alive . . . well."

"I know."

"I did everything you wanted. There's nothing between Stephen and me now—not even the real memories. You can see for yourself." Alison held her hands toward him.

Ambrose retreated. "It's not necessary," he said quickly, skirting the edge of the room to reach the door. "I believe you. I'll leave first." He shrugged and opened the door. "There's nothing to hide, after all. Is there?" He was halfway out before he looked back at them both. "Thank you, my lady."

The door closed and he was gone.

"I think he meant that, Alison," Wildecent said as they heard him join the men already on the roof.

"I thought he was talking to you."

"No, he meant letting go of Stephen. I'm sure of it. I think he understood how hard it would be."

Alison sniffed back the last of her tears. Yesterday's clothes lay on the floor. She picked up her tunic and saw it was still stained a rusty brown. Everything had happened. Somewhere there was a world where Stephen lay dead at the center of an oak grove. And somewhere there might be a world where they could love each other.

"I wonder where we'll get dyestuffs," Alison wondered aloud, trying to pick up the rhythms of mundane life. She failed and threw the garment into a corner. "It's all so strange," she muttered and went back to sit on the bed.

"We did it all, Alison, *together,* just the way we used to."

"When I saw you standing there with Thorkel Longsword's head in your hand—!" Alison shook her head. "I don't know which looked worse: you or him."

"You. You should have seen your own face."

Alison smiled wistfully. "The way it used to be . . . almost."

he sun was high overhead when the weary men rode up to the outer gate of the bailey. Five men were tied facedown across their saddles, another four sat their horses out of habit, not consciousness, and only Stephen seemed fully alert. The Englishwomen had commandeered the kitchen's largest pots hours earlier. They were lifting bandages from boiling, fragrant water as soon as the men dismounted, but Lord Beauleyas would have his say before they could tend the wounded.

"What happened?" Jean Beauleyas expressed his concern the only way he could: with a raised voice and a threatening gesture toward the two young men who had led the expedition.

"The men, Father," Eudo countered. "Let the men be treated."

Eudo's arm was bound with a leather sling, and there was a dirty bandage wrapped around his thigh. He dismounted with difficulty, placing no weight on the injured leg. Stephen waited a moment longer before swinging his leg over Sulwyn's saddle and sliding discreetly to the ground.

"It was an ambush, my lord," he explained. "Lordless men of the forest. They set a trap, and we rode straight into it. The fault is ours that we were blind and careless. There's little more to be said, and nothing that can't wait until the injured are attended to."

Lord Beauleyas regarded his nephew with a mixture of admiration and distrust. Stephen seldom was lost for words, seldom said the wrong ones, and always seemed the master of a situation—a position Beauleyas was unwilling to share. He gave the injured men leave to have their wounds treated, but he did not let Stephen or Eudo go so easily.

Eudo spoke first. He described the fallen tree and the falling net, then he hesitated. Reluctantly he recalled the ignominy they'd all felt, and the chaos of those first moments when his horse had been cut down. He acknowledged that Stephen had ridden to his aid but carefully—almost enthusiastically—pointed out that moments later his cousin had disappeared.

"Disappeared?" Beauleyas asked.

"Into the forest. It was dark before we found him again, and not a scratch on his hide."

Stephen's face was dark and resigned. He allowed Eudo his moment of glory; conceded it because there was no alternative. Now he stepped forward to face his uncle's inevitable questions.

"You ran away?"

The young man forced his tense muscles to relax. There was no easy way to explain what had happened after he'd left Eudo's side, and his cousin was going to make certain it was as difficult as possible. But there was no need to make matters worse by letting his uncle provoke him. Stephen met Beauleyas's stare and spoke in level, reserved tones. "I did not run away, my lord. We were hard pressed and driven into the forest by archers. It was every man for himself. I had just killed a man. When I turned there was another coming for me with an ax. He took Sulwyn in the shoulder—"

His uncle's scar twitched. The chestnut stallion had been as fit as his rider. "We thought it strange, as well," Eudo interjected.

Stephen's composure frayed. He raked his hair and tried again. "I *thought* it struck Sulwyn. I jumped free. I must have struck my head. I remember everything as if it happened twice—"

"Don't leave out the part about the witch," Eudo urged.

"*Deus aie,* cousin, you saw me!" Stephen put his hand to his left shoulder and pulled his hauberk forward. A long tear where the chain mail links had been smashed apart was revealed. The metal was crusted. "Did I do that myself? You found my shield. I can't explain what happened—"

"You said you met a witch and that she healed you," Eudo reminded him with a too-helpful smile.

"I was wounded—badly wounded. I thought I was going to die. The next thing I remember, the very next thing I remember, is running for my life and soul."

Eudo smirked, and Alison, who could hear them from the shelter, held her breath. Jean Beauleyas grabbed his nephew's hauberk. Flakes of rust and dried blood drifted onto his hands. He shoved Stephen away when he let go. "These English forests are strange places," he said, brushing the brown dust from his hands. "Pagan. Go to Lachebroc and see the priest. Tell him what you told me; he'll know what to do."

"There's only one thing to do with a witch's lover—" Eudo began, but his father silenced him with a glance.

"And the next time either of you comes upon a track that's tree-blocked—take the hard way 'round, the branches not the stump. If there's trouble waiting, it's always on the easy path." Beauleyas intended that bit of wisdom to be his final word on the matter, but both young men tried to follow him into the bailey.

"You, to the priest," he snarled, pointing at Stephen. "And you, have your wounds tended."

There was no room for disobedience when the lord of Torworden took such a tone. Stephen headed down the cartway without removing his tattered hauberk. But this time Eudo would not be put off. Gritting his teeth, he put his weight onto his injured leg and hobbled across the yard.

"Father!"

The yard fell quiet. Beauleyas paused. Nobody used that tone with him, not unless he was prepared to die for it. He turned slowly and saw that his son was. It was one thing to observe the rivalry between Eudo and Stephen, to watch as it sharpened both of them, but it was another, less desirable, thing to see a killing rage in his only son's eyes.

Beauleyas wouldn't be the first father to die like this, but he kept his fears well hidden behind a facade of disdain and contempt. A long moment of silence echoed through the bailey.

"You must do something!"

Torworden's lord did not move a muscle.

Sweat beaded on Eudo's forehead. "He's a coward or a witch's lover. If he does not offend your honor, he offends *mine.*"

Beauleyas hooked his thumbs through his belt. "I'll know when my honor has been offended."

"How? How will you know? Will you turn to your devil-worshipping sorcerer?"

Beauleyas unhooked his thumbs and took a step forward. He was unarmored and armed only with a knife, which he had not touched, but his son took a step backward. "I did not hear you," the old man said softly.

Eudo had gone too far, and he knew it. He looked away from his father's face. No one stood near him; everyone was watching. He licked his lips and swallowed hard. "It is a matter of *honor*, my lord . . ."

"When you have honor, it can be offended, not before. Until then there is only my honor at Torworden. And my honor is offended when my men fight among themselves, when two men lead a hunting party and one lays onus on the other for misfortune, while the other does not. *That* is an offense to my honor. Do you hear me?"

"Yes, my lord."

The confrontation was, for the moment, over. Beauleyas pivoted on his heel.

"What about the witch?"

"There is no honor regarding witches," Beauleyas said without turning.

Eudo watched his father climb the motte. He wiped

the sweat from his face and limped toward the stables. Everyone ignored him as he passed.

It was a long afternoon for Alison and Wildecent. Wildecent had been through worse, at Hafwynder Manor in the aftermath of the Black Wolf's attack. Alison had been unconscious then, and this was her first encounter with the wounds of battle.

They had Hafwynder folk to assist them, but each wound was different and, after almost two days' traveling untended, each wound was difficult. One man slipped into unconsciousness as they removed his mangled hauberk; his wounds opened and he was dead before they got the bleeding staunched. That was the curse and the blessing of chain mail: it protected a man from minor wounds, but serious wounds were worse. The women couldn't stitch the chain mail wounds closed, only cauterize them and pray.

The sun shone orange through the open sides of the shelter. It was over. The last wound bandaged; the last man sent on his way to heal. The sisters sent their helpers to the stables with the discarded hauberks. The chain mail would first be cleaned in sacks of sand moistened with vinegar, then mended, then returned to the men so the whole cycle could begin again. Alison blew her hair out of her eyes and set about restoring order among her herbs.

A shadow fell across the powders and ointments. Eudo was finally ready to have his injuries looked at. Wildecent sighed and pointed him to a table. Alison cut through the leather sling. Wildecent grabbed the shoulders of the hauberk and pulled the heavy shirt off.

"Can you take that up to the stables?" Eudo asked politely. "God knows it needs cleaning—even I can smell it—but I don't think I'll be able to manage it myself when your sister gets done with my leg."

Wildecent looked at her sister. Alison shrugged. "Go ahead. Why not?"

"You're sure?"

Eudo had shed the sweat-stained cloth and leather tunics he'd worn beneath the hauberk since leaving Torworden. Huge bruises were visible under the layers of dirt on his skin. Finally freed from the weight of the hauberk, his shoulders sagged and he seemed to have fallen asleep where he sat.

"I'm sure," Alison said.

Wildecent gathered the dangling straps of the chain mail. She and Alison had seen, but not heard, the confrontation between the young man and his father, and could feel a reluctant empathy with him. He seemed thoroughly chastened, and not even Eudo could be foolish enough to cause trouble while his wounds were still bleeding. Wildecent trudged toward the stables.

Eudo's arm wound wasn't serious—a clean gash that was already crusted over and cool to the touch. Alison left it alone. His thigh was a different matter. When she'd soaked the dirty bandage free, it was revealed as a dark honeycomb of smaller wounds from the mail surrounding the larger bite from an ax.

Alison considered the task before her. "I'll wash it first," she told him, fishing a cloth out of the cauldron. "The water will burn because of the herbs in it—but the iron will hurt less afterward."

She didn't look at him when he grabbed her tunic. Any number of men who could face naked steel without flinching cowered like children when it came time to tend their wounds. But not Eudo. He pulled her backward to the table. All signs of weariness had vanished and there was malice in his pale gray eyes.

"Heal me like you healed my cousin, witch."

His mouth was over hers before she could scream; his free hand was digging between her thighs. For an instant Alison was too stunned to resist; then she groped for the hot cloth and ground it hard against the bleeding wound. Eudo released her, but backhanded her as he did.

"You'll regret that," he snarled as Alison recovered her balance and put her hand to her face. "You'll beg for mercy—"

He was in no condition to follow her, though, when she ran from the shelter and collided with Wildecent and Bethanil returning from the stables. Alison didn't need to say anything; the blood streaming between her fingers told the other two all they needed to know.

"I'll kill him," Bethanil growled as she started forward.

Wildecent clung to the beefy woman's arm. "We don't dare. Not here," she explained. "He's Lord Beauleyas's son. We can't kill him and hope to survive ourselves—but we can make him hurt so he'll think again before bothering any of us."

All her life Bethanil had listened to the noblefolk of the manor and, though she had her doubts, she listened again and followed Wildecent into the shelter. Eudo was mopping the blood from his leg and didn't hear them until it was too late.

"Hold him!" Wildecent commanded.

Bethanil was only too happy to obey. Wildecent pulled a wide, flat knife from coals beneath the cauldron. She had it against his skin while the metal was still red-hot and held it there while he howled. He was shaking when she lifted the blade, and slumped heavily to the table when Bethanil released his wrists.

"Bleeding's stopped," Wildecent remarked as she cooled the knife in the cauldron.

For three days Eudo was confined to the long barracks. His wound healed but his pride, the other men said, was festering. Jean Beauleyas said nothing, but the fact that Wildecent went unpunished was taken to mean that Torworden's lord was not pleased with his natural son.

Alison shared Bethanil's misgivings. A man who had tried to force himself on her from the bandaging table was not, in her opinion, likely to be deterred by pain. She stayed in the donjon unless she was with Hugh de Lessay, Guy, or one of the Hafwynder men. She kept the door barred and thought of asking Beauleyas for a night guard. But one whose protection she most sought, Stephen, did not volunteer.

The priest at Lachebroc had found no blemishes on Stephen's soul, but Stephen himself had not been reassured. He could abide his shattered memories, but the image of Alison—a skeletal Alison with a sickle in her hand—haunted him.

"I must have hit my head—I was sure it was her," he said to Ambrose when they met at the hermitage.

"I'm sure it was, too," the sorcerer replied calmly. He had waited for Stephen to ask the first questions. He'd begun to hope his friend's memories were so vague the questions would never arise, but, on the proverbial third day, they had. "Alison was there when you got killed, and then she brought you back to life."

Stephen landed hard on the stone seat. He shook his head and laughed nervously. "No . . . no, this is a poor jest, Ambrose."

"It happened the way you remember it—all the ways you remember it."

The young man stared into his hand and struck his fist against the wall. "I don't know what I remember—don't you understand that? She's there; she's not there. She was in every dream, every memory, and now . . . nothing. Nothing but that nightmare beside a stream."

"Alison *did* restore you, Stephen."

"Why are you taking Alison's part now?" He jumped up so quickly that Ambrose retreated involuntarily. "You never had a good word to say about her before."

"My 'good word,' as you call it, is simply that Alison did restore you and she did remove her glamour from your thoughts. And, in honesty, I played some part in it."

"What part?"

Ambrose cleared his throat. He'd made his decision to tell Stephen everything before the hunting party had ridden up the hill. What had seemed right and rational then seemed much different here in woods above the Windraes. "I lent my power to Wildecent." He chose his words with the utmost care. "And Wildecent persuaded Alison that she must undo all that she had done."

"Deus aie! God aid me! Am I some gaming-board for all of you?"

"You know better than that," the sorcerer snapped, his own temper rising. "I do not interfere with your honor or your sword, but this was different. I could not leave you to the magic of this land!"

Stephen raised his arm and made a fist. He kept himself from lashing out, but he could not unclench his fingers. "I'm alive," he said, speaking as much to his trembling hand as to Ambrose. "I'm alive. I've lost nothing. The priest says it was a dream from God—a warning that I am too proud, too quick to battle. I didn't confess I've lived for ten years with a sorcerer who talks to the dead because *I didn't think you were involved!*"

The fist jerked closer to Ambrose's face.

"Go on," Ambrose said. "If anyone has a right to be outraged, you do. It might be the most sensible thing either of us has done in a long while." He let the tension flow from his face and made no move to defend himself.

Stephen tried, and failed. He gathered his fist against his chest and held it there. "Why can't things be simple again?"

"Perhaps if we left this island—"

"I can't leave. I can't go back to France, or Normandy, or Sicily, or anywhere else with you."

A new wave of despair had entered Stephen's voice. Ambrose came a step closer but backed away when he saw Stephen's hand clench again. "Why?" he asked. There was no answer. "If I said I would stay, would you leave then?"

"No. Yes. I don't know. You tell me. I was a dead man, Ambrose. A corpse. How am I supposed to feel? How do I know if anything I feel truly belongs to me or if any of my memories actually happened? How do I know?"

"Do you still love Alison?"

A strangled growl escaped from Stephen's throat. His fist shot forward. "I'll kill you, Ambrose." His punch went wide. "Get away from me, damn you. Leave me alone!"

Ambrose took a step backward, then another. He had his answer, though it wasn't the one he'd hoped for. He stopped in the day-village, where Bethanil had set up a provisional kitchen, and asked for bread and wine. They gave him bread fresh from the oven and ale that was left from the previous night's supper. The ale was flat and bitter. He drank it all before taking a horse from the stables and galloping it until Torworden could no longer be seen over his shoulder.

Ambrose was absent that night at supper. Jean Beauleyas stormed from one end of the bailey-yard to the other, as distraught over the missing horse as he was over his missing sorcerer. Bethanil was questioned, but as Ambrose was a sorcerer and known to do things sane men scorned, no one went looking for him. Including Stephen.

It was late the following day when Ambrose rode back. The men at the gate sent him to the donjon where he remained with Lord Beauleyas until the tables were set for supper. His reappearance was overshadowed by Eudo's return to the donjon.

The young man made a point of walking steadily to the high table. He greeted his father, leered at Alison, and gave Wildecent a look that was pure poison. No one noticed when Ambrose took his usual seat.

"You have made a bad enemy, Wildecent," he said to the pale and trembling woman.

She stared at their plate and nodded absently. "Bethanil wanted to kill him. I should have let her do it."

"I am leaving for Normandy tomorrow. Lord Beauleyas has released me from his service once I deliver certain messages to Duke William. I'm going to go back to Byzantium, and I'd like to take you with me."

Wildecent swallowed the hard lump in her throat. "Is Stephen going too?" she asked, concealing her emotions. Not that Ambrose's announcement came as a surprise. Now that Stephen was free from Alison's influence it was understandable that they would both leave England.

The sorcerer shook his head. "I don't think so. After all that's happened, he seems to feel his place is here. After all that's happened, I guess I have to agree. He doesn't need me anymore." His voice revealed his bitterness and Wildecent took his hand in hers.

"Perhaps if you waited a bit longer—"

"For you?"

"No. My place truly is here—in England if not Torworden. But Stephen . . . It's strange to say, but I think Alison would be happier if you could convince Stephen to go with you."

Ambrose smiled and shook his head. " 'Why can't things be simple,' he asked me, when the wonder is, it's simpler than it was before. Stephen cannot accept what has happened. She took herself out of his memories, but he loves Alison as much as he ever did. As I—"

"Alison and I have made our peace with each other," Wildecent said, squeezing his hand and looking away. "I wish you well, but I do not want to go to Byzantium."

"We can search for your family along the way—"

She closed her eyes and brought his hand to her lips. It was tempting. She imagined traveling with him, unraveling the mysteries of sorcery and her birth. But Wildecent had experienced all the magic and sorcery she thought she'd ever need, and she doubted whatever family she had would be particularly overjoyed to find her again. So it would just be running away. "No," she whispered as she pushed his hand away. "I don't love you"—which was a lie—"and I've got my own life" —which was not. "Let's talk about something else, if this is the last meal we will eat together."

But there was nothing more that either of them had to say. They ate in silence, oblivious of the shouting, boasting and singing around them. When the last of the food had been served and the more sober of the men had begun to leave, Ambrose escorted Wildecent to the stairway where they stood in a corner while others moved past them.

"I will talk to Stephen. I'm sure he'll agree to see Alison—and once they're together, I'm sure everything will be . . . simple. I will send someone up for her once he's agreed."

"I'll tell her. She will be glad to know you have forgiven her, too."

Ambrose looked away. "Once they are together, Wildecent. Once everything is *simple* for them, there will be no need for a third—"

"No."

He shrugged and looked much younger than he was. "I'll send someone anyway," he said and headed down the stairs.

Ambrose remembered the bright sun of the Mediterranean when he stepped out of the donjon into a misty English night. He tried to conjure its warmth as he descended the log steps, but all he could recall was the smell of the garbage in the alley where the magi had found him. He was deep in his own morose thoughts when he reached the gate. He decided to walk along the river before he sought out Stephen for the final acts of their friendship.

Something whirled close behind his ears. Ambrose brought his arm up to deflect it, but the flat of a sword caught him across the temple and dropped him, unconscious, to the ground.

hy is Ambrose doing this?'' Alison asked. Wildecent sighed and set down her mending. "He's leaving England and he wants Stephen to be happy after he's gone," she replied for what she hoped was the last time. "I trust him."

Alison warmed her hands over the brazier. "I want so much to believe you. When I saw Eudo in the hall, I almost asked Lord Beauleyas to post a guard outside our door; now I'm glad I didn't." She picked up her needle and continued fitting a band of embroidery to the sleeve of a tunic first intended for her father.

They worked quietly, pausing now and again to warm their hands or add more charcoal. Each time they heard the lower door open they would look up, but it was always someone leaving the hall, never the men Ambrose had promised. The evening stretched on until there were no more outbursts heard from the great hall.

Though neither woman said anything, each had begun to have doubts. Alison wanted desperately to make amends with Stephen, to erase the horror she saw each time their eyes chanced to meet. Her most secret hope was to start over, beginning with friendship this time, not obsession. And since all her hopes were fastened on Stephen, her questions grew there as well. She did not doubt that the sorcerer had approached Stephen, nor that he had pleaded her case in good faith; Alison doubted that anything would persuade Stephen to speak with her again.

For her part, Wildecent doubted Ambrose. They were alike, or so he'd said; so much alike that they could have become one soul if they had succumbed to their passions. And now she had rejected him. If they were alike, Wildecent knew she'd wounded him and he'd never openly reveal the pain. If they were alike, he'd have his vengeance, sooner or later. Wildecent could not imagine a better vengeance than the one he got by sending her to raise Alison's hopes in vain.

The latent tension was dispelled when voices and feet echoed up the stairway.

"I'll get your cloak," Wildecent said, dropping her work to the floor; Alison flashed a relieved smile as she headed for the door.

Alison opened the door and hailed the men from the landing. She wondered why they seemed so startled to see her, and then, more soberly, why Hugh was not among them—nor any of the men she knew. Her cheerful greeting was aborted as they began to race up the stairs. Alison retreated—but not fast enough.

There were three of them, and they knew exactly what they were about. The first shoved Alison against the wall and put his hand over her mouth to keep her quiet. The second did the same with Wildecent, though she threw Alison's cloak at him and put up a fight until she was cornered at the far side of the bed. By then the third had lashed Alison's wrists behind her back; he did the same with Wildecent. They gagged the women with the linen Wildecent had been mending, and carried their struggling but silent captives out into the fog.

The trio of abductors turned the other way at the base of the motte, heading around the practice arena, past the stone yard, to the small postern gate. Torworden expelled its most noisome refuse through the insignificant gate, sluicing it down a steep slope so a small tributary of the Windraes might eventually carry the stink and filth somewhere else. It was not a coincidence that the gate overlooked the steepest part of the natural hill, nor that it was kept carefully stripped of every tree or shrub that might provide a handhold or cover.

The guards on the donjon roof could see the entire slope by daylight. They saw less by night, and animals often came up the slope to root through the garbage, but a torch would have called forth a general alarm, whether it was headed upslope or down. The abductors did not need to move silently, but they did have to carry the women down the treacherous sluice in the dark.

Alison and Wildecent each knew where they were. Almost involuntarily each became still and quiet. Each could imagine the fate toward which they were being carried, but neither was so suicidal as to fling herself down the slope to the foul, swift waters of the creek.

Two more men were waiting on the far side of the creek. The women were quickly shuttled across and then into the forests where torches were lit. Now that they were on level ground, Alison began to struggle again. She thrashed herself loose and thudded to the ground. Before she could catch her breath or get her feet under her, they caught her again. This time they bound her legs at the ankles and carried her slung between them like an animal.

Wildecent saw her sister's fate and was more careful. She draped across her captor's shoulder like a sack of onions and lulled him into a sense of false security while they wound deeper into the Wychwood. They had begun to climb again when she put all her effort into grabbing any part of his neck or face with her bound hands. Digging her fingernails into his ear, she was ready when he let go, and kicked hard as she came free.

There was no way Wildecent could outrun five men. Her only hope was to vanish into the night in such a way that they would not consider pursuing her. She tucked her head down and her knees up while she was still in the air and began rolling downhill as soon as she hit the ground. It was what Lord Godfrey had taught both girls to do when they were learning to ride their ponies, and the saints knew Wildecent had learned the trick very well. It was harder with her arms stiff behind her back, but her hair and heavy clothes protected her somewhat. She had the breath knocked out of her when she finally came to a halt and had no trouble staying dead still, praying no one would come down the slope looking for her.

"Leave her be," a man shouted from the top of the

hill. "We can come back for her. This is the one he really wants."

"If you say so—"

"I say we're late and that she's probably dead already."

The man carrying Alison kept moving, and took the torchlight with them. The men who had carried Wildecent turned around and ran to rejoin the others. There were three men guarding Alison after that. Wildecent knew her own escape had sealed her sister's doom.

Alison sought protection in her magic, hoping that if she could not sway the minds of the men who held her prisoner, she might at least dull her own mind to what was sure to come. But she had never been good at finding peace deep within herself and was unable to do so when she was terrified. She called upon the powers of the forest, though she doubted they would hear her.

The short hairs on Alison's neck and arms stood up as the men began climbing another hill. She had no sense of where they were but she sensed the blood of sacrifices made long before the Cymry. She prayed they'd keep on going but was not surprised when she was dropped before an oak. Nor was she entirely surprised when she'd squirmed around and gotten a clear look at the torchlit grove. Eudo Beau-Bastard sat atop a flat sarsen boulder. His face held the same pig-eyed leer she'd seen from the high table.

"It's appropriate, don't you think, for a witch?" he said with an evil smile. "The peasants in Lachebroc told me about it. They say virgins were sacrificed on this very stone. Personally, I think killing virgins is a waste, don't you? Besides, you're plight-trothed and not a virgin anymore."

Alison was more enraged than frightened, but either emotion was enough to make her choke on the rag they'd shoved into her mouth. She hunched forward and fought to control her retching.

"My men tell me your sister flung herself down a hill.

Too bad. I'd meant to give her to my men. Now they'll just watch until I'm ready to share.''

Alison was breathing evenly again and stared at him with all the hatred she could push through her eyes. He still favored his injured leg, she noticed, and though she had no hopes of escaping his men, she was determined she'd hurt him before she died.

But Eudo was taking no chances. "Tie her to the tree."

He stayed well out of harm's reach while his men dragged her to one of the smaller trees. They untied her wrists, hauled her arms above her head, and tied them around the trunk. Then they laid her on her back. Eudo pulled off his tunic and loosened the laces of his braes. He knelt beside her. She tried to kick him but froze when he held his knife just above her eyes.

"I do so want to hear you beg," he purred. He slipped the knife beneath her gag and sawed through the cloth.

Ambrose rolled over and wrapped his arms over his head. His ear still rang from the sound of the sword smashing against his skull. But he was alert now, and the nausea that had wracked him when he'd begun the climb to consciousness had subsided. He moved too fast getting to his feet and lurched forward, clinging to a pile of stone to keep from collapsing again.

At least Ambrose knew where he was now—in the stone yard. He didn't remember being carried there, or how long he had been unconscious, but he doubted it was much past midnight. The sorcerer cursed himself for a fool and took an unsteady step toward the donjon. He'd need the drugs he kept in his room if he were going to rid himself of his headache. It took forever to climb the log spiral.

The donjon was quiet, as it should be at that hour. No one greeted him as he pulled open the door. No one questioned him either. If anyone had noticed his absence, they'd thought nothing of it. Ambrose put his shoulder against the wall and shoved himself up the stairs to his chamber. He hoped the women were asleep.

The door at the top of the inside stairway was closed, but not latched from the inside. He pushed it open and knew something was wrong when he fell across an overturned stool. Moving slowly through his own room, he found a lamp that hadn't been broken and lit it from the brazier. He blinked dumbly at the wreckage. Alison and Wildecent were gone—the fact hammered in rhythm with his headache, but it made no sense to him.

There was a chest beneath the washstand. Ambrose withdrew a wax-stoppered flask from its disordered depths. He broke the seal and held the glass beneath his nose. The fumes burned his nostrils and made his eyes water, but his head began to clear. He shook a few drops onto his tongue and tucked the flask inside his tunic. The drug hit his blood with a jolt.

He saw the smaller details of the struggle now. A half-sewn tunic lay on the floor, the outline of a muddy boot across its sleeve. Alison's cloak trailed from the bed, also marred by footprints. Both women had been carried off.

Gods knew, he'd been careless, making promises to Wildecent without looking to see who might be listening. He'd seen the looks on Eudo's face; he knew the sisters had an enemy who would stop at nothing. And because Wildecent had trusted him—had left the door unlatched—they were both in mortal danger.

Ambrose took a step toward his sanctum; he'd need sorcery if he had any hope of finding them alive. His next step was toward the outer door; Stephen should be here—he owed his friend that much. Another step toward the sanctum; the next toward the door. The drug he'd taken set his mind racing, and with what was left of his rational self he knew he'd need to hear another voice before he could trust his judgment.

Delving under his bed, Ambrose retrieved his sword and slung it below his waist. He didn't expect there was anyone lurking in the darkness between the donjon and the barracks where Stephen slept, but this time he was taking no chances.

He clamped his hand over his friend's mouth. "Get your boots and sword."

The younger man's eyes were huge and white-rimmed in the dim light of the barracks, but he obeyed quickly and without questions until they were outside.

"I expected you earlier. You said we should talk—"

The drug made the sorcerer reckless. "Not now," he said, grabbing Stephen's sleeve and pulling him toward the inner gate. "We've got to find our ladyloves."

Stephen jerked free. *"Ladyloves?* Are you drunk?" he demanded while stamping his feet into his boots and knotting the laces of his braes.

Ambrose related the events of the evening as he knew them in a few short sentences. The recitation sobered them both.

"You didn't sound the alarm?"

"I . . . I thought it would be better this way. If the world doesn't have to know about it. I wasn't thinking clearly," Ambrose admitted. He turned away before Stephen answered, and headed up the motte.

Stephen paused, agreed, and caught up with Ambrose just outside the gate. "You're right you're not thinking clearly. Why're you going back up there? You've got your Greek sword—we should be on our way."

"I'm thinking clearly enough. They could be anywhere. We'll never find them without help—and help is in my chamber."

Stephen reluctantly agreed. He swallowed his aversion to sorcery and followed Ambrose up the log steps.

"We'll need something personal. A piece of their linen. A lock of hair would be best if we could find it." Ambrose pulled the blankets back and shook the pillows. He found two long strands of golden hair, but nothing of a deeper brown.

"We're in luck," Stephen called from the doorway,

where he'd found a half-dozen golden strands caught on a splinter.

They had enough for the sorcery Ambrose had in mind, though he'd hoped to have hair from both of them. But the women had been abducted together. Finding one would be the same as finding the other, or so he told Stephen as they entered the sanctum. Stephen stayed pressed against the wall while Ambrose made a loop of Alison's hair and used it to suspend his talisman in the basket of light.

Ambrose pointed to the geometria. "That is Torworden. I've been building it since we got here," he said with evident pride, though Stephen saw no resemblance at all. "Now watch!"

Stephen didn't want to watch, but it was Alison they were looking for and, as Ambrose had learned, Stephen's love for the English heiress wasn't rooted in his memory. "Can I help?" he asked, as he had never asked before.

Ambrose looked away from his sorcerous engine. "Just watch," he said compassionately.

The crystal hung motionless for a moment, then began to rise along the wires. It drew its power from Ambrose's drug-heightened senses. It moved so quickly the wires began to glow and there truly was a basket of light in the upper room of Torworden's donjon. The wires sang, a diminishing chorus until only one clear tone remained and a single beam of light descended to the geometria.

"Do you see it?" Ambrose asked, and Stephen said that he did. The sorcerer stood up and the room went dark except for the oil-lamps.

Ambrose studied the place Stephen indicated and unhooked Alison's hair from the wire. He wove the hair loop through a longer loop of silk and pulled both taut between his fingers. He'd created a cat's cradle, save that the hair loop moved along the silk, and when it stopped the crystal began to glow.

"Out past the day-village," Ambrose said, collapsing

the figure. He snapped the talisman, silk and hair still attached, onto the gold torc he wore around his neck and led Stephen back down the stairs.

Wildecent had remained crouched below the path long after the forest had become silent. She'd scraped her face against the hard earth until she'd loosened the gag, but she didn't try to unbind her hands or find her way out of the forest until she heard Alison scream. Her sister was far away, which made the sound that much more blood-chilling. She found a jagged stone and rasped the rope across it. When that failed she knelt down and caught the thickness of her skirts with her teeth. It was like being gagged again, but at least she could walk—after a fashion.

There wasn't anything she could do for Alison except survive and return for vengeance. She set off in the opposite direction, continuing to scrape with the stone as she did. Wildecent's goal was the day-village, where Bethanil slept close by her pots. She'd trust only folk from Hafwynder Manor now that she and Alison had been betrayed.

She had fallen more times than she could remember when the rope frayed loose. Walking was no problem then, but direction was. She'd climbed several hilltops and discovered that at night all hills looked like Torworden. She didn't even know if she was walking in the right direction. Nor would she appeal to magic. If the greenwood could protect anyone, Alison needed it most. Sorcery was out of the question.

Some sort of luck remained with her. She found the cartway between Lachebroc and Torworden. Wildecent belted up her skirts again and found the strength to run up the hill. Bethanil's suspicious face, peering out the window, with a cleaver in one hand and a lamp in the other, was the most wondrous thing Wildecent had ever seen. She stumbled across the threshold and threw herself on the cook's mercy.

* * *

"It was Alison he wanted all the time. I heard the men say so," Wildecent said as she concluded her tale of horror.

"Aye," the Hafwynder woman said, nodding as she slapped the cleaver flat-bladed across her hand. "I heard the sorcerer go by a bit ago. But he wasn't alone. The other one, Stephen, was with him. I never forget a voice." She set the cleaver aside and bustled about the makeshift kitchen. "I'll find Eodred. He'll have an idea what to do. You drink this while I'm gone."

Wildecent took a cup of heated honey wine from Bethanil's hands and stared into it. *Stephen?* She sat down on an overturned kettle. Suddenly nothing made sense. Stephen's complicity was harder to accept, and there was certainly no reason for him to carry Alison off into the forest. Even the timing seemed wrong. Bethanil had heard the pair "a bit ago," when it had been hours since the three men had burst into their room.

Her hands began to shake. She took another sip and set the cup down beside her. And yet Bethanil *had* heard the two of them going by. There was no good reason for them to be out unless they were involved.

Wildecent repeated her story when Eodred, still barefoot and his braes billowing wide around his knees, followed Bethanil into the room. When she finished, the old hawkmaster said that Jean Beauleyas should be awakened.

"For what?" she snarled. "It's way too late now."

But Eodred was adamant. "He's lord here. He must be told. It's the only right thing to do," he insisted.

Wildecent looked into their faces. They both believed, even Bethanil believed, that men were wiser than women, and that lordly men were the wisest of all. It didn't matter that Jean Beauleyas was a Norman and a foreigner, or that his nephew and his sorcerer were the ones who stood accused. It was enough that he was a lord.

"All right," she conceded. "Go. Tell him. But I don't want to talk to him or see him—make certain he understands that. Tell him I've fainted or that I'm overwrought. Better yet, tell him I'm already mourning for my sister.''

"You should pray that she's safe," Bethanil whispered.

Wildecent remembered the screams and shook her head. "They didn't mean for either of us to survive. I just hope she hurt them—cursed them—before she died.''

Both Eodred and Bethanil were aghast at Wildecent's heresy, but the dark-haired woman stared them into silence. She'd started to change the night she'd worked sorcery with Ambrose; the night she'd offered Thorkel Longsword's head to the Cymric gods. The change was complete now, and there was nothing of meekness or timidity left in her.

"I'll go tell Lord Beauleyas now," Eodred muttered.

Moments later he was racing into the bailey-yard, shouting that the Englishwomen were missing. Bethanil put another ladleful of warm wine into Wildecent's cup, then stropped her cleaver with a whetstone like any warrior. Her eyes never left Wildecent, and it was clear she, at least, had no difficulty believing the dark-haired woman was dangerously overwrought.

It was not long before the assembly gong clanged into the night and Eodred came running back.

"He's waking them all to see if anyone else's gone missing," Eodred said softly once the door was barred behind him. "Lord Beauleyas was wondrous angry when I told him what you said and what Bethanil had heard. He means to see justice done. He's promised gold to the man who finds 'em and death to 'em once they're found.''

The hawkmaster had taken time to get his boots. He paused to pull them to and to bind the loose cloth of his braes. "Lord Beauleyas said I could ride with 'em too. Says there's a priory not far from here, and it's there he wagers they're taking her. Says if we ride hard we can be there first and bring her back—''

"Don't you fools understand! They weren't planning to marry us!" Wildecent raged.

The hawkmaster looked to Bethanil, who shook her head slowly, then he rested his hand gently on Wildecent's head, as if she were his own child. "Don't worry, little one. Lady Alison's a beautiful woman with property and fortune; no real harm will come to her."

tephen and Ambrose made slow, sure progress through the forest. They followed no easy path, but moved in straight lines guided by the crystal talisman suspended from a loop of Alison's golden hair. Then one time the crystal glowed red and Ambrose put it quickly away.

"We're close, now," he said to Stephen, pointing in the darkness. "Over there a bit, I think." He tossed his torch to the damp ground and stomped it out.

Stephen extinguished his torch as well but put a hand on his friend's shoulder before they continued. "Why did it turn red?" he asked.

Ambrose was grateful for the darkness between them. "She's hurt . . . bleeding."

"Alison?" Stephen asked, though he knew they had only golden hair in the loop.

The sorcerer grunted and started moving slowly uphill through the fog. Like Alison, he could sense the power of the place they approached. It was older than the oak above the Uffington chalk carving; perhaps older than the carving itself. Ambrose couldn't guess how Eudo had found the place, but he had, and now he was abusing it and the last Cymric priestess at the same time. Alison was bleeding, but it was the hill that made the crystal glow.

They went more slowly without the torches and with the need for quiet. While they had been searching, Stephen had been content to listen to Ambrose. They had their goal now, and Stephen took command effortlessly. He chose their pace and their approach once they saw torchlight spilling out of the grove.

Alison wasn't screaming anymore, but when they heard her moan Stephen charged up the hill. Ambrose dove for his friend's knees and wrestled him to the ground.

"You blundering oaf!" he whispered loudly. "Do you

think he's up there alone with them? Do you think his men will stand aside and let you run him through?"

"I'm sorry."

But the moans continued and fueled Stephen's rage. It was Alison whom his cousin had brutalized. Not the leering crone Stephen had beheld by the stream, or the fey maiden of his dreams, but the flesh-and-blood Alison whom he had promised many, many times to protect. When they'd left Torworden Stephen had thought only of rescuing her; now there were two thoughts: rescuing her and killing each man who had hurt or touched her. Stephen said nothing of this to Ambrose. It didn't particularly matter if his friend agreed; he'd prefer to spill their blood himself.

Four men lingered at the edge of the grove. They stood with their backs to the scene and well away from each other, though they were not guarding anything. Their clothes were disheveled and watermarked, but they winced when a woman's moan reached their ears. Belated guilt would not be enough to save them. Stephen grasped Ambrose's arm, then drew his finger across his friend's neck. He felt Ambrose nod and released him. Taking his knife from his belt, Stephen approached the nearest man.

Ambrose removed the silk loop from his talisman and threaded it through a wooden toggle. The magi did not approve of killing, but the gutter-rat they'd brought into their community had survived by tooth, claw, and knife. The child would not purge himself of violence, but clung to it with a stubbornness that unnerved them. So Masianos, first among the magi, hired a tutor to teach the boy the ways of death; a magus could never be too well educated. It was true that Ambrose could not couch a lance or fight encumbered with a helmet and hauberk, but only because his Saracen tutor considered Western ways unrefined, and had taught him the civilized ways of the Orient instead.

Ambrose slipped the strong silk around his victim's neck and jerked it tight around the toggle. The man clutched his neck, but the silk bit deep. He made no sound; not even a death groan could leak past the pressure on his throat. His body spasmed once, then relaxed. Ambrose lowered him quietly.

Stephen had also been successful, but slightly less skilled. His man thrashed the grass as he collapsed with Stephen's dagger shoved high under his ribs. Alarm was shouted and the two other men had time to draw their swords. Eudo and his last man abandoned their raping and looked about for their swords.

The Beau-Bastard did not fight. He met Stephen's eyes but once, as he knotted the laces of his braes, and quickly descended into darkness on the far side of the grove. He was grinning as he left.

His men outnumbered Stephen and Ambrose; he had no reason to fear. Stephen was a worthy opponent with a sword, but not so the sorcerer. The knights had little respect for a curved, watermarked sword, and less for a man who shrieked like a demon while fighting with it. Eudo's three cronies divided themselves two and one, with Stephen facing the pair—which was just the way Stephen and Ambrose wanted it.

Stephen had fought with Ambrose against his back before. Like Eudo and the others, he would not touch a sword that could not be thrust deep into an enemy's gut, but he was confident nothing would strike him from behind. He took a step forward, giving Ambrose and his manic sword a bit more room, and met each heavy thrust with a solid parry of his own.

This night, however, Ambrose had the advantage. His sword was best suited to long, deep cuts through cloth and the muscles around a man's ribs. The man he faced wore nothing more substantial than a woolen tunic. The sorcerer did not waste his strength absorbing the mighty swings with the steel of his lighter sword, but swept them aside. Ambrose waited until the man grew careless and enraged by a handful of small gashes, then he drove in for the kill and proved that the point of his sword was as sharp as its edge. When Ambrose's shouts turned jubilant, Stephen knew only his pair was left—and his cousin.

"Finish them," he shouted to Ambrose. "I'm going after Eudo."

Dark steel swooped in from Stephen's left. There were small notches set along the back of Ambrose's sword. He could make the sword sing as it sliced through the air. Stephen's opponents pulled back a fraction, suddenly convinced they faced a demonic blade. Stephen had the moment he needed to escape the combat, and Ambrose drew his knife left-handed to parry the second blade.

Stephen looked down as he ran across the clearing. His eyes saw her clothes torn to either side; her bloody, glistening skin; the dark, splotchy bruises—but his mind did not. He slowed only enough to sheathe his sword before charging into the brush.

There was little light beneath the forest's canopy of new leaves. Stephen stumbled a while before he found the path Eudo had used to bring Alison to the grove. He paused, and listened, and heard his cousin's heavy stride not far ahead. Eudo's thigh was far from healed. Stephen made haste as he followed the overgrown path, but not recklessly. He'd catch up with Eudo soon enough.

"Put up your sword!" he shouted when he could see the black outline of his cousin moving against the grays of the forest. His own was already drawn.

"Is that you, little cousin?" The sound of metal scraping as Eudo cleared his sword. "I did not expect you so soon."

"You did not expect me at all, coward."

They swung at each other. Darkness undercut their skills, and the swords did not touch. Stephen stepped in and swung again.

"I hardly expected you to pass so tasty an opportunity," Eudo called from just beyond the range of Stephen's sword.

Arm braced for a mighty thrust, Stephen lunged toward Eudo's voice. And swept an armful of leaves from their branches with his efforts. He'd lost his cousin in the darkness. He froze, knowing the next move could come from anywhere, but the next sounds he heard were Eudo's stride retreating along the path.

Only a fool would charge through unknown forest with three feet of honed steel at the end of his arm. Stephen resheathed his sword and followed. Twice more he caught up with Eudo, and each time his cousin goaded him into a precipitate attack. Finally, when Stephen stood alone and panting, he realized Eudo had no intention of fighting him but was simply luring him farther away from the grove—and closer to Torworden.

The next time when he caught up with his cousin, Stephen shouted no challenge but drew his knife and sprang at Eudo from behind. He plunged his knife deep, but Eudo had a coward's luck and a coward's defense. The Beau-Bastard squirmed at the last moment, and the blade sliced through the soft flesh of his upper arm, scarcely hurting him at all.

They wrestled on the ground a moment, then broke apart, Stephen without his knife and Eudo with his hand clapped over his naked shoulder. This time the heavier man did not retreat down the path.

"Why fight with me?" Eudo asked the darkness. "She's a witch—you said so yourself. I've done you a favor; you should thank me—"

"Shut up!" Stephen barked back. He'd drawn his sword again and was crouched forward. He'd forgotten everything he'd ever been taught about keeping his mind clear when there was steel in his hand; all he wanted was more of Eudo's blood.

Eudo knew it—knew his younger cousin was incompetent with rage—and goaded him again. "A sorry plight-troth you made," he said with a sneer Stephen could hear rather than see. "I had the virgin's flower from her, Stephen, that she wouldn't give to you—"

Stephen's sword was not properly raised when he

leaped across the darkness. Eudo parried it effortlessly, spinning the weapon out of Stephen's hand. But the younger man had not been thinking with his sword when he began the attack; he scarcely noted it was gone. He pushed Eudo off-balance with a flying tackle, and brought his knee hard into his cousin's crotch as they fell. Eudo gasped and released his sword, then got a handful of Stephen's hair and rolled on top of him.

He smashed the back of Stephen's skull against the ground. The younger man seemed properly stunned, and Eudo reached for his knife, only to have Stephen's hand lock over his wrist. They rolled through the dirt, the single knife braced four-handed between them.

Stephen was incoherent with a rage that would have shamed him at any other moment. Eudo was fighting a madman, and fighting for his life. The Beau-Bastard poured all his strength into the arm that still held his knife, and slowly forced it around until the steel pointed down to the hollow of his cousin's throat. He drained himself and the point began to descend.

Eudo was prepared for almost any counter-assault, but not for his cousin to rise into the attack and bite down on his wrist. He blinked. It was over for Eudo—but not for Stephen. The madness that had been rising within him since he first heard Alison's moans was not sated by simple death. The young man withdrew the knife and plunged it back into Eudo's chest not once, but again and again.

Stephen stood up, gasping for air and sanity, his hands hot and wet. There was no honor in what he had done. Then he thought of Alison, and Ambrose's crystal glowing red with her blood, with her pain. An anguished, unwilling cry came from the depths of his soul. He fell to his knees. The knife began to rise and fall again.

It was not long before the madness faded. A shaking young man got unsteadily to his feet. He surveyed his butchery with disbelief and revulsion. The knife fell and he staggered to the bushes. It had been a madness, like

the *berserkerang,* and his remorse was blunted by the certain knowledge that it had not truly been him wielding the knife. And yet he could not return to the grove. He could not face Alison, even though it was her rapist's blood that soaked his clothes.

Stephen wiped his hands on the grass and wished for a stream to wash the blood and bile away. He retrieved his sword and knife; they'd had no part in his madness and he put them carefully away. Before he could stare at the corpse or sink into despair, the forest revealed the sound of a stream not far away.

It was knee-deep and bitter cold. Stephen laid his weapons on a rock and stripped to the skin. He splashed into the stream and let the icy water cleanse the bloody heat from his body and soul. He dragged his clothes in and pounded them against the rocks, then he climbed out and, shivering and shouting, put them on again. He was cold, but he was clean, and he started back up the path to the grove.

Ambrose had killed the last of Eudo's men. His sword—which was black Damascus steel and had never been in Greece—sang as he whirled it clean of blood. He replaced it in its scabbard, but he did not bind the scabbard shut. He trusted Stephen to do what he'd sworn to do, but Ambrose took no chances on trust alone.

The grove was quiet as he stood by the sarsen stone and glanced over every part of it. He'd already seen Alison sprawled beside the oak; he looked for a second woman, and could find none. His desires urged him away from this place in search of Wildecent; then Alison moaned.

It was not easy, but he forced Wildecent from his mind; he would not leave this place until Stephen returned. Bile rose in his throat when he saw what they'd done to her. Alison was still conscious: battered, bleeding, almost naked but able to see that yet another man walked toward her. She had screamed herself hoarse an eternity before. She moaned, and tried to writhe away from him.

Eudo's tunic lay where he had discarded it. Ambrose almost scooped it up, but he could not bring himself to cover her with the Beau-Bastard's clothes, so he loosened his belt and pulled off his own tunic instead. He did not consider the effect this would have on Alison. She kicked the cloth away after he draped it over her, and he had to wait until she'd exhausted herself again before he could replace it or unbind her bleeding wrists.

Ambrose folded her arms beneath the tunic and tried to ignore the wild hatred in her eyes. He could not comfort her. She was like an injured animal that must be terrified further before it can be helped or healed. He turned away and Alison became quiet.

He was not always gentle; it was not natural to his childhood, nor to any later part of his life. The women who gave themselves casually to warriors and other travelers were seldom gentle in either birth or manner themselves. Taking a woman cooled a man's blood; it had nothing to do with the exotic emotion called love. In the most tortured moments of his forbidden love for Wildecent, Ambrose had never once considered *taking* her.

It came to Ambrose that he'd been wrong about love, and that it was the *taking* of a woman whose mind meshed with his own that was dangerous. Sorcery was only indirectly involved. Ambrose swallowed hard. Accepting what he felt for Wildecent seemed far more frightening than resisting it.

Ambrose looked down at Alison. Her eyes widened and she held her breath. The sorcerer resolved that Stephen would never see his beloved like this. He would do the one thing he had sworn he would never do; the very thing Alison believed was the heart of sorcery. He unhooked his talisman and held it before her eyes. They both stared into it, and it built a bridge of light between their eyes.

The shafts of light had faded, but the crystal still glowed

when Stephen raced across the grove. The younger man fell to his knees and spread his arms to embrace her, then pulled away. Alison did not writhe or moan as she had with Ambrose; she did not seem to see him at all.

"Oh God—no-o-o," he cried, unashamed of his tears.

Ambrose reattached his talisman to the torc. "Wait," he counseled.

"What have you done? What did you have to do?"

"I—I entered her mind."

"You made her forget?" Stephen's voice was almost grateful.

The sorcerer shook his head. "I dulled her memories, but I could not remove them." Ambrose saw the questions in Stephen's face and smiled sadly. "You, of all people, should understand. Love and hate have very little to do with mind or memory. She'd go mad if I took her memories away completely, because her heart will always remember. But I think she might begin to heal if you stay beside her until the sun comes up, and carry her home gently."

Alison said nothing but lifted her hand so Stephen could hold it.

Ambrose stood up. He saw his friend's wet clothes and did not ask what had happened to Eudo. He stripped the tunic off the man he'd garrotted and draped it over Stephen's shoulders. Then Ambrose picked up Eudo's tunic and pulled it on. He wrapped his belt below his waist and hung his sword from it. "Take care of her," he admonished, when Stephen finally looked up. "There's someone else I must find."

efore dawn Alison began to shiver. With Stephen's help, she put on Ambrose's charcoal-colored tunic and wrapped the remnants of her clothes around her. She let Stephen hold her in his arms until it was light again in the grove. When he lifted her up and said he'd carry her home, Alison leaned her head against his shoulder.

"I have no home," she sobbed in her cracked voice.

He set her down and knelt beside her. "You have Hafwynder Manor."

Alison made a strange sound that might have been a laugh. "Do you consider I might be with child from—from one of those—" But she couldn't bring herself to complete the thought.

"I could not love such a child," Stephen admitted, having considered the matter while he'd held her during the night. "Male or female, I would give it to the Church, but such a child does not change my love for you." He paused and took her hand between his. "Not even *you* could change my love for you," he chided, not knowing if she would appreciate the irony. "My memories cannot tell me if we have known each other forever or if we met for the first time by a stream. But my heart knows . . ."

She looked away from him, but her fingers closed tightly around his. "There will be a stream around here," she said after a moment of silence, a faint glimmer of her old self in her eyes when she looked at him. "I would like to wash myself."

Stephen grimaced, though he knew there was. "A stream?"

"I feel water beneath this grove. There will be a well, or a stream somewhere nearby."

Stephen shrugged. Alison would always be Alison, and if he would live with her and love her, he would have to

accept her magic. He set off and found where the stream
came closest to the hill, then he carried her to its banks.
He waited with his back to her while she bathed and tore
her clothes. There were flowers on the bank. He picked
a handful and held them nervously.

"I am ready to go back."

He held the flowers out to her and stared.

Alison's hair was damp, but carefully rebraided. Ambrose's tunic came only to her knees, but she'd made an
underskirt out of what remained of her linen, and was
decently covered as any honorable woman ought to be.
Her lip was cut and swollen, and there was a cut beside
her ear where Eudo had slipped while removing the gag.
All other signs of her ordeal were hidden until she took
a step toward Stephen. Pain tightened her face and
showed in each slow, cautious gesture.

Stephen handed her the flowers and lifted her into his
arms. "I'll carry you."

"It is a long way—"

"We're in no hurry."

He carried her along the stream until the grove was far
behind them and there was no chance she would see
Eudo's mangled corpse where he'd left it sprawled beside
the path. They had to stop often, and at each resting
place Stephen shouted Ambrose's name.

"They'll be all right," Alison would whisper each time
the forest birds alone answered Stephen's call.

It was midmorning when another voice shouted back
to them—not Ambrose, but Hugh de Lessay. There'd
been little doubt as to what had happened once Beauleyas's muster had shown both his nephew and his bastard son were missing. The only question was who had
survived, and de Lessay was unabashedly happy that it
was Stephen.

Hugh offered Alison his horse, but she could not ride
alone. Stephen held her before him in the saddle and
suffered Hugh to lead them. The other two men with
Hugh were sent ahead with the news that six men were

dead—including the lord's natural son—that Alison was safe, and that Ambrose was still searching for Wildecent.

Jean Beauleyas was waiting at the outer gate when Hugh led them through the day-village. Stephen would have fallen to one knee before his lord, but the sight of so many people—so many men—had frightened Alison, and he could not entrust her to any other arms. Then Bethanil came forward, and Stephen's problems appeared solved.

There was so much natural emotion in the cook's plain face, no one would have thought to look for guilt. She took Alison in her arms. Stephen knelt before his uncle.

"I have killed my cousin," he began, reciting the words he'd chosen in the night. "He took the lady I would call my own from your protection and assaulted her with no thought for her honor—"

"Or mine," Beauleyas interrupted wearily. "Get up. Nothing more will come of this at my hands. I've lost my son; I'll not lose you as well."

All those who believed from the beginning that Jean Beauleyas was biding his time to see which of his possible heirs proved strongest could not tell that day or any other if the lord was happy with the outcome. He ordered Stephen to lead another party back to the grove to reclaim the bodies, but when they came back Beauleyas did not descend from the donjon to view his son's remains.

Alison had been put to bed in Ambrose's room and given one of her own sleeping draughts. Bethanil sat beside the brazier when Stephen entered the room. Guilt was now more evident on her face and in her knotting hands.

"She's resting, Lord Stephen," she said as he pulled back the bedcurtains.

He winced at the unaccustomed title. Alison lay curled on her side with her hands beneath her cheek. She sighed when he touched her cheek, but there was nothing fearful in the sound and he let the curtains fall back.

"Have they found Wildecent, or Ambrose?"

It seemed a perfectly natural question to Stephen, but it brought the cook to her knees in tears. She grasped the hem of Stephen's tunic and pressed it against her lips and forehead. Her wailing awoke Alison, who got to her feet unsteadily.

"It be all a terrible mistake, my lord," Bethanil said many times. "She came to us in the night—to Eodred and me. She said it was your witch-friend who'd carried them off—"

Alison blanched and clung to the curtains, fearing the worst now that she'd heard the beginning; Stephen didn't notice.

"I'd heard you go off earlier with him—" Bethanil let go of Stephen's tunic and sat crying on the floor.

"What happened to Wildecent?" he asked, firm but calm and squatting down beside her.

"We said Lord Beauleyas must be told, and she agreed. She wasn't herself and we did not argue when she said she'd have naught to do with the lord once he was roused. She gave little hope of finding Lady Alison alive. After Eodred returned saying the priory was empty, she turned away from us completely. Toward dawn I fell asleep myself . . ."

"And?" Stephen encouraged.

"She must have wakened Eodred, and persuaded him that they must leave. Hafwynder horses were gone from the stables, and bread from the hearth. I'd hoped she'd taken him to search for her, but now I think not. There was an anger in her like I'd never seen before . . ."

Stephen tried to coax the big woman back into the chair. "It is unfortunate, nothing more," he said. "She'll be found. She may have found Ambrose, and they may not be ready to return."

He stood and noticed Alison for the first time. Now there were two distraught women. He despaired of calming Bethanil and tried his luck with Alison. "Wildecent was safe, but it seems she ran off this morning," he said, feeling foolish when the concerned expression did not fade from Alison's face. "Well, she must be looking for us—one of us, at least?" Alison shook her head.

"It is not so easy," Alison said, seating herself gingerly in the chair. "Wildecent thinks Ambrose betrayed us—"

"A mistake. A simple mistake." But he noticed that Alison's face did not lighten at all. "Alison," he said more seriously. "It was Eudo's men who attacked Ambrose as he left the hall. I'm sure of it. You don't think—"

She shivered and shook her head. "No, not once I saw . . . *him*. I was afraid when Ambrose came out of nowhere, but . . . no, I know I was wrong about him from the beginning. I—I shall have to find words to thank him—but Wili knows only what we knew last night, and what she heard from Bethanil."

"But once she knows," Stephen said, still thinking it was simple. "Surely she'll forgive him. I mean, there's nothing to forgive him for—is there?"

"No." Alison stopped and put her hands to her face. In the end it had been Wildecent who made the sacrifice. Now it would be Wildecent who paid the price for being used by the gods. It wasn't fair, but it seemed inevitable. "It was all a mistake," she whispered and began to cry again.

Bethanil laid her head in Alison's lap and they sobbed together. Stephen stood up and glowered at them both. Women and simplicity didn't mix well. "You!" he shouted at Bethanil. "Put your lady to bed!"

Faced with a sharp-voiced man and a simple task, the cook got to her feet. She carried Alison to the bed. Stephen went off in search of his uncle.

Wildecent woke up on the hard dry ground where she'd fallen asleep shortly before dawn. Sunlight made rainbow shapes as it penetrated the tree branches far above her. She raised her arm to block the light and squinted. For a moment she did not know where she was or why it seemed so strange, then everything flooded back. She let her forearm fall back to cover her eyes again.

Too much had happened. In the passing of a few days she had gone from betrayed to betrayer. What else could Eodred think when he awoke and found she'd run off with their supplies during the night? Yet it seemed she had no choice. The path of vengeance was all downhill and very steep; it allowed no deviation or escape.

With a loud, unappreciated sigh, Wildecent got to her feet. Her pony and the donkey were cropping grass near where she'd left them. Her saddle and the donkey's pack were heaped on the ground, also where she'd left them. In the predawn darkness, she'd told herself that she was too tired to make a proper, secure camp; the fact was, though, that she really didn't know how. All her life there had been menfolk and servants to take care of such things.

She'd gotten the bridles off the two animals, but she knew she'd have the devil's own time getting them back on. It had been years since she'd groomed her own pony. For that matter, Wildecent could not remember being so totally alone before in her life. Not even her nightmare journey through the realms of magic and the Cymric gods had felt so strange as knowing there was no one at all to talk to.

Reflexively, Wildecent reached up to tuck her braids behind her ears, and touched instead the tight band of a peasant's cap. Her hand dropped to her side and she stood, trembling, beside the tree. In every sense she was not the person she'd been just two short days before. That timid, anxious young woman had been replaced by someone who trekked alone along the cartways and wore a young man's clothes.

I had to do it, she told herself again. *There is no one else who can avenge the wrongs done to Alison . . .*

Digging through the packs for bread, Wildecent considered her plans—such as they were. At their core was anguish; her heart could not yet accept that Ambrose had betrayed her love and that Alison was dead—raped and, no doubt, sacrificed to the darkest aspects of sorcery. Her heart counseled grief and the rituals of mourning; but her mind counseled vengeance and drove her onward. In the middle of nowhere, in borrowed clothes and with only the animals for company, Wildecent clung to the strident demands of her conscience.

The sorcerer must be made to pay the highest price for his treachery. Without his now-broken promise, she never would have opened the door. His henchmen could never have broken through that door without arousing the whole donjon. Alison would still be alive . . .

Wildecent thought of Alison's glowing face as it had been, moments before betrayal—and, later, as she had heard of her, upside down in torchlight with a dirty rag tied across her mouth. Cold hysteria closed over Wildecent's heart: she had to believe that everything was Ambrose's fault, lest the burden of guilt descend upon her own shoulders. She had been Ambrose's willing dupe. *She* had opened the door; *she* had allayed Alison's rightful suspicion of the sorcerer; *she* had made her sister's horrible death possible.

This realization of her own culpability had burst upon Wildecent the previous afternoon while she and Eodred were riding east toward King Harold. She had been rehearsing her impassioned pleas, painting a detailed portrait of Ambrose's misdeeds, when she heard the echo of her own thoughts. What justice could a Christian king mete out when he heard such a tale of sorcery and magic? What justice that would not condemn her and Alison as surely as it damned Ambrose?

Indeed, as the crystal voice of Wildecent's conscience pointed out, Harold's justice could *only* fall upon her. Ambrose was a deacon of the Church. Any and all of his crimes would be judged in the bishop's cloisters—and, though vengeance thrilled to the thought of what he would endure in their hands, there was much it was best the Christian Church never suspected. So, Ambrose could never be *brought* to justice; justice—vengeance—would have to find him in some out-of-the-way place.

Wildecent finished her bread and picked up the pony's bridle. Her notions of what must be done were much more sharply defined than her notions of how to accomplish it. She had to kill Ambrose, she was sure of that, and he had to die in full knowledge of his crimes, but Wildecent wasn't ready to plunge a cold dagger into his breast. There was still the anguish in her own heart to deal with.

She would have to make herself heartless before she could become vengeance's weapon. It wouldn't be easy, and it would certainly involve a measure of black sorcery—but deep within herself Wildecent knew that she must suffer almost as much as Ambrose, if she were to redeem herself at all.

And so she had left Eodred while he slept and turned southward toward Hafwynder Manor. There were things there that she needed, and a place—the abandoned chapel where the Black Wolf had made his camp—where she could stay while she purged herself of softhearted feeling.

Ambrose returned to Torworden as the sun descended into the treetops. He was tired and dirty, but paused to cast Eudo's tunic into the mud before opening the door of the sunken hut.

"She's safe," Stephen said, springing to his feet as soon as the door was open.

The sorcerer reeled backward. He hadn't expected to find anyone waiting for him; the good news took a few heartbeats to settle in his mind.

"Wildecent? Here? You found her?"

"Not here . . . but safe, I'm sure," Stephen began. He told his friend the story, as it had been pieced together during the day, concluding, "And you're to see my uncle, once you're presentable again."

Ambrose went to the table, where Stephen had thoughtfully provided wine.

"I'll ride out tomorrow—"

"He's sent riders out, but he also said you were already planning to ride out tomorrow." There was a note of hurt accusation in the younger man's voice.

Ambrose pulled his braes. Standing naked in the center of the hut he poured a ewer of cold water over his head and wiped away Eudo's smell. Then he answered Stephen. "Yesterday. Yesterday it seemed the wisest thing to do. By the Two, it would still be the wisest thing, but I won't be going. Not until I find Wildecent; not without her." He sat on the edge of the box bed mopping himself with the castoff linen, wincing when he probed the sore spots on his temple and neck. "I tried to convince her to come with me. She wouldn't—no more than you would. And she told me how miserable Alison was, thinking that you no longer loved her. I thought I might at least set *that* to rights before I left.

"More the fool I was, I stood in the stairway pleading with her and promising I'd send for Alison once I'd talked with you—"

Stephen swallowed Ambrose's words and thought on them awhile. "Alison says 'thank you.' "

Ambrose let the shirt fall to the straw. "How is she?"

"I took your advice; it worked, as usual. Just as you were right when you said I still loved her. I think I shall become the lord of Hafwynder Manor when all this is over, and I think I shall like it very much. But I think I would like it even more if you didn't need to leave."

"I should leave," Ambrose said as much to himself as Stephen. "If I listen to my mind, I should leave because, my friend, magic's not done with this land. If I listen to my heart, I should leave because I've made a fool of myself with Wildecent, and I doubt she'll forgive me—"

"Even Alison has forgiven you, as if you needed it. What happened wasn't your fault."

"Ah, but I made a fool of myself before that—"

"It is not a fatal affliction, Ambrose. Most men are

fools. I've heard you say that dozens of times. Stay at least until we're back at Hafwynder Manor?''

The sorcerer sighed and stood up. ''Secretly, I'd always hoped I wasn't like most men. I'll stay.''

LYNN ABBEY was born in Peekskill, New York, and earned her undergraduate and graduate degrees in history at the University of Rochester and New York University, respectively. She spent several years working as a computer programmer and systems analyst in New York City, during which time she began to attend science fiction conventions and met her husband-to-be, Robert Asprin. In 1976 she moved to Ann Arbor, Michigan, to pursue a full-time writing career.

Ms. Abbey is the author of the historical fantasies *Daughter of the Bright Moon* and *The Black Flame,* as well as UNICORN & DRAGON and its sequel, CONQUEST: UNICORN & DRAGON VOLUME II. She is perhaps best known as the co-creator and co-editor (with Robert Asprin) of the *Thieves' World* anthology series.